Also by Donna Small

from Indigo Sea Press

Just Between Friends

A Ripple in the Water

www.secondwindpublishing.com

Through Rose Colored Glasses

By

Donna Small

Perseverance Books
Published by Indigo Sea Press, LLC.
Winston-Salem

Perseverance Books
Indigo Sea Press, LLC
302 Ricks Drive
Winston-Salem, NC 27284

First Perseverance Books edition published
September, 2015
Perseverance Books, Logo and all production design are trademarks of Indigo Sea Press, used under license.

For information regarding bulk purchases of this book, digital purchase and special discounts, please contact the publisher at
www.indigoseapress.com

Cover design by Pan Morelli
Manufactured in the United States of America
ISBN 978-1630662622

During the writing of this novel, I spoke to countless women who had experienced some version of the story you are about to read. Each woman's story, though different in some way, was eerily similar. It pained me to hear it, though I'm sure not as much as it pained these women to tell it. Not only were they betrayed by their husband, partner, or significant other, they were betrayed by a friend; someone they had shared with, confided in, and most of all, trusted. In addition to mourning their now dead relationship, they had to mourn the loss of a friend. That being said, I feel certain not one of these women feels any sadness today at the loss of that particular friendship.

This book is dedicated to all of these women. I hope I have accurately conveyed your stories and appropriately captured your voices in Abbie Hamilton.

And for all those women who saw a man through their own "Rose" colored glasses...

Shame on you.

—Donna Small

Rose

The first time I saw Reid Hamilton, I might have actually gasped.

The moment that man walked into my line of vision I felt things I'd only read or heard other women talk about when they spoke of the rush they felt when they met the man of their dreams. Although my experience with the crap found in romance novels is slim, I've had countless friends who spoke of the man who took their breath away, caused their pulse to quicken and made their nether regions actually ache with desire. And while I've had my share of boyfriends, none of them, despite countless dates and too may intimate sessions to count, never made me feel anything close to the instantaneous, powerful attraction I felt when he walked into the room. Truth be told, I felt like I'd been hit by a ton of bricks.

Reid is beyond striking. He is well over six feet tall and his suit simply cannot hide what I felt certain was a better than average physique just lurking beneath his overly starched shirt and crisp pants. But besides that, there's something much more intriguing about him—something that drew me to him immediately. It was his confidence. When he strolled into the room that first day, I knew he was a man who was very comfortable in his skin. And when his eyes met mine as he reached out to shake hand, I felt the strength there and immediately began to fantasize about what those hands would feel like roaming my body.

But, since Reid was interviewing me for a position in his department, I forced myself to table my fantasy for the moment.

A difficult task, to say the least.

Reid sat down across from me and began to ask several

questions about me and my expectations for the job I was interviewing for. A job that suddenly, I was desperate to have.

What I didn't know then was that there were several openings in the company for the position I was interviewing for. The four hiring managers were meeting with the candidates to determine which of us would be best suited for each team. Had I known just how slim my chances of working for Reid were, I would have been even more nervous than I already was.

Reid asked me several questions to which I'm sure I gave appropriate answers—though I can't remember one bit of what I said. I was too busy watching his lips move around as he spoke. After the interview finally ended, he stood up and grasped my hand with the two of his, enveloping my hand within. Despite the warmth of his hands wrapped around mine, I shivered.

When I got the call two days later telling me I would be working on Reid's team, I nearly wept with joy. The thought of working with him all day, every day was more than I could've ever hoped for. I envisioned the two of us working long hours together and developing a friendship that would, inevitably, turn into something more. After all, most workplaces nowadays, are more like your own personal Match.com than they are a place to build your career. More and more people are falling for people they work with, simply because of the amount of time they spend working and getting to know their co-workers. I felt certain that would happen with Reid. Needless to say, I couldn't wait to begin my employment.

Now, the fact that he was going to be my boss might pose a bit of a problem but I was willing to overlook this tiny, insignificant detail. If things progressed with Reid (and I hoped they would), I'd simply transfer to another department. But I'd worry about that later. Right now, the only thought I could focus on was the fact that I'd be in close proximity to Reid Hamilton for the better part of forty hours every week.

I was grinning from ear to ear.

When I arrived at work that first day and discovered that my cubicle was a mere ten feet from his office, I nearly did a cartwheel. I contained myself; not wanting to appear giddy and immature and probably lose my job before I'd even sat down in my chair. So I gathered up my giddiness and stored it for a more appropriate time. I did, however, find it rather difficult to wipe the smile off my face the entire day.

Once my cubicle was identified, I got to work organizing it so that I could stealthily glance at him over the top of my computer if I stood, or simply lean back in my chair and glance into his office.

Since that day nearly two months ago, I have spent countless hours monitoring his movements as well as all things Reid Hamilton. From in the safety of my cubicle, I can casually glance his way and watch him cross and uncross his legs, stare at his computer screen or stand and walk around his office. Even the simplest of tasks are made sexy when performed by him. It's ridiculous really. The other day I lost complete track of time watching him slowly sip on his coffee.

By now, I know his routines so well by now that I can predict within three minutes when he's going to grab that next cup of coffee, where he's going to eat for lunch, and even when he's going to take a restroom break. I have been known, on occasion, to time my trips to the rest room or break room so that I can walk with him part of the way

By now, you might think that I'm a bit obsessive and that I'm not able to complete my work because of this...er, hobby, but strangely enough, I find that because I am so excited when he's around, I have an abundance of energy that makes me incredibly efficient. I only wish this enthusiasm bled into my personal life. I could use some of it to clean my apartment, which, at the moment, could be condemned if anyone were to step inside of it. But frankly, who has time to clean their apartment when there is so much work to be done? Not work, work. Reid work—not that I'd call it work...more like the best hobby in the world.

When I'm at home, my time is spent doing any number of productive tasks. For instance, Reid is a Yankees fan so I make sure to watch any game that is on TV so I can mention it to him the next day. And I have to watch the *whole* game. No highlight shows for me. That just won't do. As a matter of fact, I consider it cheating. How can you possibly speak about a professional sporting event when you haven't watched the entire thing?

Why do I spend my time watching any number of sporting events, you ask? It's simple really. Men love their women to be interested in sports, and particularly, be a fan of the team they cheer for. They imagine her beside him at an outdoor arena. She is wearing her ball cap, her ponytail peeking neatly through the hole in the back. He is wearing the team shirt and she's wearing one as well, though not the same exact one. Men never want to do the matchy-matchy thing. They think it's cheesy and I have to agree. There is nothing...NOTHING worse than seeing a couple walking together wearing matching outfits. I mean, what other indication that a man is pussy-whipped than walking around in public wearing an outfit your significant other clearly picked out to match hers.

It's sad, really.

In addition to watching the sporting events that are favorites of Reid's, I've made it my mission to discover all I can about him and his interests so my office, as a result of this research, is littered with Pearl Jam concert ticket stubs, Big Daddy Love paraphernalia, and anything New York sports related. I purchased a Yankees mug recently and it's the only mug I will drink out of when I'm at the office (It's a *great* conversation starter).

I've also begun to watch his favorite shows - The Soprano's and Breaking Bad - repeatedly, so that if I find myself in his office (as I do quite regularly), I can prolong our little visits by discussing the shows.

You might think my interest in Reid is a bit extreme, but I have to disagree. All smart, goal-oriented women do this type of research when they find a man they are interested in. It's just part of the process. You've got to show the man in question that the two of you have so much in common, you'll never run out of things to talk about.

Now, you might think all of this "work" isn't necessary but I assure you, it is. It's all part of the game we call dating. I mean, I'm only doing what any smart women do. It's not as if I'm taking advantage of him somehow. I'm just doing my best to show him how much we have in common.

So far, however, all of my work has produced very little results. Granted, I've been moving slowly and cautiously so as not to scare him away. Men like Reid tend be skittish. Conversations between the two of us are kept to "safe" topics; the weather, the latest project we're working, or as previously mentioned, the game that was on the previous evening. Occasionally, I'll ask about what he did the night before or what he did over the weekend. In turn, he'll ask about my evening or weekend, as the case may be, and that's an opportunity for me to allow him to get to know the outside-of-work Rose. I reply politely but I'm cautious not to bore him with the minutia of my life. Everyone knows that men really don't have an interest in the things we women do so I simply answer Reid's questions with as few words as possible, then turn the conversation back toward him. He is always very pleasant and professional in our exchanges and I'm certain that as of right now, he has no idea how I feel about him.

And that's just how I want things…for now.

I have to admit, when I first started working here, I wasn't entirely sure this was what I wanted to do with my life. After all, marketing isn't what you think it is. It's not coming up with the next greatest Super Bowl ad or finding a new Chihuahua for Taco Bell. Sure, some people do those things but most of us are simply trying to find a new way to describe orange juice or a pen. To make matters worse, our advertising company only focuses on print work, we're never looking at hot actors or cute little dogs.

It's boring. Well, mostly it is. Admittedly, Reid and I spend a lot of time together discussing ideas and possible slogans and that part of my day isn't boring at all. Still, mainly we're just trying to write a paragraph or two for a local business to use in their advertising and despite ogling my boss during the entire time I'm seated in his office, even I have my limits.

He does his best to keep me entertained though, and without even really trying. Reid is hopeless at typing. He's one of those hunt-and-peck typists, only using his index fingers. We always start out with him trying to type but then I end up pushing him out of the way and sitting down at his desk to take over. It's like we have our own little joke between us.

Now, don't for a minute think that I'm not aware my quest with Reid isn't without its hurdles. I'm fully aware that the man is my boss. If…when, *when* we are finally together, I will get another job. And of course, I'll do this before we tell anyone about it. If I can't find something here in Winston Salem, I'll look in another city nearby. Like Greensboro. Heck, that's only thirty minutes from here. Besides, while I don't know Reid's actual salary, I'm certain he pulls in a sizable one. It just wouldn't make sense for him to find another job; not with all the years of service he's got with the company.

Oh, and there's one other teensie-weensie bump in the road that prevents Reid and I from being together.

His wife.

Abbie

"I'm in the kitchen!" I call out to my husband when I hear the front door open. I'm standing in the kitchen rifling through the day's mail when Reid walks in and greets me with a smile that never gets old, even after fourteen years of marriage. I grin right back and lean in for our customary kiss. Since the children aren't around, he reaches around me and pulls me closer to him by grabbing my ass with his hand. He deepens the kiss and murmurs a hello into my mouth.

"Well, hello to you too," I whisper back. "Long day?"

"Eh, not too bad." He looks around kitchen and nods to the pans I have on the stove. "Want some help? It looks like you've got a lot going on here."

I look at his crisp white shirt and think of the spaghetti sauce simmering on the stove. There is no way I'm letting him near it. A spaghetti sauce stain is the one item I've never been able to successfully eliminate from any article of clothing and I feel certain that if Reid were to stir a rather large pot of bubbling red liquid, his shirt will end up with the spatterings of said liquid, which will remain there for eternity, thereby ruining the shirt. And that is something I can't bear to think of. With his height and build, his shirts cost a fortune and I don't want to have to replace it. Besides the cost, trying to find shirts that have a 17 neck size with a sleeve length of 37 takes up more time than I'd like it to. Apparently the clothing industry feels that if you have a larger than normal size neck, your arms must be really short. And conversely, if your arms are long, your neck must be tiny. Searching for shirts for Reid is a nightmare that normally takes the better part of an afternoon. You'd think I'd get smart and just order ten shirts when I find one but I can't do that either. If a store happens to have Reid's size, they'll most likely only have one or two. Needless to say, Reid will not be getting anywhere near the red sauce simmering on the stove.

"Go on and get changed," I reply, shaking my head from side to side. "The girls are upstairs if you want to see them."

He waves over his shoulder as he leaves the room and I know that tonight will be like most every other night. Reid will change into comfortable clothes—shorts and a t-shirt—then he'll head up to see our two daughters who will, the moment he enters the room, climb on top of him as though he were a human jungle gym. After several minutes of giggling and screaming (mostly by the girls but some by Reid) he will come downstairs with one daughter strapped to his leg and the other strapped to his back like a monkey. This chain of events is such a normalcy in my home that I wonder how he'll manage to carry those two girls downstairs when they're fifteen and thirteen. Thankfully, now they're only ten and eight and are probably as light as a feather to my husband, a former football player.

The pan holding the spaghetti sauce begins to make a noise that tells me I should turn down the burner as it's nearly ready. I lift the lid of the other pot and see the tiny bubbles in the water and know that within a minute or two, it will be a full, rolling boil. Placing the cover back on the pan, I reach into the pantry and try to find some pasta. Unfortunately, I'm only able to locate whole wheat pasta, which Reid dislikes tremendously, despite my numerous attempts to get him to eat healthier. I sigh, knowing that the girls also prefer regular spaghetti. Unfortunately, this is all I can find and I'm not about to drive to the grocery store now. I'll have to cook the pasta longer than usual and cover it with extra sauce to mask the chewy texture of the whole wheat. Maybe I can get away with it.

Nah. Not a chance.

I lift the lid once again and pour the entire content of the box into the pan, knowing that my intention is to have some leftover for snacks and perhaps another dinner later in the week. Because of Reid's work, he travels frequently so if he's out of town, the girls are perfectly content to eat pasta with butter and parmesan cheese. It's only when Reid's home that I tend to make it more of a production, making my own meatballs, a salad, and garlic bread.

I stir the pasta, watching it soften and become fluid as the water returns to a boil. From up above, I hear the sound of laughter and shrieks and I know that this is the girls' favorite part of the day. They love their father, as most young girls do and I'm so thankful that I married a man who relishes being a father as much as Reid does. I'm sure all the traveling he does wears on him at times. I would imagine it's frustrating to miss dance recitals, soccer games, or school plays. Thankfully, he more than makes up for it when he's home; both with the girls and with me. I can't tell you how many weekend nights the four of us have sat together for a marathon of movies the girls have watched more times than I care to remember. And Reid does it. Without complaint. Even I'm sick of watching The Little Mermaid and can't help but sigh softly and roll my eyes discreetly when the girls offer that particular movie up as a suggestion. I'm not sure why, but the replaying of this movie over and over doesn't seem to bother Reid. He knows all the words to "Under the Sea" and will dance around the living room while singing it. On occasion, he will grab salad tongs and pretend to be Ariel's best friend, Sebastian. While the movie tends to wear on me, the sight of my husband pretending to be a snarky crab never does.

On those nights, the girls will beg to stay up well past their bedtime, which we allow, given the fact that no one needs to get up early the next morning. The girls will start out the evening full of energy, determined to stay up well past midnight. But by eleven-thirty, they're both fast asleep, which means Reid must carry them to bed since I can no longer lift them when they're dead weight.

Once the girls are tucked safely in their beds, Reid will shut off the television and sit beside me. He'll open his arms wide, an indication I should curl up next to him, and then wrap his arms around me and pull me close. So close in fact, that it's hard to discern where his body ends and mine begins. We'll sit in the semi-dark room, only lit by the lamp on the other end of the couch and sip the glasses of pinot noir that I poured for us while he was putting the girls to bed. We'll each talk about our day, him telling me about any new clients or proposals while I tell him about homework, projects, or anything child related.

It is then, in the near darkness that we're able to, once again, be the couple we were before our two hurricanes came along.

I've always thought this time we spent together was key to our successful marriage. Of course, successful is a relative word. We are like most every other couple I know in that we are, for the most part, happy, but have those stupid little idiosyncrasies that drive the other person crazy. In our case, the fact that I hardly ever clean the fridge drives Reid bananas. I will continue to cram food onto the shelves, neglecting the sticky, dried juice, yogurt, or God-only-knows what else that has been spilled. It is only when I need to tug something out of the fridge using all my strength because it's attached to the shelf by the aforementioned sticky substance that it occurs to me to get out the soap and warm water and clean up the mess.

On the other hand, I know for a fact Reid hasn't once, during the course of our marriage, replaced an empty toilet paper roll with a new one. He will put out a new roll of toilet paper but instead of placing it on the holder, he will put it on the back of the toilet, on the floor, or (my personal favorite) vertically on *top* of the empty roll. To further add to my frustration, when I consistently point this out to him, he remains in a state of total and absolute denial. While this tends to make me want to scream, (and I'm sure my lack of fridge cleaning has the same effect on him) overall, we're good together. I think a good part of our relationship is this knowledge that we have these characteristics that drive the other person insane, but we also acknowledge them and on a good day, we will poke fun at them.

The thing is, I figure if the only thing we're fighting about is an empty toilet paper roll or an unclean fridge, we're doing pretty good.

The other part of our success is that we both give each other this one on one time. Reid could spend countless hours working in his office and there are a million things I could be doing—laundry, making lunches, cleaning the fridge (Well, I could!) or the counters, prepping a grocery list - but this is our time. It's our time to reconnect and unwind and become a couple again and neither one of us would forego that time for something as unimportant as a load of laundry or yet another email.

Besides, this time with Reid is the one time that my world resumes its sanity. We are sitting on the couch, whispering about our day, our plans for the weekend, or any number of things—basically doing nothing.

But it is this time of day that all is right with the world.

Rose

I read once that while filming his movies, Harry Connick Jr. would have his assistant hold his wedding ring so that he could put it back on between takes. He was so committed to his wife and his marriage that he didn't want to ever go without his wedding ring unless he was in character.

Seeing Reid every day—well, seeing the damn ring on the third finger of his left hand—reminds me of that story. Doesn't he ever forget to put it on? Leave it in the shower? Drop it down the drain? It's infuriating really. Like a beacon highlighting his unavailability.

Besides, it isn't as though some cheap band of gold is going to prevent me feeling what I feel. If anything, that shiny band has the opposite effect. It only makes me want him more. He's someone who is not commitment phobic or "emotionally unavailable" like most of the guys I've met recently. Reid had proven he can commit to someone; he just made that commitment to the wrong woman.

Still, staring at that gold band on his finger is enough to drive me insane. It's all I can do not to rip the damn thing off his finger. It seems like whenever he's typing or moving his hands in the slightest, any light in the room bounces off of it and shards of pain rip right through me.

Seriously, it's like taking a bullet.

What's even more frustrating is that the ring looks as shiny and perfect as the day it was put there. You'd think that after all this time, the gold would have dulled or it would have gotten scuffed up...something! But no. It still rests on his hand all shiny and perfect.

I just hope his marriage isn't all shiny. I hope his relationship with her has a few scuffs and dings. They must.

Everyone does. There's got to be something missing in their relationship. I mean, think about it. Who doesn't wish for what they don't, or can't, have?

"Rose?" I finally got Reid to call me Rose instead of my given name, Rosemary. I really don't know what my parents were thinking giving me such an old name. And who wants to be named after a spice, anyway? It's not even one of the good spices, like Saffron. Now that's a cool name.

I look up to find Reid leaning against my cubicle wall rifling through a folder. I didn't even hear him approach, which is odd because as we have previously established, I always know where he is. Always. As I look at him, I feel a flutter inside of me. He looks confused and utterly adorable. "Do you know what we decided on for the closing line of that Apple Festival ad?"

I stifle a giggle. He's helpless without me. "Come on," I say, standing up. "Let's see if we can figure this little problem out."

I grab the file from him and lead him into his office, sashaying ahead of him so that he has a full view of my bottom, which is cleverly wrapped in a snug pencil skirt. It occurs to me that I should 'accidentally' drop some papers on the floor in front of me so that I have to bend over in order to pick them up. I smile, thinking of Reese Witherspoon in Legally Blonde demonstrating the "bend and snap" and wonder if I could pull it off without looking like a complete idiot. Knowing my luck, I'd "bend" gracefully, but the "snap" part would look like I was having a seizure or something. I quickly dismiss the idea and continue to walk towards Reid's office.

I guess things at the office are progressing nicely, but truthfully, I wish I had more to report. We get along just fine, Reid and I, but that's just it. We work well together but as far as anything other than an employee/boss relationship? Nada.

A good part of each day is spent in Reid's office and I can tell we're becoming closer, but let me explain so there aren't any misconceptions here. He relies on me, trusts my opinion on pretty much anything work related and knows that if he asks me to do something, I will ensure it gets done. On very rare occasions, he will ask my opinion on what his daughters might like him to bring them on his next business trip, particularly if he's going to be away from them for several days. It's a very comfortable, compatible working relationship, but nothing more.

Yet.

Reid still possesses a reserved and (If I'm being completely honest here) somewhat standoffish and distant demeanor, but I can tell he's loosened up quite a bit over the past few months. When we used to meet, he was incredibly stiff and it was borderline uncomfortable; he'd barely crack a smile. Now, he's a bit more relaxed. I think all of our conversations about sports (Go, Yankees!) and mutual interests in TV shows have really brought us closer.

Again, in the work sense only. *Sigh...*

I wonder if the warmer weather has helped him loosen up a bit. He's only recently ditched the button down dress shirts and spends most of his days in golf shirts. Come to think of it, I don't believe I've ever seen the same one twice. The man must have dozens of them. Yesterday, he came in wearing a new pink one which I thought looked incredible on him until he told me his wife bought it for him. That sort of ruined it for me.

Reid's attire has changed and so has mine. I've got to step up my game. I've put away all my wool pants and bulky sweaters and brought out strappy sandals, flowing skirts and sheer, chiffon blouses. Button down, of course. And if I were to happen to leave an extra button or two undone, leaving a generous view of the delicate curve of a breast? Well, all the better.

Today, in addition to finalizing the local Apple Festival marketing paraphernalia, we're meeting to discuss a new client K&M recently signed. I'm not too familiar with the client at this point. All I really know it that it's a local juice company—one of those knock-off Gatorade type of drinks. Apparently, the hope is that one of the big juice companies will notice our little Winston Salem juice and purchase it for millions, allowing the owners to retire immediately. Reid got word about this new client and apparently got to work on it last night while at home. I have to admit, the thought of him working at home instead of spending time with his wife makes me smile with just a bit more enthusiasm.

Knowing he's probably gotten a good start on the direction of the ad, I figure our time together will be more personal than work since knowing Reid probably has a pretty good idea of where the ad is headed.

I walk into Reid's office and sit in my usual chair, the burgundy chair that is farthest from his desk. While this might seem an error on my part, I can assure you the selection of the chair was completely intentional, since the distance enables Reid to have a complete view of my legs as I cross and uncross them while I'm seated there.

As I sit, I watch as he walks around to the other side of the desk, pulls out his chair and sits at his desk. Like usual, he barely glances at me as he's very one-track minded and, quite frankly, a little over-focused ADHD when work in involved. I can't help but wonder if this attention to detail and desire for perfection carries over into other, more intimate, areas of his life. Hmmm…

But I digress.

I had hoped that Reid would notice the new skirt have on-not that he'd mention it. Like I said, Reid tends to be *extremely* professional at the office and it would be completely out of character for him to mention my clothing, even if it is an adorable Banana Republic pencil skirt that fits snugly to my size 6 frame and ends just above my knee. The navy blue looks perfect against my skin, which has just recently begun to get a little color thanks to the warmer days. The white shirt I've paired it with is loose fitting and makes my dark hair shine. The delicate pearl earrings and stunning bubble necklace I have on make this one of my favorite outfits.

I sit silently while Reid moves his mouse around and clicks on several file folders, trying to locate something. His shoulders are hunched forward as he concentrates and his left hand rests comfortable on the side of the desk. The fingers of his right hand tap the keyboard a few times and I have to suppress a grin. Not only is Reid one of those 'hunt and peck' typists, but his desk has one of those keyboard trays that pulls out from underneath his desk, which means that he has to hunch over even further when he types, given his height. It's almost comical.

"Help me out here, Rose."

"Of course," I reply.

"Where did I save the file?"

He doesn't even have to tell me which file. I know exactly which one he's referring to. Just last week, he and I sat in his office for the better part of an afternoon and worked on the brochure for the festival. We just about had it completed and now, the poor man can't seem to locate it. Thankfully, he has an employee who truly understands him and has organized his files into a system that is completely user friendly.

I cross my legs and lean back against the chair. "You want me to find it for you?"

He leans back in his chair and sighs softly. "Please."

I stand up and walk around to where he's sitting. I bump his chair with my hip, nudging him back from the computer so I can squeeze by. I reach over him and grab the mouse. It only takes a few clicks but once I'm done, the brochure for the festival is in front of him in all its mega-pixel glory.

"Thanks."

"No problem," I reply. It suddenly occurs to me that I am quite close to Reid and I'm not ready to leave his side. I quickly figure out a way for me to stay longer, even if only for a few moments. I rest my hip onto the edge of his desk and lean closer, pointing to the screen. "I've been thinking about this part here," I say reaching for the mouse. "Let me show you what I had in mind."

I make a few adjustments to the color and the size of the graphics, then sit back onto the edge of his desk. "Whaddya think?"

He's staring at the screen and nodding, which is good, but I'd rather he be staring at me. Finally, he looks at me and grins. "I like it. Nice work."

"Thanks." I reply more calmly than I feel. Though it's hard to suppress the fact that hang on his every word and am starving for any positive words from this man, it is imperative for me to maintain the appearance of indifference.

I'm still perched on the edge of the desk and I realize I should probably return to my chair on the other side of the office but I can't seem to make my legs work to push myself up. Suddenly, an idea occurs to me and I reach behind me to grab the file for the new client. Opening the manila folder, I begin to review the ideas Reid has prepared, most likely the evening before. Absently, I chew on my lower lip as though I'm in deep concentration. Once I'm certain Reid has gotten an eye full of my soft lips (Thanks Babylips!), I look up.

"This is really good," I say.

"Thanks."

We're silent for a few seconds and I realize we're bordering on having an awkward moment. Can't have that, now can we? I stand quickly, move away from him, then head over to the chair. Once I'm seated, I almost feel the tension dissipate and I begin our daily chat.

"Watch anything good last night?"

"Nah," he replies. "I worked on this for most of the night, then crashed late."

Once again, I suppress a smile knowing that he spent the night working instead of spending time with his wife doing

God-only-knows-what. A shiver runs through me as I picture Reid embracing what I imagine to be an overweight, mousy wife who doesn't wear makeup because she's so stressed and has no time for such luxuries. I'll bet she wears track suits every day because nothing in her closet fits and she's desperate to hide the sagging skin and stretched out midsection she now has after giving birth to two children.

Most likely, her hair hangs limply down her back or she pulls it up into a ponytail that she thinks look chic but really just looks messy. Of course, she may have cut it short like most moms do because they know they're just too busy to worry about blow drying and styling their hair. And without a doubt, she's got big circles under her eyes from years of not getting enough sleep, which also means she's been too tired exercise and lose the last twenty pounds she gained from her pregnancies.

Well, that's how I picture her anyway.

What can I say? It's the little things that make me smile.

"I watched that episode of the Soprano's where Tony comes home with the fur for Carmela. You remember that one?"

He grins and nods.

"God, that's a great show." And I'm thankful it is such a good show because I've spent a small fortune buying every damn season of it on Blue-ray. But hey, if spending that money gets me some results with Reid, then it will all be worth it.

We chat for a few more minutes talking about the Soprano's and how the Yankees are doing—too early in the season to tell—and then I feel as though I've spent just the right amount of time with him. It's tricky. You've got to stay long enough so that when you leave, they're sorry to see you go. But you've got to leave without staying too long so they miss you a bit every time you leave.

Tricky…very tricky. And I can't afford to make any mistakes. This is one man I don't want to let slip through my fingers. I've got to make sure that every step I take is perfectly planned out.

I smooth my hands down the front of my skirt, then stand. "Well, if you're all set with that," I say, nodding toward the colorful brochure still displayed on his computer screen. "I guess I'll head back to work." *Tell me to sit. Tell me to stay.*

But Reid doesn't say anything. In fact, he's already shifted his focus to the papers on his desk and simply nods as I turn to walk out of the office.

When I sit back at my desk, I can't help but run through my entire conversation with Reid in an attempt to determine if I said or did anything wrong. I can't think of anything but still, I wonder what I need to do to get this man to notice me as anything other than one of his employees. Surely he must think I'm attractive. And I've shown him that we have so much in common. What else can I possibly do?

Trust me on this; I have laid the ground work. I've tilted my head, tossed my hair and set him up for any number of sexual jokes with an endless supply of suggestive, yet ambiguous, comments.

But nothing. Our conversations, even after these few months, are still very…well, friendly and professional. Sure, he's pleasant and all, but something tells me that he's the same way with anyone he works with, and that just won't do.

Somehow, I need to figure out a way to get him to see me as the woman I am and not just his employee.

As an idea comes to mind, a slow smile spreads across my face.

Abbie

The end of the school year is always hectic for me. The girls are counting down the days until school lets out for the summer and it seems as though there is an "end of year" party every day. For me, this means baking cookies, preparing goodie bags, and volunteering as the classroom mom for countless hours.

Honest to God, I don't know why each and every year I think I'll have the time for this.

In addition to all of those duties, I find myself doing all the things that need to be done before the girls are at home with me for the eight weeks of summer. Once that happens, my time will be limited since we'll be heading to the pool most days, planning day trips, and doing our annual family vacation at the beach. This year, we've selected Oak Island for our beach destination. Though we've never been there, we heard it's not as commercialized as Myrtle Beach but still provides enough activities that will prevent boredom from setting in.

For the girls that is. I can think of nothing I'd like better than a week of sheer boredom.

True to North Carolina weather, the temperature outside made a quick shift from cold to hot and humid, thereby ensuring the Hamilton home once again goes from using the heat to immediately using the A/C. I have to admit, this is my favorite time of year. I love to work outside in the yard, planting and weeding, then coming in to feel the cool air on my skin.

Reid, surprisingly, has been home steadily for two weeks, which is practically unheard of. The girls love being able to spend this extra time with him, though I think even they realize it can't last forever. Travel is a part of Reid's life. Always has been, always will be. So although we have adjusted to him being gone frequently, we all seem to cling to him a bit more when he is home.

Despite his being physically home each night, mentally, he's somewhere else. He follows the same routine each evening and plays with the girls, then joins us for dinner. But once we're finished and the table is cleared, he heads into the office to work and stays there until well after I've gone to sleep. Last week, I grabbed a magazine and joined him in the office but after several moments, I could tell the sound of the pages crinkling as I flipped through them was just about to drive him batty. After giving him a kiss on the forehead, I crept out quietly, leaving him to his work.

I worry about him. I worry that his job is stressful, that he's working too hard, and that it's only going to get worse but when I visit him in our home office and reach around to hug him, he tells me I'm just being silly. I suppose I am. Reid loves his work. And I think there is a part of him that loves the challenge of taking on a new project and coming up with just the right words to advertise it. The juice campaign he's working on at the moment is especially enticing to him because he knows the company is hoping to be bought by a larger company. Reid feels the pressure of gaining the attention of that big company with his ad.

I pile the last of the dishes into the dishwasher and start it, then store the leftovers in the fridge. I glance down the hall and wonder if I should go into the office and see Reid or if I'd just be an annoying distraction. I decide that distraction or not, I'll peek in just to see if he needs anything.

When I open the door, I find my husband hunched over the computer with his head resting in his hands. He's staring at the screen as though hoping the words will simply appear. I wish they would. Then he could relax, until the next project, that is. I step into the room quietly, trying not to disturb him.

"You need anything?" I ask, rubbing his shoulders with my hands.

21

"You," he replies, grinning at me.

I chuckle. "You've got me."

"Then I'm good."

Even now, after all this time, I still think my husband is the most handsome man I have ever seen. I lean in closer to him and wrap my arms around his neck. He takes my hand and kisses the palm of it, then nudges me to a standing position while he spins his chair away from the computer and pats his lap. I sit down and wrap my arms around his shoulders and nuzzle his neck.

"You sure you don't need anything?"

He squeezes me. "Nope. I have everything I need right here."

I sigh contentedly. These times we have together where it's just the two of us, even if it's for only a few moments are all I need to feel loved and cherished. And I do. Reid can work and travel all he wants but as long as I'm held in his arms for a few moments, life is good. We are good.

From down the hall, I hear something that sounds an awful lot like the beginnings of an argument. I sigh softly, knowing that Reid probably can't afford another interruption tonight and these few stolen moments will be the only ones we share tonight. Reluctantly, I pull away from him.

"I guess I should go out there and referee before things get out of hand."

He kissed me gently on the lips and nods. "Go get'em tiger."

"Come to bed early tonight?"

"I'd come to bed now if I could," he replies, grinning.

I laugh, and head toward the door. I jump and shriek when Reid's hand smacks me on the ass. "Reid!" I say sternly, though we both know I'm not the least bit upset.

He giggles - yes, he actually giggles - before returning his gaze to the computer.

The rest of my evening passes by swiftly. I manage to

referee several arguments, though none of them warranted the level of screaming I heard, managed to bake a batch of cookies for the girls to take in for snack each day, and put the girls to bed on time. Overall, a very productive evening. Also an evening that wore me out. Skipping the glass of wine that earlier sounded so tempting, I choose instead to head to bed, anxious to change into my pajamas and curl up with a good book before nodding off to sleep. My plans are diverted, however, when I walk into my room and see Reid lying on our bed looking utterly relaxed. He's lying against the headboard with his hands folded behind his head. I see the look in his eyes and know that I won't be going to sleep anytime soon, and that's just fine by me. As I walk toward him, he opens his arms to me and holds me tight. I lean into him and he gently lays me down sideways on the bed.

"I love you, Abbie," he says softly.

"I love you too."

And I know he does. The one thing I have never doubted is that Reid loves me. Our marriage is a good one, I think. Sure, we have our problems just like most everyone but we are more happy than sad and we get along more than we argue. And in this day and age, I think that's pretty damn terrific.

Reid slowly pulls my t-shirt over my head, then unhooks my bra and tosses it onto the floor. He takes each nipple into his mouth and sucks on them until they form taut peaks, which takes mere seconds since Reid knows my body nearly as well as I do. While he pays close attention to my breasts, he slides off my jeans with such ease that I barely even notice. When he slips a finger inside of me, I gasp. His fingers work their magic until I am writhing beneath him, moaning his name softly. He leaves me for only a moment while he removes his own clothing, then returns and covers my body with his own. He slides into me, filling me and begins to move slowly, knowing that this is what I crave. My breathing quickens, telling Reid to quicken his pace, which he does. I cry out as my orgasm rips through me and Reid thrusts into me one final time, coming mere seconds after me.

We both lie on the bed breathing heavily. He is still inside of me. I know once he's there, he doesn't want to leave. After years of being with this man, I can practically read his thoughts.

"You know, you're going to have to get up sooner or later," I whisper, trying to hide a chuckle.

"Later," he replies. "Much later." He nuzzles his face into the crook of my neck and kisses me gently. Slowly, he pulls out of me and I hear the tiny sigh that always follows. I have grown to love that sigh, the significance of it. It tells me that the love of my life would rather be inside of me than any place else in the world.

As I stroke his back and knead his shoulders, I think about how lucky I am. So many of our friends have fallen victim to divorce. We've seen it happen time and time again. Marriage is tough, no doubt, but Reid and I seem to grow closer with each passing year. I know that I can count on him for anything and I know he feels the same. I guess that's what marriage is all about; knowing the person you've chosen to spend your life with will do anything in their power for you.

Reid is a good guy. From the first moment I met him, I knew it. I could just sense it. And during the past decade or so, he's proven it to me over and over. When Hannah came along, he was so tender and caring with her that it nearly brought me to tears. He was so gentle with her, always picking her up carefully so as not to jostle her in any way. With Caroline, he was exactly the same but with the confidence that comes with knowing you've been down this road before. And seeing Reid with our girls makes me fall in love with him a little more each day.

Rose

I lift my long, dark hair off my neck as I walk across the parking lot toward the office. The summer is in full swing, which is great since it means I have pulled out my shorter skirts, sleeveless tops, and much cuter strappy sandals than I wear in the spring when it's cooler in the mornings. Now that the heat of the summer is here, humidity has arrived as well. Humidity and naturally curly hair do not get along with each other, which means I have a battle to fight each and every day.

Today, I've taken the time to blow it out straight and I'd rather it not turn into a frizzy, curly mess before I even make it into the building.

In other news, Reid and I have been spending a good deal of time together lately, but I don't feel as though I've made much progress. Despite spending hours talking, there still has been no sexual banter and not a single sexual innuendo despite my many attempts. It's like there's this line with Reid and he simply won't cross it.

Well, I've determined that today, he's either crossing the line or I'm going to move it.

For today's mission, I've chosen a skirt that admittedly is a bit snug. I've gained a few pounds over the past few months, which, now that I think about it, makes me wonder if this is why things have not progressed. I make a mental note to hit the gym more frequently and drastically reduce the amount of my daily carb intake.

All things considered, the extra pounds aren't entirely bad. They've added just a bit more oomph to my A-cup chest and just enough around my hips to make my skirt hug my frame enough so that when I sit down, it slides up and inch or so on its own. If a certain individual were to look at the skin said skirt

25

will reveal, then so be it. I've also worn my tallest heels today, thinking that they might accentuate my legs and make them appear longer than they actually are. At five feet, six inches, I'm not short but I'm not considered a tall woman either. I've always wanted to be just a few inches taller, since I do have this penchant for tall men, but this is all I've got. I think it was God's little joke on me.

At last, I reach the office and pull open the door, feeling the coolness of the air conditioning as it surrounds me. I keep my hair lifted off my neck for just a few minutes longer so that the cold air can cool me there and eliminate any perspiration before I lay my hair back down. I pass the security desk, flashing my badge and then stroll down the hallway to my cubicle.

After stowing my purse in the bottom drawer and giving my hair a final once over, I head into Reid's office, anxious to begin the day's festivities.

"Reid?" I ask, leaning against the door jam.

He is facing away from me and it takes me a second or so to realize that he's on the phone. I can't quite make out what he is saying but he's speaking so softly that I can only assume he's on the phone with his wife. I feel a twinge of jealousy but quickly push it away knowing that it's me he's with all day long.

He hangs up the phone and then turns to face me, surprise registers on his face for a quick second but he quickly replaces it with a smile.

"Rose. Come in. We can get started."

Yes. Let's.

As I move toward the round table in his office, I manage to eek out a tear. I let it fall from my eye and slowly roll down my cheek. Just as Reid notices the tear, I angrily wipe it away and sit down heavily in the chair.

"Rose? Are you okay?" He looks so concerned for me that I almost feel bad for tricking him. Almost.

"Oh, I'll be all right," I reply softly. My voice is scratchy and thick, a sure indicator that I've spent the night crying.

As expected, Reid persists in asking me about what has upset me. He's just too much a considerate person not to. So, I unload. I tell him how I'd been dating a great guy—a resident at the local hospital. I explain that things were going great for a few months and I thought things were progressing nicely, blah, blah, blah. Then I tell him how much I cared for this guy only to be dumped tragically the night before.

Lies. All of it just a bunch of lies.

But at this point, I'll do anything to gain a little progress in my mission to have this man to myself. Tears are a surefire way to get a man to see you as vulnerable. Which, in turn, spurs on their desire to care for you and protect you. I'm hoping my little performance will do just that. I imagine it perfectly in my mind. As I tell him about the jerk who dumped me, Reid will come and sit across from me. He'll reach over and take my hand in his as if to provide me comfort and help me through this horrific day. At the same time, he'll appreciate my dedication to my job and the fact that I was able to come into work today despite being so obviously distraught. His fingers will begin to caress my hand. At first, it will be simply to comfort me; to let me know he's there for me. But after a little while, he will begin to notice how soft my hands are, how smooth my skin in. He will begin to look at me differently— like a woman instead of just his employee. I, in turn, will start to feel better knowing Reid is the one who is giving me the strength to make it through this horrible (and completely fake) breakup. Reid will look into my eyes and it will occur to him that he is attracted to me. I'll gently wipe the tears from my eyes in order to show him that I'm feeling better simply because he's near. The vulnerability I'll be showing him will throw him over the edge. I'll thank him for being so supportive and then, for reasons he can't quite understand, he'll realize he wants to kiss me. Still sniffling just enough to show I'm not completely over my previous relationship, I will look at him as

27

he leans in toward me. I too, will lean forward and wait for his lips to reach mine. When at last our lips meet, we will realize our passion for each other. He will then wrap his arms around me and never want to let me go.

Of course, none of this actually happens.

Then again, nothing ever goes the way you think it will, does it? But even given the reality of that statement, what happens as I'm telling my story is something I could never have imagined.

As I begin to tell my story about the idiot that dumped me, Reid stays firmly seated behind his desk. Initially, he is looking at me with concern; his brow is furrowed and his hands are clasped gently in front of his mouth while he listens to me silently. The look of concern quickly fades and is replaced with what appears to be discomfort. He begins to shift in his chair every so often, almost as if he can't quite get comfortable. And then, much to my dismay, I watch as he pushes the home button on his iPhone and discreetly glances at it to check the time! By now, I'm certain he's wondering just how long I've been sobbing in his office and how soon he can ask me to leave.

This is not going how I'd planned it at all.

Realizing my plan is a complete and total failure, I switch tactics. Time to stop being the vulnerable girl who is distraught because she got dumped and time to be the woman who can handle anything. I wipe the tears from my cheeks and clear my throat. The moment my cheeks are free of tears, I can see Reid visibly relax. His shoulders drop several inches and he leans back against his chair. For a minute there, I think he just might sigh with relief.

"Sorry about that," I say. "It won't happen again."

"No, no," he says, waving his hand around dismissively. He clears his throat, then reaches for a pile of papers on his desk. He stacks the papers into a neat pile, then looks at me as though he's surprised to see me still sitting there. He's silent for a few moments and then just when it's about to get extremely uncomfortable, he begins to speak.

"I'm sorry you're having a rough time," he says. "Men can be jerks."

I smile. "I know."

"Present company excluded, of course," he says, grinning.

"Of course!"

And then something entirely unexpected happens. Reid actually invites me out to dinner. I'm thrilled. Thrilled, that is, until I realize it's a group going and said group includes his wife.

"You should go," he says, nodding. "A night out will do you some good. Abbie and the girls are coming...Oh! Jim and Natalie are coming too. You know Jim Cooper, right? Works in accounting? And Steve and his wife said they might show up...and..."

Reid rambles on, telling me who is coming and what department they work in while I sit there staring at him with a grin on my face, unable to do much more than nod. My first inclination is to politely decline. After all, who wants to sit there and watch him interact with his wife? Then I think that meeting her might be a good thing. You know what they say...keep your friends close and your enemies closer.

And Abbie Hamilton is definitely the enemy, even if she doesn't realize it. After all, she is the only person standing between me and Reid.

"So, you'll come?" He's looking at me expectantly and for a moment, I think he actually wants me to come. I feel a little tingle inside of me and know that there is no way I'm going to decline this invitation.

I smile. "Sounds great!"

"Excellent," he replies. He reaches for his cell phone and looks up at me expectantly. "What's your cell number?"

Without even a second thought, I blurt out the digits to my cell, thrilled I'm going to be added to his list of contacts. I actually speak so fast that I have to repeat it because Mr. Hunt and Peck can't type that fast.

"Okaaay," he says, typing what I'm assuming is my contact info into his phone. Finally he looks up. "I've just sent you a text so you'll have my number. If you get lost, just text me."

"All right," I reply. I'm completely dumbfounded. I'm now going out to dinner with Reid (and several others) and we've just swapped phone numbers. How the hell did I manage to do this?

Reid must interpret my stunned expressed to mean that I'm still upset over my recent "breakup" because he looks at me and tilts his head to the side. His brows come together in a frown. "You know what? This can wait until later," he says, gesturing to the papers scattered all over his desk. "Why don't you get some coffee and we'll regroup this afternoon. Sound good?"

"Sure," I reply. I stand up on unsteady legs and slowly walk out of his office. What the hell just happened? I honestly have no idea. But I do know that now I have Reid Hamilton's cell phone number and we are going out to dinner later this evening.

Life is good.

Abbie

"Girls! Are you coming?"

I'm standing at the bottom of the stairs waiting for the girls to come down so we can leave. Of course, my eldest cannot leave the house unless every hair is in place and her entire outfit is coordinated, right down to a scarf that she has most likely snatched from my bedroom closet. My youngest on the other hand, can't even be bothered to comb her hair so I have to wonder what is taking her so long.

I walk upstairs, frustrated and impatient, and walk into Hannah's room. As expected, she is standing in front of the mirror holding two scarves up to her chin, trying to decide which one to wear. She turns to me, still holding them up.

"Mom, which one?"

I squelch a sigh and do my best to offer her an honest opinion. "The yellow one. It looks great against your skin." Though I have to wonder why in the world she wants to wear a scarf in this heat. She is such a diva.

She turns back to the mirror and inspects herself with only the yellow one close to her body. She nods, apparently satisfied with my opinion. As she's wrapping the scarf around her neck, I turn to leave, intent on finding my youngest daughter.

"Caroline? Where are you honey?"

From deep in the play room, I hear her sweet voice. "In here, mommy!"

It takes me a moment to locate her within the dimly lit room but when I finally do, I have to giggle. She has buried herself underneath a mountain of stuffed animals and all I can see is her head sticking out from between last year's Christmas Belkie bear and a ginormous rabbit that she got last year from the Easter bunny. I whip my phone out from the pocked of my

31

shorts and slide my finger across the screen to unlock it and find the camera.

"Hold still," I say. "Lemme take a picture."

She giggles, but remains still enough for me to catch this moment and preserve it digitally. I help her out of the pile of softness and give her a hug simply because she is just so darn cute.

"You ready to go?"

She nods. "Can I get a cheeseburger?"

"If they have them," I reply cautiously. One of the first lessons I learned as a parent is to never promise anything you can't be 100% certain you can deliver. Since I have no control over the menu at the restaurant, I'm not about to promise anything, lest it be held against me for days.

"Why wouldn't they have cheeseburgers?" Her face scrunches up in confusion since her mind simply cannot comprehend the fact that any restaurant would opt to not serve her favorite food.

"Well, this place is known for its chicken wings, so I'm just not sure. Most likely they'll have cheeseburgers but I don't want you to be upset if they don't. I'm sure they'll have something you'll like."

She ponders this for a moment and then nods. "Okay," she says.

The girls and I load somehow manage to climb into the minivan and as we wait for Reid to join us, the fighting begins.

It's Hannah who begins this round.

"Caroline, didn't you brush your hair?" Instead of sounding like a simple question, her tone is accusatory and filled with disgust. I groan inwardly, knowing this is the tone that sets her sister off every single time.

"We're only going out to eat. It's not a fancy place. Right mom?" And there it is: Tag, you're it mom. Step in and take sides. Tell one of your children that they're wrong and the other they're right. The only problem is, in this case, Hannah is right. Caroline should probably have brushed her hair but quite frankly, it wasn't a battle I was willing to fight today. I fumble through my pocketbook and locate a scrunchie. Reaching back toward Caroline, I place it into her tiny hand.

"Here," I say. "Put your hair in a ponytail. Then we don't even have to have this discussion."

Unbelievably, she does as I ask without another word. Reid hops in the driver's seat and we're off. When we pull into the restaurant, I take Hannah off to the side while Reid walks slowly ahead of us, Caroline skipping along beside him while she holds onto his hand.

I lean down to Hannah so that we're eye to eye. "I need you to stop mothering her, all right?"

"But-" I know what she's going to say. That Caroline needs to comb her hair, and I know that. But that's not the issue here.

"Stop," I say, holding up my hand. "I'm the mother, all right. I've been doing this job now for ten years. I've got this. If I ever need an assistant, I'll let you know. But for now, you need to monitor yourself, not your sister. Got it?"

She nods.

"Now. Let's go get something to eat."

We walk together into the restaurant, Hannah walking beside me. She doesn't hold my hand as Caroline normally does and it saddens me. This is a relatively new thing and I feel the pinch of it every time we walk side by side. She feels old enough to be embarrassed to be seen holding hands with her mother. Thankfully, I have another child who still lets me.

I lead the way to the back of the restaurant, following the boisterous noise that can only be a large group of people. Sure enough, we walk into a small room just off the main bar section and there is a group of people seated together at a large table. Reid and Hannah are seated together at one end of the table and there are two empty seats across from them. We walk over and join the group.

I catch Reid's eye and he raises his eyebrows, asking me if

everything is okay with Hannah. I smile and nod, telling him that I've got it under control. As we sit, Reid begins the introductions. Closest to Caroline is Jim Cooper, who works in accounting at K&M. Beside him is his wife Natalie. At the far end of the table, Steve Baker sits beside his wife Carol. I move closer to Carol and give her the hug I always greet her with. She and Steve have only recently moved here from Michigan and the four of us have become quite close, going out to dinner on more than one occasion.

"Carol," I say warmly, "How are you?"

"I'm good," she replies. "How are the girls?"

"They're wonderful. Though Hannah continues to think she's the mother in the house."

She smiles at me and her expression tells me she understands all too well. Though her children are older and have moved out of their house, I'm certain a mother never forgets the years when fighting between siblings runs rampant. "Have you met Rose?" She asks, indicating the woman sitting beside her.

"I don't think so," I reply. I extend my hand to Rose and she shakes it. "You work for Reid, right? Wait. You're Rosemary, aren't you?"

She smiles and nods. "Yes. But please, call me Rose. When you say 'Rosemary,' people tend to look for a condiment."

"Well, Rose," I say, repeating her name so I can remember it. "it's always nice to meet the people that somehow manage to put up with my husband all day long. I hope he's not too hard on you." I giggle, knowing that Reid is perhaps the nicest person in the world to work for, as evidenced by the fact that when we do go out, it's normally with several of his employees. It seems they all generally like him.

"Well, he can be tough," she says, smiling. "But somehow I manage to make it through each day."

"Ah," I reply. "Well, it's very nice to meet you." I then pull out a chair and sit down beside Rose, who is on my right.

Hannah is to my left and Reid and Caroline are across the table from me. We pick up our menus and peruse the selections. I quickly glance to the children's section and see that they do, in fact, offer a cheeseburger and I sigh with relief. Reid catches my gaze when he hears my sigh and he smiles, knowing that I've just located one of the few items on the menu that our daughter will eat without complaint. I make a few suggestions to Hannah that are quickly dismissed. I give up and focus on the menu in front of me, trying to figure out what I'd like to eat.

The conversation swirls around me. Because these people all work together, the topics stay focused on work for several minutes. Carol takes this opportunity to lean forward and strike up a conversation.

"What's new with you? Anything?"

"Well," I say, smiling. "I did find another house that I think might make an ideal project for me."

"Really?" Carol squeals. "Where is it?"

"It's over off Smithfield Road, just before you get to the section that's really rundown."

"Abbie flips houses," Carol says to Rose, who up until now has been reviewing her menu. She looks up and me and smiles.

"Really," she says. "You actually buy run down houses and fix them up? What are you, a contractor or something?"

"God, no!" I'm quick to answer. "Nothing like that. I honestly think I just got lucky with my first flip. Carol is being a bit overzealous in her description."

Carol jumps in. "Don't let her fool you, Rosie. She may have only done one house but it was gorgeous!"

I feel my cheeks redden as I'm not accustomed to hearing accolades. This whole house flipping thing was just a chance thing. Reid and I happened to be driving around town one Sunday afternoon and spotted the dilapidated old house. Knowing my love of all things HGTV, he dared me to flip it. When I researched the house and found out how little they were asking for it, I thought I might give it a shot. Luckily, the structure of the house was sound and all I really needed to do was cosmetic work.

I turn back to Rose. "I'm really just starting to get into it," I explain. "See, this is what happens when you're a stay at home mom and you watch too much HGTV."

"Come on," Carol interjects, "Your first flip was incredible! You know it was." She turns to Rose and begins to tell her about my first flip, waving her hands around excitedly. "Abbie found this run down house over by the office. It was in an older section of town and it had been neglected for what? Three years?"

She looks at me for confirmation and I nod.

Carol continues. "So this house had apparently been sitting there unlived in for all that time. The outside was horrific—weeds, dirt piles, long grass, dilapidated fence—just awful. The inside looked even worse. But the thing is, it was all cosmetic. Abbie went in there over the course of a couple of months and repainted everything, put in new laminate flooring on the first level and worked on the yard. Before she knew it, she had a buyer!"

"Really?" Rose asks, turning to me. I nod. "That's pretty impressive."

I wave my hand around dismissively. "Anyone can do it if they have the time."

"I doubt that," Carol says, "I saw what you did to the inside of that place. It was gorgeous when you were done with it. When Steve and I finally buy our house, you're helping me decorate."

"Deal," I reply, smiling.

The waitress comes to take our order and since the place appears to be getting busy, we order our drinks and food at once. Once she takes our menus away, Rose angles her body to me.

"So," she says, nodding to Hannah and Caroline. "These

are your daughters?"

"Yes," I reply. "Hannah is ten and Caroline is eight."

"They're gorgeous." Rose says, smiling at them.

"Thanks. I think so but I'm biased."

She chuckles.

The waitress places our drinks in front of us. "So how long have you worked for Reid?"

"Umm…about six months."

"And do you like it?" I pause, almost cringing. "I'm sorry. That came out all wrong. What I meant is do you like marketing, not whether or not you liked working for my husband."

"It's fine," Rose replies. "But yes. I do like marketing. And I actually like working for Reid. He's got so much experience in this field and I've got a ton to learn."

As Rose is speaking to me, I notice her glance down the table at Reid. Her gaze lingers on him for just a fraction of a moment longer than I'm comfortable with. And if that weren't enough, her eyes soften ever so slightly and it's then that it occurs to me that maybe, just maybe, this woman is attracted to my husband. I follow her gaze and glance down the table at my husband, who is oblivious to the stares from this woman and I feel myself calm. The feeling I have is fleeting, barely more than a second or so but in that instant, I begin to look at her differently. I look at her as an attractive woman instead of just another one of Reid's employees. And while I've done my very best to keep myself looking good, I've realize I've only maintained the status of "looking good for my age" as opposed to simply looking good. Gone is the youthful, smooth skin and effortless slenderness I had in my twenties. Not that I'm complaining mind you. I have two beautiful children and the battle wounds to prove it. But still, when faced with someone who is much younger than me, spends nearly every day with husband, and looks at him with the awe and admiration of someone who has never cleaned his clothes, been with him during a road trip or seen him sick as a dog and unable to make it to the toilet to vomit, it gives you just a moment when you wonder, "Do I need to worry about this?" But then I glance back at Rose and see that her gaze has left Reid and she's smiling at me so genuinely that I actually feel guilty for thinking my earlier thoughts. This woman is lovely. She really is.

I'm just being paranoid.

I turn my attention back to Rose and the conversation at hand. "Reid has been doing this for close to twenty years. And he loves what he does. I'm sure he's a great person to learn from."

She nods. "Absolutely." Rose takes a small sip from her glass. "So tell me about the house-flipping you're doing. How'd you get into it?"

"Well," I say. "I've been a stay at home mom since Hannah was born and now that the girls are getting older, I wanted to do something with my time but didn't want to return to work full-time. It was actually Reid who suggested the whole house-flip thing."

Rose raises her eyebrows and I chuckle.

"I know, right? But once he suggested it, I kept thinking about it and it seemed like a good idea. When the girls are in school, I can do all the work on the house. I spent all my time at Home Depot, looking at light fixtures, flooring, tile…you name it. I just worked on the house, trying to make it livable and before I knew it, I had a buyer."

"So, you're doing another one now?"

I nod. "We just found another house and made the purchase. I'm not sure what's involved yet and that's the scary part. Whenever you do something like this, you never know what you're going to find. There may be structural damage, electrical issues, foundation cracks. If there's any of those things, it'll cost me more to fix and then I need to sell it for a higher price in order to make a profit."

"Wow," Rose says. "Sounds stressful."

"It is at the beginning," I reply. "But once I'm in the thick of decorating it, it's really more fun than stress."

"Gotcha."

Our food arrives and I busy myself with making sure the girls have all they need. Caroline's cheeseburger needs to be cut in half and Hannah requires ranch dressing—for what, I have no idea since she ordered pizza.

"You're Caroline, right?" Rose asks my youngest.

Caroline nods, knowing not to speak when her mouth is full. She chews vigorously while she nods, a sure sign she's got something to say. She swallows, then takes a sip of water. "I'm eight."

"Wow," Rose replies. "You're almost to double digits."

A look of confusion crosses Caroline's face and she glances toward me, looking for an explanation. "She means you're nearly ten years old. Two numbers—one and zero."

"Ohhhhh," she replies, and a look of understanding crosses her face.

"Do you like cheeseburgers?" Rose asks, pointing her Caroline's half empty plate.

Caroline nods vigorously. "They're my favorite, right mom?"

I smile. "Right." Turning to Rose, I say, "She'd eat them every day if I let her."

Rose grins, then returns her gaze to Caroline. "I'll tell you a secret," she says.

Caroline looks at her, eyes wide and thrilled to be included.

"Cheeseburgers are still my favorite," she says. "In fact, I eat them every chance I get."

"Why didn't you get a cheeseburger tonight," Caroline asks, glancing down at Rose's plate.

Rose looks side to side surreptitiously, as though about to reveal some deep, dark secret. She leans closer to Caroline and whispers. "I ate one for lunch. Extra cheese."

Caroline smiles at her and I know she's thrilled to have something in common with an adult.

Rose turns to me and claps her hands together as she squeals. "She's is so adorable!"

"Thanks," I reply. "You just made her night, by the way. She's thrilled to have something in common with one of the grownups."

"Really?" She says. "That's awesome." She reaches across the table at holds her hand, palm up to my daughter. "To cheeseburgers."

Caroline raised her hand to slap Rose's palm and repeats, "To cheeseburgers!"

"I think you and I are going to be great friends," Rose says to Caroline, which prompts the biggest smile I've seen all day. My daughter returns to her cheeseburger and fries and Rose turns to me.

"Are you on Facebook?" she asks.

I nod. She pulls out her phone and opens her Facebook account. She searches my name and then taps her finger to the screen. "There," she says. "I just friended you."

"Okay." I pull my phone out from my pocket and swipe my finger across the screen so that I can 'friend' Rose back.

Her phone pings and she looks down at it, then back up at me. "Awesome. Will you post pictures of the house you're flipping?"

"Sure," I reply.

"Great. I really want to see what you're doing with this one. I watch HGTV all the time too and I'm always amazed at the stuff they come up with."

I nod. "Honestly, that's where I get most of my ideas from. I don't have the imagination to come up with stuff on my own. I need someone to get the idea first, then I either copy it or tweak it so it works for my project."

"Do you think I could come out sometime and see the house?"

Carol leans in. "Ooh! Can I come? I want to see it too!"

I laugh. "Sure. You can both come. But give me a bit of time. It's still in an unlivable state. Let me work on it for a month or so, then I'll take you there."

"Sounds like a plan," Carol replies.

"Let me give you my cell number," Rose says to me. "What's your number? I'll text you and you'll have my number."

I tell Rose my number and shortly thereafter, my phone pings, alerting me to a new text. "That you?" I ask.

"Yup. Just call or text if you ever feel like showing off the house. I'd love to see it."

"Hey," Carol interjects. "You wanna go shopping with us next weekend? We're heading to Greensboro to check out the Christmas Tree shop."

"Christmas Tree shop?" I ask. "But it's July."

Carol and Rose look at each other knowingly. "No," Carol explains. "The store isn't just for Christmas stuff; it's all sorts of stuff for the house—curtains, lamps, knick-nacks, small furniture, food - all at unbelievable prices."

I shrug. "All right. I'm game."

"Great!" Rose says. "I'll text you the deets once we figure it out."

"Deets?" I ask.

Carol chuckles. "Youth," she says, nodding toward Rose. "When she talks like that, I realize how old I am."

"You are not!" Rose cries, wrapping her arm around Carol's shoulders. "Age is a state of mind and you are most certainly not old."

Carol looks at me and grins. "You see why I like her so much? She keep me young."

I laugh as I look at these two women, separated in age by more than twenty years and I silently chastise myself for my earlier thoughts. Rose has been nothing but nice to me and I can't help but feel guilty for thinking she might have any sort of feelings other than respect and admiration for my husband.

I find I'm looking forward to our shopping day the following weekend. It will be great to spend some time with Carol and I think I'm really going to enjoy getting to know Rose.

The remainder of our dinner passes swiftly. The men continue to talk about work until I notice Caroline nearly falling asleep at the table. I catch Reid's eye and nod toward our daughter. He smiles at her and then nods at me, telling me he's ready to go. We pay the bill, say our goodbye's, and then get up to leave. Reid picks up a very sleepy Caroline and carries her to the car. Much to my delight, Hannah is feeling tired as well and walks with me toward the car with her arm wrapped around my waist. Though I know it's because she's tired, I'm thrilled. It's so rare than she leans on me for anything that I've learned to savor these moments as they come. Reid gently places Caroline into her seat and pulls the seatbelt around her and snaps it into place. She adjusts herself in such a ways that is a clear indication she'll be asleep before we even leave the parking lot. Hannah climbs in next to her sister and leans her head back against the seat. While she may not fall asleep in the car, I can tell putting her to bed tonight will be quite easy and without any sort of argument. Reid climbs into the driver's seat and turns the A/C on full blast, wanting to rid the car of the humidity.

"Did you have a good time tonight?" He asks.

"You know, I really did. It was great to see Carol again. We need to have her and Steve over again soon. And I chatted with Rose a bit. She tells me you're a bit of a slave driver."

"She did not!" He says, pretending to be appalled.

I grin back at him. "She said you're pretty good to work for. That you know a lot about the field and she can learn a lot from you."

I can see him smile in the darkness and I know he's flattered. "I hope she doesn't think I'm going to reveal all my secrets. Wouldn't want her to think she can have my job or anything." He turns to wink at me and I chuckle.

"Like that's gonna happen. We both know that no one is taking your job unless you decide to give it up, which you won't. You love that job and you're great at it."

Reid is silent for a moment. "I hope you don't mind that I invited one of my employees."

"You mean Rose? Not at all. Why would I mind?"

He shrugs. "Oh, I don't know. Maybe having an employee there would change the dynamic? Might make dinner a bit less comfortable?"

I shake my head. "Nah. It was fine. Rose seems very nice. Actually, she and Caroline bonded over cheeseburgers."

"Really?" He says, glancing at me out of the corner of his eye. "That's good. " He pauses for a moment as though pondering something. "Yeah," he says nodding, "I'm glad I invited Rose. Poor girl has been through a bit of a rough patch recently."

"Really? How so?" I ask.

"She was dating some intern and she thought things were going really well. I guess she really liked him but then he dumped her last night. She was in my office today crying."

"Oh no," I say. "Poor girl."

"God, it was awful," Reid says. "I wanted to review some of the things I worked on last night and before I knew it, she was sobbing. Tears were streaming down her face and she was telling me the whole thing. I didn't know what to do so I just sat there."

I nod knowingly. Reid is one of those strong men who relishes in his ability to fix a problem. If one of the kids breaks a toy, he can fix it. I need something done, he's right there. But the one thing he's helpless with is someone crying, especially one of his children.

Several years ago, Hannah had one of those fighter fish—the one that can pretty much survive for weeks in a cup of moldy water. The only thing you really need to do is feed the damn thing—and not even all that often! But that is something Hannah neglected to do. When the fish died, after God-only-knows how long of going without food, she was inconsolable. I'd never seen Reid so distraught. Simply not being able to fix something for his child was nearly unbearable for him.

"God, Abbie. You should have seen her. She was a total mess. I seriously considered calling you but I wasn't sure how to pick up the phone and call you without looking like an insensitive clod. But really, what did she think I was going to do?"

"Who knows," I reply. "Maybe she just felt the need to explain to you what had happened so you'd understand if she wasn't quite herself today?"

"I have no idea. I just hope it doesn't happen again. I have no desire to have a sobbing employee in my office."

"We can only hope."

We complete the drive home and as expected, Caroline is sound asleep. Reid picks her up gently and carries her into the house. Hannah is groggy but I manage to coax her out of the car and help her into the house. Once she's settled in bed, I check on Caroline who, while under the covers, is still in the clothes she wore to dinner. I kiss her gently on the forehead and make my way back downstairs to find Reid pouring two glasses of wine. I take one from him and walk into the living room. Reid follows me and sits down beside me, wrapping one arm around my shoulders and pulling me close to him.

"I'm sorry I've had so much work lately."

I place my glass on the coffee table in front of us and curl my knees underneath me so that I'm tucked in closely beside him. "It's okay. I know you're doing all of this for us."

"I am," he says. "I hope you know that."

"Of course I do. Besides, when you work a ton, you always make it up to us. I know that. The girls know that. Believe me, we know how hard you work."

"I just miss all of you so much when I have to travel. But there's no getting around it. If I'm the lead on a project, they need me there for the presentation, the signing of the contract, every time there's a change in the campaign…"

I sense there's more to this than he's letting on. "Is this your way of telling me you've got a lot of travel coming up?"

He sighs softly. "I'm afraid so. It's going to be pretty bad for the next few months. You up for it?"

"Do I have a choice?" He looks at me with such an expression of sheer horror that I feel bad for joking about it. "Reid," I say, taking his face in my hands. "I'm kidding. You know that when we got married, I knew you'd always have to travel. It's fine. We'll manage."

"I know you will," he says, pulling me in for a kiss. "It's just for a little while, all right?"

"I know, babe. Just don't worry about us when you're on the road, ok? Focus on what you're doing and then you'll be home before you know it."

"Yes ma'am!" He replies, grinning.

We sit there silently for several moments while we sip from our glasses. I'm not sure what Reid is thinking but I'm hoping he's not still worried about his upcoming travel. This is one of the reasons we decided that I would stay home with the girls. He travels. Always has. Always will. Many days, he just can't call in sick to stay home with one of our kids. It's not like if he's in California, he can make it home early. He's at the mercy of the airlines, and they really don't give a shit that he's got a sick kid at home. Our set up may not work for everyone but it works for us. I pull all the shifts when he's out of town or working on some major project and he pulls any shift I need him for when he's home. Like next Saturday, when I'll be shopping with Carol and Rose, which reminds me…

"Oh, I forgot to mention…"

"Forgot to mention what?"

"Carol and Rose invited me to go shopping with them next

Saturday. I hope you don't have any plans then."

"Nope. I'll be here. Maybe I'll take the girls to a movie or something."

"Perfect. They'll love that."

"And then the travel begins…"

"So you're here all week?" I ask.

He nods.

"Good," I say, snuggling closer into his chest. "We'll have all week before you take your tour of duty. I can get my fill of you before you take off." I begin kiss his neck and nibble on his ear. When I hear him moan, I know that he's on the same page as I am. Together, we stand and walk toward our bedroom. I lift my shirt off over my head and toss it playfully in his direction. When I pull my bra off, he growls, then tosses me onto the bed. He makes quick work of eliminating me from the rest of my clothing. As he stands to remove his pants, I sit up and take him into my mouth, causing him to shudder.

"Abbie," he says, "if you keep that up, I'm not going to last."

I smile, but release him and lie back on the bed. Reid kneels in front of me and begins to kiss me from my inner thigh upward. When he reaches the center, I gasp. He brings me to brink of orgasm and then pulls away, leaving me wanting more. Within mere seconds, he is inside of me and his lips find mine. I wrap my arms around him as he moves inside of me, slowly at first, then quicker. As our breathing quickens, so do our movements. Reid thrusts inside of me one last time as he comes and I follow only moments after. Our breathing is labored and we sound like we've just run a marathon. He looks down at me and smiles, then kisses me gently on the lips.

"I love you, Abbie Hamilton."

"And I love you, Reid Hamilton," I reply.

Like every other time we've made love, Reid stays inside of me for several moments. It in only because I feel the urge to pee that I shift my hips slightly to let him know I need to move.

"Gotta pee?" He says.

I chuckle. God, this man knows me so well.

"Yup."

And then I hear it, the tiny sigh that I have become so accustomed to hearing. The sigh that tells me still, after all these years of marriage, that my husband does not want to leave me. It is that sigh that tells me we are still strong, we are still together, no matter what.

Rose

Despite my initial reservations, dinner last night with Reid, his family and the others from K&M was actually quite fun. Though I didn't get to speak to Reid much –Okay, not at all—I did get to spend a good amount of time talking to his wife.

It was somewhat of a surprise to finally meet her. I mean, obviously I thought she'd be this overweight, unkempt woman who'd latched onto Reid and now that she'd had his children and had lost any attractiveness, was now clinging to her marriage with both hands. Truth be told, my assessment couldn't have been further from the truth.

Dammit! But that only means I've got to step up my game even more.

Abbie Hamilton was put together quite nicely and even I had to admit that the large, silver hoop earrings she wore were a nice touch. Though I did wonder if it was merely her attempt to draw attention away from her face and the tiny wrinkles I spotted around her eyes.

She's tall, probably three or four inches taller than me with dark brown hair that, despite her advanced age, shines when the light hits it. Well, she probably colors it to hide all the gray she has. Still, though. She manages to clean up nicely. Her body isn't bad either. She's managed to keep herself in pretty good shape but then again, I'm sure she's lost some of the flexibility those of us still in our youth seem to hold onto effortlessly.

But what was so striking to me was how she looked when she stood next to Reid. It was weird and I hate to admit it, but the two of them looked…well, nice together.

It nearly made me vomit. Seeing the two of them walking together with their two perfect children was nearly unbearable. I'm just glad she didn't sit beside him all night. I can only imagine what it would feel like if they held hands or even worse, if she placed her hand on his arm or (gasp!) his thigh. I most definitely would've had to leave. That would have been the breaking point for me. I mean, knowing he's married is one thing. I know she exists. But to see them together in the flesh? It's just too much to take.

I have to admit that the Facebook thing was pure brilliance on my part. Since we are now friends, I can look at everything she's ever posted on her page. And if she's like most people, I can tell by her posts what kind of mood she's in, or even if she's fighting with Reid. That type of information would be just what I need to make headway with him. I mean, it doesn't take a genius to figure out that if she's pissed at him for traveling too much, I just have to say something like how beneficial it is that he travels. If she's pissed at him for something, you just need to subtly show him that it wouldn't bother *you*. I don't think there's a woman out there who hasn't seen or heard of "that guy" who complains about his wife. The woman he chooses to spend his time with next is the woman who can sympathize with him and show him that whatever it is that's bothering his wife surely wouldn't bother *her*....

So after I arrive home, I toss my purse and keys on the table and grab my laptop so I can do a little reconnaissance work on her facebook page. First, I create a post about my great dinner and tag Abbie and Carol. Then, it's time for my research to begin. I check out all her pictures and find more pictures than I care to recall of she and Reid. It seems they somehow manage to take a vacation alone at least once a year. Even I know that's bad news for me. We all know those couples who manage to vacation alone simply for the purpose of reconnecting with each other and keeping the flame alive or whatever crap they tell themselves. Unfortunately, it does tend to work and I'm going to need to work even harder to get Reid to notice me.

In addition of the pics of Abbie and Reid in numerous vacation spots, there were several photos of the two of them with their daughters. There were pictures of them cutting down a Christmas tree each year, the four of them at the beach, at Hannah's soccer game and even some of them at Caroline's school. It seems like the four of them pretty much do everything together. This makes me think that when Reid is home, he spends all his free time with his family.

Once I've gone through every picture (and several bottles of beer) Abbie has posted to her page, I begin to look at her posts. I spend the better part of an hour reviewing every post she's made for the past three years. While I do realize there are some people who don't post much of their personal lives on Facebook, I'm still dismayed to realize that Abbie has never posted a single irritation she might have about her husband. There are none of those cartoons that poke fun at lazy husbands, or bad fathers. Nothing that even hints at how great women are and how they'd be just fine without their men. There isn't a hint of that Susan Faludi crap anywhere on her page! I mean, come on. Not even a joke about how men are helpless without their women? Is this woman for real? Is it possible that she's still in love with her husband after…what? ten or so years of marriage?

Then a thought occurs to me. Is it possible that Reid feels the same way? Does he actually love his wife? Find her attractive? Enjoy spending time with her?

God. That would suck.

It never occurred to me that Reid might be on Facebook as well but as I look through Abbie's friend list, I find him. I click on the 'Add Friend' button knowing that once he accepts, I'll be able to review his page as well. Then I'll have an even better understanding of what makes him tick.

I realize that Reid may not respond right away since it's the weekend. Besides, after getting a good look at Abbie's Facebook pictures, I feel certain he's spending time with his family. Then again, he does have a smart phone, which means that the Facebook app is probably on it. If so, he may see the friend request at any moment since I know Reid doesn't even go to the bathroom without his phone. (Hey, it's all part of the due diligence process. Don't judge!)

While I'm waiting to receive the notice that Reid has accepted my friend request, I begin to peruse Abbie's pictures again. I go back to the earliest ones and find pictures of Hannah and Caroline from when they were both just babies. As I scroll through, I find a picture of Reid holding one of his children when they are teeny-tiny. I'm guessing whatever kid he was holding was only a few days old. He's holding her in his hands away from his chest so that he can look down at her. She appears to be so tiny and delicate in his large hands that I have to chuckle. It's almost comical how small she looks in those hands.

Then I look at the expression on Reid's face as he is looking at his newborn daughter. His face is gleaming with so much love for this little person that it makes my chest squeeze and though I didn't think it possible, it makes me love him just a little bit more. This is a man who loves his children. How can I not be completely in love with him? How can I not want to spend the rest of my life with him? After seeing that picture, I realize I will never give up pursuing him. I love him. We are meant to be together and I'm going to do everything in my power to make sure we end up together.

Abbie Hamilton be damned.

Abbie

Hannah and Caroline have been at each other's throats all week. It's all I can do to referee their arguments. By Friday night, I'm frustrated and exhausted and after putting the girls to bed early, I find myself in the kitchen pouring a rather large glass of wine. Reid comes up behind me and wraps his arms around my waist with his palms flat against my stomach, which reminds me of how he used to hold me each time I was pregnant. His hands would cover my entire belly, that is, until my belly grew to ten times its normal size.

I sigh, then lean back against his chest and close my eyes.

"Rough week?"

"Yeah. The girls have been fighting non-stop."

"I'm sorry. I guess I've been pre-occupied with all the work I have."

"You have been in your office a bit much this week." I turn to face him and wrap my arms around his neck.

"I'm out now," he replies, grinning. "And I can't help but notice the children aren't around."

"I put them to bed early," I whisper. His arms reach up under my shirt and work their way around to my chest. He takes each of my breasts gently in his hands and squeezes.

"Reid," I giggle. "I just put the kids to bed. They're probably still awake."

"They you'll just have to be quiet," he replies as he gently nibbles the sensitive skin on the side of my neck.

I lean my head back in order to give him easier access and whisper, "I shall do my best."

There is something a bit different when we make love that night. It's almost imperceptible and perhaps I'm being a bit paranoid but I feel as though this week—the final week Reid will be home before his hectic travel begins—is the end of something. I'm not even sure what I mean by all of this—like I said, I'm probably just being paranoid—but tonight, I cling to him just a bit more tightly and when we finish, I let Reid stay inside of me for as long as he wants. After several minutes of silence, he looks at me questioningly.

"You all right?" He asks.

I nod. "I'm just feeling a little off with all the travel you've got coming up."

Slowly, he pulls out of me, pulls on his boxers and sits on the bed beside me. "I won't go," he says. "Abbie, if you're not feeling good about this, I won't go."

I sit up abruptly. "No, Reid. That's not what I meant at all. I guess I'm just…I don't know, a bit worried maybe? I mean, I'm used to your traveling all the time. I really am. It's just this time, I'm feeling a bit sad. Like you're going to be gone longer than before maybe?" I sigh heavily. "Oh, shit. Who knows? Maybe I'm just getting sappy in my old age."

He grins, then pulls me into his arms. "Maybe you just love your husband so much that you can't bear for him to be out of your sight for even a moment. Maybe the thought of him being away from you is just too much to bear, maybe-"

"Nope," I interject, giggling. "That can't be it."

"No?" He asks. He makes a mock look of confusion and scratches the top of his head with his finger. "Huh. I felt certain I'd nailed it."

"Oh, you nailed it, all right," I retort, thinking of the mind-blowing orgasm I'd experienced moments ago.

At hearing that, his chest puffs out. He lifts up his hand and blows on the tips of his fingers, then mimics wiping them off on his chest. "Yup," he says, "I've still got it."

"Oh my God, Reid! You are impossible!"

"But you still love me, right?" He asks.

"Sadly, I do."

He pulls back the covers and crawls under, then motions for

me to do the same. He holds his arms out, indicating I should curl up next to him, something we only do when neither of us has to wake up the early the next morning. While the position is comfortable and enables us to share pillow talk, it's not really conducive to a good night's sleep since Reid snores horribly when he lies on his back. I lie down beside him and rest my hand across his stomach.

"You sure you're okay?" He asks.

I nod. "Don't worry about me. I'll be fine. Really."

"Promise?"

"I promise."

"I love you, Abbie."

"I love you more," comes the automatic reply. I smile because I know what's coming next. "I'm bigger."

Rose

I can't stand this fucking heat.

It's the middle of September and still the simple act of walking into the office from my car causes my hair to frizz and my face to look like I've bathed in olive oil. It makes me wonder why I moved to North Carolina when New Jersey was much cooler.

Oh, right. My hometown was a hell-hole, filled with nothing but tattoo parlors and liquor stores. I couldn't wait to get out of there. Plus, there was that little incident with one of my former teachers. Apparently having sex in the classroom of one of your college professors is frowned upon. And when your professor's wife walks into the room, sees her husband having sex with one of his student's, then files a complaint with the Dean of Students, you're lucky to graduate. And said professor is lucky to have his job at Starbucks.

I can't say that if I were in her shoes, I wouldn't be upset. Of course, I would be. But would I have made all the fuss she did? I doubt it. I, at least, would have maintained a bit of composure and not gone off my rocker like some crazy person. Man, the way she screamed at me? Completely ridiculous. Besides, her anger should have been focused on her husband since he was one who pursued me. Okay, maybe I was a little bit more receptive to his advances than I should have been but who can blame me? I happen to find older men attractive. Besides, if he was happy at home, he wouldn't be looking elsewhere, now would he?

But I digress. The fact of the matter is that I did move to North Carolina and I'm not going anywhere anytime soon—not while Reid Hamilton is in my line of vision each and every day.

God, that man is so fucking sexy. I really don't know how Abbie lets him go to work every day looking like he does. But I guess she's got to. After all, someone has to bring in a paycheck. It's not like she's going to provide for her family doing that silly little house-flipping thing she does. She might as well run a bake sale every week for the amount of money she'll bring in.

Despite the oppressive heat, I manage to walk into the office without melting but I can feel the wetness between my thighs and under my arms. I simply cannot have pit stains when I'm about to see Reid. I take a slight detour and head into the ladies room to check my reflection before heading to my desk. When I see what I look like, I'm grateful that K&M has a restroom just off the front lobby, which enables me to check my appearance before any chance run-in with Reid.

When I left my apartment this morning, I was a reasonably attractive woman. My hair was straight, thanks to a recent flat-iron purchase and my skin was free of any blemishes and was looking rosy and delicious. Now, I see my brown hair has started to frizz at the ends and my forehead and nose are so shiny, I swear I can see my reflection there. But not to worry. I reach into my purse and pull out a clip for my hair. I twist it up and of my neck and secure it with the clip. I pull a few loose strands out around my ears and my neck, trying to make it look natural and sexy at the same time. The restroom unfortunately has those hideous brown, horribly scratchy hand towels so I pull out a few of those and use them to blot my skin, trying to absorb as much oil as I can. When I'm somewhat satisfied with my attempt, I retrieve my compact from the inside pocket of my purse and begin to blot my forehead and nose, taking extra care not to leave it looking caked or flaky. I add a touch of gloss to my lips then survey myself in the mirror, nodding at the improvement I've made with just a few simple steps. Now I'm ready to head to work.

Because I work so closely with Reid, I'm privy to his

schedule. I basically know where he is at all times. I find this unbelievably advantageous. Of course, because I'm privy to all this information, I also know that this week will be his last in the office for a good deal of time. Sure, he'll be in the office for a day or two here and there but for the most part, he will be on the road, traveling to all parts of the country, flying home each weekend to spend time with his family.

That just doesn't work for me. It doesn't work at all. I simply cannot stand the fact that Abbie will get to spend more time with him than I will. Having him in the office with me every day means I know what he's thinking and what he's doing. I know what sort of day he's having and what I can do to make his day better. The more time I spend with him, the better I get to know him, and that's the ultimate goal—to know him better than anyone.

This whole travel thing is just throwing a wrench into my plans. Not that my plans are going anywhere, mind you, but I'm not ready to give up. All I need is more time with him. More time to get to know him, to show him how much we have in common, more time to show him how great we'd be together. Clearly, this spending time in the office together thing isn't working as I'd like it to. Reid and I are still exactly where we were when I started working for him nearly six months ago. Sure, we talk and spend countless hours together but there still has not been a single episode of sexual banter. Not a single lingering gaze. Not even the tiniest hint of sexual innuendo.

What the hell is wrong with him? Despite my constant vigilance, we're still sitting pleasantly at DEFCON 5. All is stable and peaceful in the land.

Well, this just won't do. Clearly, I'm going to have to step up my game. And first things first: I've got to figure out a way to be with Reid outside of the office.

And I think I just might have an idea.

Abbie

The past few weeks have been incredibly hectic in our house. Reid has been traveling to so many time zones, I can't even believe he knows what day it is. Hannah and Caroline don't seem to be too affected by his travel but I think it's mainly because most nights he's away, we all pile into the king sized bed in the master bedroom to sleep. We all gather together under the comforter and find ourselves all bundled together in a tangle of limbs. I've just found it's easier to get the kids up for school in the mornings if they're both lying right beside me. Of course, this arrangement isn't ideal for our English bulldog, who likes to sleep under the covers with plenty of space. When there's too many limbs for him to deal with, he gets a little cranky and sounds like a grumpy old man who's trying to get up after being seated for too long.

After non-stop travel for the past three weeks, Reid arrived home late last night instead of the usual mid-afternoon arrival time. The girls were already in bed and while he missed seeing them and putting them to bed, their need for sleep allowed us to reconnect with each other after him being away for several days. We sat on the couch for an hour or so while he told me about his travel for the week. After we'd had a glass of wine, we realized it was past midnight so we crawled into bed and both slept soundly all night.

It always surprises me that Reid and I can just sit together in a quiet room talking about pretty much nothing. It might sound silly but I like to hear about the minutia that occurs to him while he's traveling—the funny looking guy at the car rental place, the weird mints that were left by the maids in his hotel, even the snotty baby that was in the seat beside him on the way home. I guess it sort of makes me feel like I'm there with him.

We speak often about what it will be like when the girls are older and I'm able to travel with him. That's the thing about Reid; he's a planner. He's got goals that reach out ten and twenty years. The one goal he's committed to involves us moving to some sort of beachy, golf community. And while that sounds unbelievably perfect, I don't want to wish away one minute of the time I have with my girls. I know that if I blink an eye, they'll be heading off to college or getting married. I can't think that far ahead. Right now, I'm just trying to get through each day. Between lunches, after school activities, and trying to flip this house, I'm swiftly running out of steam.

Hannah and Caroline have really taken an interest in the house I'm flipping. Yes, I'm still flipping the same one I've been working on since the spring. The summer came and went and very little progress was made. Having the girls with me all day during those weeks really limited the amount of time I could spend on it. And I need hours of uninterrupted thought— something practically impossible around here - to figure out what I want to do with this house.

Now that they're back in school, things are moving along nicely. Over dinner each night, I tell the girls what part of the house I'm working and what I'm thinking of doing. If the discussion item sounds the slightest bit appealing to them, they beg me to wait until they are out of school so that they can come with me to pick out paint samples, flooring, or even a new sink. And I don't mind at all. I know that in only a few short years, Hannah will not want to be in the same room with me and Caroline will do the same a few years after that.

As I've worked on the house, I've been taking pictures and posting them to Facebook. When Carol, Rose and I went shopping before the summer, Rose had the idea to post tons of before and after pictures of each room. I have to admit, it was a great idea. Not only will I have the pictures for my own benefit but when someone comes to look at the house, my realtor will be able to show the prospective buyers what it looked like *before*. It seems everyone likes a house all the more when they're able to see the train wreck it used to be. And while once again, I got lucky with my purchase and found no structural problems, this house has been a bit of a nightmare. Probably more the timing than anything else.

Note to self: Do not attempt to renovate a house while your two children are home for the summer. It's not humanly possible.

So while the pictures of the house have been few and far between over the summer, I did manage to post a few. Each time, Rose and Carol would comment on how run-down the place used to be and how much it's improved since I started working on it. They've really been quite encouraging. I'm honestly a bit surprised at how well the three of us get along given the fact that we're all so far apart in age. Rose is in her mid-twenties, I'm in my late thirties, and Carol is well into her fifties. I wonder if we all get along so well because of the industry we're familiar with. Surely the fact that Rose, Reid and Carol's husband work in marketing gives us a common interest. We're all accustomed to the lingo and terminology and can empathize with the stress associated with the quest for new clients and the ever present push to achieve greater notoriety for an ad campaign you had some involvement in. But besides that, we all seem to have the same taste, which was demonstrated during our shopping trip in the spring. Throughout the day we all continued to gravitate to the same items. Rose would pick up a picture or finger a carpet and either Carol or I would be holding the same item the next aisle over. The three of us giggled like a bunch of high school girls each and every time. Since that initial shopping day, the three of us have gotten together for lunch quite a few times and we continue to find we have many of the same tastes. I wonder if I were to visit Rose in her apartment or Carol at her place if we have the same place settings or throw pillows.

While I've known Carol for some time and had her over to the house on several occasions, I didn't really know Rose all that well. But between shopping, dining and her encouraging comments on the pictures of the house I've posted, I'm beginning to like her very much. And I'm glad Reid has her in the office with him because she seems extremely organized. I adore my husband but I also know him extremely well, faults and all. That man would lose his head if it wasn't attached to his body. Having an employee in the office that has a good head on her shoulders will ensure he stays organized. I've even teased Reid on occasion about Rose being his "work wife." I don't think he really appreciated my humor there.

Now that I think about it, I haven't seen either Rose or Carol in a few weeks and I wonder if they'd like to visit the house and see what I've done thus far. Though they've seen the pictures, you can't really gauge what a house looks like until you walk through it. I've got a couple rooms nearly completed and I'd love to see their reaction firsthand.

While I have the thought, I whip out my phone and send a text to both of them asking if they'd like to visit the house and perhaps grab lunch afterward. I toss my phone back into my pocketbook and decide to go upstairs to check on the girls. Before I even make it out of the kitchen, I hear a sound from my phone that tells me that I've gotten a text. Pulling the phone out from my pocketbook, I see the text is from Rose telling me she'd love to see the house. Now hopefully, Carol can join us as well.

As I toss the phone back into my purse, I hear the low rumbling sound our garage door makes and smile as I realize Reid has returned home. He woke up earlier than usual this morning with the grand idea of heading out for donuts for the girls and coffee for the two of us. I thought it was a splendid idea, even better since I rolled over and pulled the covers tightly around me as he got dressed and headed out for the coffee.

Reid walks through the door and sees my still fresh-from-sleep hair and grins at me. He knows I can barely function without caffeine in the morning. Now that I think about it, I may need to re-read the messages I sent to Rose and Carol since I feel certain they're riddled with grammatical and spelling errors. I push that thought from my mind as I take the warm cup from Reid and smell the aroma.

"Ahhh," I say. "I knew there was a reason I kept you around. You bring me coffee. You are a good man, Reid Hamilton." I reach up and pat him on the top of his head, 'good dog' style and walk into the living room, knowing he'll follow.

"You know," he says, sitting down beside me, "I may have to take offense with that statement. I don't only bring you coffee."

I take a long sip from my cup and realize it's exactly the way I like it—extra cream, no sugar—and I grin at my husband. "Even if this is all you did, I'd keep you. This is *delicious* coffee."

"The girls upstairs?" He nods toward the ceiling.

"Yeah." I reply. "Give me another minute before you call them for the donuts. I just want to make sure I have enough caffeine filtering through my veins."

"You are such an addict," he says, grinning.

I hold my hand up to him. "I am a mother of two. Let me have my vice."

He laughs out loud. "I'm going to head up and gather the troops."

I scooch down onto the couch and lean my head back. In this position, I can simply tip my cup of coffee forward in order to drink from it since my head is just above my hips. I rest the cup on top of my chest and take several sips from it, knowing that once the girls arrive, slowly sipping from a cup will become a distant memory. Sure enough, within moments, I hear the unmistakable sound of children's excited feet on the steps. They skid into the kitchen and I hear the sounds of delight as they open the box.

"Chocolate frosted!"

"I want one!" Caroline cries.

"We'll see…." Hannah retorts, a little too quickly for my taste and I can tell she's getting ready to tease Caroline and will most likely suggest that perhaps she won't allow her to have the one donut she has selected. With a groan, I lean forward and propel myself off the couch so that I can referee.

Still holding onto my coffee, I round the corner into the kitchen and see Hannah doling out a donut for herself. Just as she's about to shut the box in an attempt to prevent her sister from getting one, I intervene.

"Hannah, would you get your sister a plate, please?" I fix her a gaze that tells her I knew *exactly* what she was about to do.

She looks back at me with an expression that says "What?!" and I continue to glare at her, then nod to the cabinet where the plates are kept. "Don't give me that look," I say. "Just get your sister a plate so she can have a donut and please, *please,* don't irritate your sister. It's too early for that."

"Too early for what?" Reid asks as he comes into the kitchen. He reaches over Hannah, pulls out a plate and sets it in front of Caroline. She grins, then reaches into the box for a donut.

"Too early for the bickering to begin," I reply.

"Your mother's right," Reid says, taking a large bite of a frosted donut. "Whaddya say we have a moratorium on fighting for today." His mouth is covered in white powder and when he talks, little bits of it float around him, making it look like it's snowing, if only for a second or two.

"What's a 'mor-tor-ium'" Caroline speaks the word slowly, rolling around the syllables in her mouth.

"Moratorium," I reply. "It's when something isn't available."

"Like fighting. For today," Reid interjects. "No fighting today. Can we do that girls?"

They both look at their father and nod. Just then I notice a wad of toilet paper on the counter behind Reid. "What's that?" I ask him, nodding to it.

He looks over his shoulder, then returns his gaze to his donut and takes another large bite. "Dog poop," he replies.

"What?!!? Why is there dog poop on my kitchen counter?!"

"Finley pooped upstairs."

I nod. "Okaaaayyy. But why did you bring the poop down here? Why not throw it away upstairs in the toilet?"

He shrugs.

"Reid," I sigh. "Get the poop off the *counter!!!*"

He grins at the girls, shrugs his shoulders and then grabs the wad of toilet paper and carries it out of the kitchen. I shudder. "Gross…" I mumble as I reach for the gallon jug of bleach I keep beneath the kitchen sink.

Just another day in paradise.

Rose

Sometimes I wonder about myself. I mean, really. How is it that I overlooked the need to travel with Reid? It's the perfect solution, really. I'm actually a little embarrassed with myself for not coming up with this idea sooner.

Traveling together.

Once again, I shake my head. Why it took me so long to figure this out is beyond me. Reid has been traveling so much lately that I've barely gotten to see him. Occasionally, he'll swing by the office in the morning just to check up on things but mostly, he's out of the office. When he arrives back home, he normally heads straight home. There have been weeks—literally weeks—that I've not been able to see him. And with this sort of mission, that just won't do.

The more I think about it, the more sense it makes. If we travel together, we will spend countless hours together where we can get even closer than we already are. There will be dinners in different towns, long flights together where we sit side by side, delays, perhaps long layovers where we could drink horrible coffee while we bond in some overcrowded airport, making up stories about the people that cross our path. And then there are the nights….Countless nights where Reid is across the hall from me or right next door. We could be sharing a wall! Maybe we'd even get connecting room so that we could meet in the comfort of our rooms to review whatever agenda we have prepared for the next day.

And if we were to…I don't know…snuggle on the couch while reviewing a presentation…all the better!

The possibilities are endless. I just need more time with this man; preferably out of the office.

I have to prep myself for the discussion by laying out all the reasons it would be beneficial for me to travel with him. Given the extra cost of a hotel room, flight, and food, I need to make this good.

Then again, perhaps in time we'll only need one room....

After spending an evening at home trying to determine my reasons for travel as well as responses for when he says it's just not possible, I head into his office first thing the next morning, prepared for battle. You can only imagine my shock and delight when I'm not required to go through a single reason why I should travel with him. He simply sits behind his desk, ponders it for a moment, and nods.

Holy shit! Before the end of the day, I have a plane ticket to Atlanta, a hotel room booked, and an itinerary of our meetings for Thursday.

Let the games begin.

Abbie

"So, you'll call me when you land, right?"

I'm seated on our bed, watching Reid fold his best suit carefully into his garment bag. His duffel bag, which holds his casual clothes and toiletries, is on the floor at the end of the bed.

"Of course I will. I land around by 7 so I'll be able to talk to the girls before they go to bed."

"Good," I reply. "They'll love that."

Reid has come home to pack before heading out on yet another business trip. For some reason, I miss him already. It's not that I'm not used to him traveling, because I am. He has traveled on business the entire length of our marriage so it's not that I'm not accustomed to it. But today's events caused a shift in my emotions. Normally, Reid will pack the night before so that when he leaves for work, he doesn't need to swing by the house for anything. Today, instead of going to work and then heading to the airport after, he opted to come home to pack prior to leaving. It's almost like seeing him immediately before he leaves has shifted something inside of me and I'm not ready for him to go. I watch him walk into the closet, then come out holding two ties. He places them against the shirt he's packed and looks up at me.

"Which one?"

I point to one of them half-heartedly, barely even glancing at the options. "That one."

He looks at me for several moments. "You okay?"

I nod because I am okay. But I'm feeling something that I can't quite put into words. I wonder if the simple fact that he has come home after work to pack instead of heading to the airport has really thrown me for a loop or if I've suddenly become one of those people who knows when something bad is about to happen, which is stupid. I've never been one to believe in all that crap. The people who instinctively know when a plane is going to crash and warn their loved ones to get off at the last minute always give me the creeps. I grin, realizing how silly I'm being. Reid is just going on a business trip like he's done countless times before.

"I'm fine," I reply. "I think I'm just a bit sad watching you pack. I don't normally see it because your flights are at some ungodly hour and you wind up packing before I'm even awake."

He grins at me, then pushes the garment bag to the side so he can sit down in front of me on the bed.

"Are you saying that you're actually going to miss your wonderful, handsome, intelligent husband?" He wraps his arms around me and begins to nuzzle my neck.

"No," I reply, giggling. "I'm saying that I'm going to miss you."

He looks up at me with a pained expression. "I'm hurt. Terribly hurt. Wounded actually."

I poke him. "I'm sure your ego can handle a little bruising. Now finish packing so you can get the hell out of here."

He grins at me, gives me a quick kiss on the lips, then stands up. "What else do I need…" I watch as he walks back into the closet to see if he's forgotten anything, which he normally does. Reid is famous for forgetting something essential to his attire for these trips - like shoes (Really? There's not a woman alive who would forget to pack shoes!) - and winds up running out to the nearest mall in order to purchase a pair that will match whatever he's packed. I've often thought about simply packing for him but I refuse to turn into one of those women who mothers their husband. I figure at some point, Reid will learn from his mistakes.

Nearly fifteen years in, though, and I don't see a learning curve.

Sure enough, he comes out of the closet holding his dress shoes and shoves them into the side pockets of the garment bag. "Okay," he says. "I think I've got everything."

I stand up and survey his two stuffed bags and suddenly am overcome with just how much I'm going to miss my husband. My expression must tell Reid exactly how I'm feeling because he takes my hand in his and pulls me toward him.

"Hey," he says. "I'll be back on Friday. It's only two days."

"I know," I reply. "But I'm still allowed to miss you."

He grins. "Of course you are. I wouldn't have it any other way." After he kisses me gently on the lips, he turns to leave but then at the last moment, turns back. "I love you, " he says.

"Love you more," comes my automatic reply.

"Nope," he counters, grinning. "I love YOU more. I'm bigger."

This exchange is something we've said for years. And though I'm still anxious about this trip and don't know why, the familiarity of the exchange gives me just the amount of comfort I need.

But let me clarify. He is bigger. The man towers over me by a good six inches. But just because he's bigger doesn't mean he loves me more than I love him.

I know that's just not possible.

Rose

I'm seated at the gate with my purse tucked into the chair beside me when I see Reid walking swiftly through the airport. He looks extremely relaxed in a pair of jeans and a button down shirt while navigating through the crowd like he's done this a million times before, which of course, he has. Just the sight of him nearly takes my breath away but I somehow manage to calm myself before he reaches my side.

"Hey, Rose," he says. "You ready to go?"

I nod and stand. We walk together to security and hand our licenses and tickets to the security person before walking to the security checkpoint. Together, we empty our pockets, take off our shoes and then Reid takes off his belt. We slide our laptops out of their cases and place everything into those horrid, gray bins. Once we walk through the body scanner, we put our shoes on, Reid places his belt through the loops on his jeans, and we walk silently to our gate. I'm just about to feel some discomfort when he slows and points to an area that looks an awful lot like a bar. The inside is filled with more brass than any should ever be in one place and from where I stand, I can see the handles to several drafts of beer.

"You want to grab a drink? We've got time."

Stunned, it's all I can do to move my head up and down to indicate my willingness to join him for a drink. We walk into the bar, crossing the threshold from the smooth white tile of the airport terminal to the dark brown wooden floor of the bar area—expertly placed so that one might forget they're actually in an airport. The only available table is along the back wall so we head there and place our bags beside it.

"What would you like?"

"A beer is fine."

"Any preference?"

"Nah," I reply, shaking my head.

Reid is a beer drinker, something I noticed at dinner all those weeks ago. Though I've never been much of a beer drinker myself, I knew that I'd need to become one swiftly if I was going to show him something else we had in common. Besides, everyone knows that men like for their women to drink beer. No man wants a woman who when going to a bar orders a glass of wine or (Gasp!) a frothy concoction with a fruit speared on top of it. Women who drink beer are perceived by men and much cooler and laid back than their wine-drinking counterparts.

Sorry, I don't make the rules; I just abide by them.

So, over the course of the past few weeks, I've made it my mission to sample a bunch of different beers in the hope that at least one of them would be to my liking.

No such luck.

I did however, realize that with each sip of beer, I hated it a little less. And now I find that I can at least drink an entire beer without making a face while holding that crap in my mouth. Well, as long as it's not something dark, like Guinness.

Dear God, please don't let Reid come back to this table with a dark beer. I'm not sure I would be able to get it down.

I spot him at the bar and breathe a sigh of relief when I see him carrying two tall glasses of light amber liquid. He catches my eye and smiles as he walks over to our table, lifting up the glasses in a mock salute.

"Here you go," he says, placing the glass in front of me.

He sits down across from me and lift his glass, taking a large drink from it. "So," he begins. "You've got the agenda for tomorrow?"

I nod. "Nestle in the morning and then Coke in the afternoon."

"We should probably review the Coke proposal later on. I want to make sure we've got it down pat. It's a long shot, I realize, but I still want to make sure we make our best attempt."

I suddenly realize how important this trip is to Reid. K&M has been trying for years to take on Coke as a client. Rumor has it they have literally millions to spend on advertising and if K&M could take on even a small portion of that, it would put us on the map.

I lift my glass and take several large gulps of the beer, trying to give myself courage. I reach across the table and pat Reid's forearm in a friendly gesture. "Don't worry. We'll review it all night if we have to and you'll be great when you present tomorrow."

"Thanks," he says, taking another drink.

Several moments later, I realize that my hand is still on his forearm. It's almost as if he doesn't realize it's there. Or maybe he has realized it and doesn't want to be rude and remove his arm from underneath my arm.

Then again, maybe he wants it there.

Not wanting to push my luck, I remove my hand from his forearm and place it around the glass in front of me. We sit in silence for several moments and I realize Reid is mentally preparing for tomorrow's meeting. Nestle in the morning will be a breeze. They've been our client for years and always love our ad work. It's the Coke meeting he's worried about.

Well, not to worry. I'll stay up all night reviewing the Coke proposal if I have to.

All night.

Abbie

I glance at the clock once again and see that it's well past nine. Though Reid hasn't called yet, I'm not too worried. There are occasions, albeit rare ones, when his flight is delayed and he's simply unable to call. Plus, he knows I'm in bed by 9:30 most nights so even if he were able to call sometime soon, he probably wouldn't, knowing he'd most likely wake me. While I miss not being able to speak to him, the fact that he wouldn't call even if he could because he might wake me is so utterly and completely my Reid, that I have to smile. He's always been quite considerate where me and the girls are concerned and this is yet another example of that. Since he assumes I'm in bed and knows need every last minute I sleep I can get, he'll forego a phone call so that I can sleep for as long as possible. I still feel the need to have some contact with him, however impersonal it might be so I rummage through my pocketbook in order to find my phone.

Girls and I miss you! You'll be great tomorrow! Love you MORE! XOXO

Smiling, I hit send feeling a bit better knowing that Reid will receive my text whenever he turns on his phone and he'll know we were thinking of him. I toss my phone back into my pocketbook and head into the bedroom to join the girls.

When I walk into the room, I have to smile. I can make out two small forms on the bed thanks to the Christmas night-light emitting a soft glow from my side of the bed. The night light was a gift to Caroline last Christmas and she loved it so much that I was never allowed to put it into storage with the other holiday decorations. So now, her room is lit each night by an extremely fat Santa clause even in the heat of the summer.

The comforter is angled off the bed with half of it on the

floor. Hannah is holding tightly to a corner of it as if to keep the rest of it from falling off the bed. At her feet lies her baby sister who, for whatever reason, felt the need to crawl underneath the blankets and curl up in a ball at the foot of the bed. There is a round lump in the middle of them that looks unmistakably like an English bulldog curled up comfortably between the two children he loves most in the world. For a moment, I'm tempted to retrieve my phone and take a picture of this scene. Then I realize that I am perhaps the only person on the face of the earth that hasn't yet figured out how to take a photo in a dimly lit room with an Iphone. Instead, I opt to stand there for a few more moments, etching the scene into my memory.

After I put my pajamas on, wash my face and brush my teeth, I adjust the comforter by tugging it gently back into place so that I don't wake Hannah. I slide under the covers and attempt to find a comfortable spot in the little amount of real estate left for me thanks to a ten year old at the foot of the bed and English bulldog near my hip who doesn't like to be disturbed. I nudge Finley with my hip, ignoring the sort of growl-moan he makes which tells me doesn't appreciate being disturbed. Though no one can see me, my eye roll is both automatic and immediate. My dog doesn't want to be disturbed. Classic.

I roll over onto my side and tuck my hand underneath Reid's pillow. His scent lingers there and knowing I'm sleeping where he normally lies causes my chest to constrict ever so slightly. Despite his horrendous travel schedule, despite the fact that it has always been this way, and despite the fact that I'm really quite used to him being away from home, I still miss him.

Each and every time.

It is odd though, that even after all this time, I still don't sleep as soundly when he's not beside me. It's almost as if my body has become accustomed to having him next to me even if

I don't consciously realize he's there. I can't tell you how many times I've woken up when Reid is out of town because of the tiniest sound outside our house or the sound of a distant car driving by. It's almost as if I'm on edge when he's away. The first night he returns home after a business trip, it's almost I'm as jet-lagged as he is, simply because I haven't slept as well.

We're an odd pair, Reid and I. He doesn't sleep well when he's not in our bed and while I can sleep fine anywhere, I can only really sleep if he's lying beside me. It's like I've gotten so accustomed to having his warmth beside me that without it, I feel as though something is missing; something that prevents me from truly falling asleep.

I toss and turn for several moments, trying to find a comfortable spot in between Finley and the tangle of limbs that surround me. It's in these hours of the evening that I tend to miss Reid the most. The house is quiet, I'm desperately trying to fall asleep, and I have two of the most precious people lying beside me. But because of that, the absence of one makes it all the more pronounced. I love sleeping with my daughters. I mean, I really love it. But I chose Reid and he chose me. We're a team. And there's no one I'd rather have lying beside me while I sleep than him.

Actually, there's no one I'd rather have beside me at any time of the day or night.

Rose

Tonight, I may not sleep at all. Instead, I may lie awake replaying the events of the past few hours over and over in my head.

We landed in Atlanta as scheduled and then got our luggage and rental car. On the way to the hotel, we chatted as we normally do at the office. Football season has begun so Reid was chatting animatedly about the Giants and how they'd played the first few weeks of the season. The Yankees, unfortunately, didn't make it to the playoffs so they're done for the season. Never having been to Atlanta, I was blown away with the intense traffic. Reid however, seemed to take it in stride and weaved his way around the city like he'd been here dozens of times, which of course, he has.

Once we arrived at the hotel, we checked in. I was pleased to discover that our rooms were not only on the same floor, but directly across the hall from each other. The ride in the elevator was uncharacteristically silent and lacking the easy conversation that normally flows between us. When we finally located our rooms and separated at our respective doors, Reid looked back at me as he slid his card into the reader.

"Want to grab dinner downstairs in a bit?"

"Sure," I replied. "Are we going to review the Coke proposal?"

He nodded. "Ten minutes? I'll come get you."

"Okay." I slid my card into the slot and opened my door. Once the door shut behind me, I tossed my suitcase onto the bed and rummaged through it, looking for my makeup bag. Finding it in the bottom corner, I yanked it out and headed toward the bathroom where I spent the next few minutes running my fingers through my hair and touching up my eyeliner and blush. I wanted to look relaxed and attractive without trying too hard. This was going to be the first time Reid and I were together outside of work and there would be no interruptions.

Exactly ten minutes after I'd last seen him, Reid knocked on my door and we headed downstairs for dinner. I was pleased to notice that he seemed back to his old self and was talking to me as if it were any other ordinary day. It made me wonder once again why he was so quiet earlier. I just chalked it up to him still worrying about the Coke presentation tomorrow.

Though we both had our notes for the next day's meetings, neither one opened them or even referred to them during dinner. It was almost as if we were both trying to forget we were here on business. I know I was desperately trying to pretend that the two of us had simply gone away together and were enjoying a quiet dinner with each other.

"Do you want something to drink?" He asked me.

As always, I deferred to his judgment. "Whatever you want."

"We could split a bottle of wine if you like. One of Abbie's favorites is this Bogle merlot," he said, pointing to the menu. "I've only had it a couple of times but she raves about it."

I had to admit, the mention of his wife's name gave me a bit of a jolt. Was he mentioning her name to me to remind me that he was, in fact, married? As if I could forget that fact. I quickly squashed the tiny surge of jealousy I felt and focused on the present. He was here with me at the moment and she was five hundred miles away. I quickly opted to split the bottle of wine.

Her favorite, I might add.

We both ordered steaks because despite what little I know about wine, I do know that red wine is the perfect complement to red meat. Besides, men like a woman who eats. None of that 'I'll-just-have-a-salad' crap for me.

Though I left half my steak and Reid left some of his baked

potato, we somehow managed to finish the bottle of wine. I was feeling a little buzzed and Reid appeared to be a bit more jovial than normal, which was fine with me. After Reid signed for our dinner (company card, of course) we began to head to our rooms. I think we both knew that after a bottle of wine, we weren't going to be getting any work done.

We began to walk out of the restaurant and found myself leaning into Reid for support. Initially, I placed my hand on his upper arm to steady myself but then worked it up so that it was resting on the top of his shoulder. Almost instinctively it seemed, his hand found its way to the small of my back. Once there, I couldn't help but lean in just an inch or so closer to him, leaning against his chest as though I was unsteady.

I was, but not for the reason you might think. While the feeling of warmth emanating from his hand was more than enough to sober me up, the thought that he had actually reached out and touched me made me dizzy. I held onto him because I was afraid I'd trip over myself, but also because I thought it I were move away in the slightest, the spell would be broken and he would remove his hand from my body.

I wasn't about to let that happen.

We walked toward the elevator with my body still pressed against his. There was an elderly couple getting off just as we approached so we walked in and Reid pressed the button for our floor. He glanced at me out of the corner of his eye but when I turned to meet his gaze, he looked away. Once we reached our floor, the elevator pinged and the doors opened. I'm not sure what exactly it was but at that moment, he removed his hand from the small of my back and looked straight ahead. I removed my hand from his shoulder and turned to look at him questioningly. I wasn't sure what I was asking.

"Well, this is us," he said, stepping to the side to allow me to exit first.

"Yes," I replied. I rifled through my pocketbook looking

for my room key as we walked down the hall. I was walking slowly, determined to prolong my time with him. When we finally approached my door, I pulled out my key as though I'd only just located it and handed it to him, asking him with my eyes to open the door for me. I could almost hear him sigh with frustration and I could tell he wanted to leave me. He was torn. I just knew he was. He was attracted to me but his conscience wasn't going to let him to do anything that would cross the line he'd established in his mind.

When he unlocked my door and pushed it open, I knew I had only mere seconds to change his mind. I stepped close to him, placed my hands on his chest gently, and looked into his eyes. He looked back at me for a moment, then quickly looked away.

"Rose," he said sternly.

I knew what he was about to say. I could hear the anguish in his voice. But we were so close. There was no way I was going to let him go. I stood up on my tippy toes and gently placed a kiss on his neck. I felt his entire body tense as if he were readying himself for battle, which of course he was. But the battle was internal only. God knows I wasn't going to put up any sort of a fight.

I slid my hands up and wrapped them around his neck in order to pull him closer to me. I began to knead his neck and shoulders while kissing and licking the soft skin just beneath his ears. I could feel the stubble that was beginning to form on his jaw line and the roughness of it made me want him all the more.

I felt the tension is his body ease just enough for me to tug him gently into my room and allow the door to close behind us. I pressed him against the wall, still kissing his neck and kneading his shoulders. Finally, it was as though he gave in to his desires and he placed his hands on my hips and tugged me closer to him so that I could feel his erection through his pants. It was all the encouragement I needed. I removed my hands from his shoulders and dropped them to his waistband. I undid his belt and wrenched it from his pants so that I could undo the button and the zipper. I reached into boxers and held his hard length in my hands, stroking it up and down. His breathing was now coming in short gasps in that moment, I wanted him desperately. More so than ever before.

And given the firmness of his erection, I knew he wanted me too. But I also knew he was conflicted. I knew he loved his wife, but I also knew he wanted me. He gripped my hips firmly and pushed me away from him but his effort was a weak attempt at best and lacked any strength I knew he possessed. I knew the push was simply so that later, he could tell himself he'd made an attempt to stop things before they went too far.

But before he could make another attempt to push me away, I dropped to my knees and took him in my mouth, loving the sound of him gasp in pleasure as I took in every last inch of him. I teased him mercilessly, taking him deeper and deeper into my mouth until he gripped my shoulders and bucked hard.

Knowing he was about to climax, I took in the full length of him slowly, reaching around to grab his ass in order to hold him in my mouth while he came.

"Christ," he whispered.

I held him in my mouth, sucking his erect penis until the throbbing subsided.

Then something changed. He looked at me, kneeling on the floor in front of him, then at the room we were in and I watched as his expression changed. Gone was the relaxed look he'd had all through dinner and the look of utter contentment he'd had only moments ago. Now, his lips were pressed into a thin line and his brow was furrowed, making him look almost angry. He glanced at me, still kneeling on the floor in front of him, then his gaze traveled further down to where his pants were bunched up around his ankles. When my gaze finally met his, I nearly gasped. He looked both angry and shocked and I felt certain he was wondering just what the hell happened.

I stood up in front of him and reached out to take his hand. "Reid?" I whispered.

"Don't," he replied. He pulled his hand from mine and bent over to pull up his pants. He quickly zipped, buckled and tucked his way back to neatness, then was out of my room before I knew what had happened.

You'd have thought there was fire or something.

Slowly, I made my way over to the bed, which is where I now find myself. Though I'm surprised with Reid's swift departure from my room, his behavior isn't entirely unexpected. I'm certain he's going to feel at least some small measure of guilt at what's brewing between us. But he can't feel too guilty.

I mean, it was bound to happen.

I'm too wound up to sleep so I kill some time by hanging up my clothes for the next day and organizing my makeup on the counter in the bathroom. I had just finished washing my face when I heard the sound of an incoming text. Tossing the towel onto the counter, I skip out to the bedroom where my pocketbook rests on the bed. When I pull out the phone, I see that the text I received is from Reid. Relief washes over me.

You asleep?

I nearly laugh out loud. Like I'm going to fall asleep any time soon after what just happened between us. I quickly text back.

No. Need to chat?

Perfect, I think. Not too pushy. I'm not asking him to come back. I'm just offering my friendship if he wants to chat. Of course, if he takes me up on my offer, he will be in my room, late at night. My phone is silent for several moments. I keep clicking the phone on and checking our conversation scroll to see if I've missed anything but there is still no reply. I can just picture him in his room; he's seated on the end of the bed, tie loosened, and he's staring at his phone trying to determine whether or not he should come over and talk with me. He knows it's late. I know it's late. And chances are, if he comes over, he won't return to his room until much later, if at all.

Finally, my phone lights up and I see the text from Reid.

Ok. Coming over.

I grin. It's all I can do to hold back a fist pump and give a little cheer but I've got to control myself. He's probably already out in the hall. Sure enough, only a moment or two later, there is a soft knock at my door. I untuck my blouse from my skirt and kick off my shoes before walking over to the door and slowly pulling it open.

I lean against the half-open door, trying to make it appear as though I'm concerned about him. I look at him and take in his mussed up hair and unbuttoned shirt. He looks distressed and for just a moment, I feel sort of bad for him. He's obviously wracked with guilt.

"Hey," I say. "Come on in." I step back and allow him entry into my room. The only sound I hear is the scruffing of his shoes on the carpet. Finally, he makes his way across the room, bypassing the two queen beds and making his way over to the small, round table in the corner. He pulls out one of the chairs and sits down heavily into it, then leans forward, elbows on thighs and looks up at me.

"Rose," he begins slowly. "I can't...We can't..." He's stumbling over his words and I know that the guilt he feels is much worse than I thought. It's really going to take some effort to get past this. I realize it might be time to take a direct route with him and push him in the direction he needs to go.

Slowly, I walk over to the bed closest to where he is sitting and I perch on the end of the bed. I cross my legs, not bothering to smooth down my skirt.

"Are you attracted to me?"

He looks up abruptly. "What?"

"Are you attracted to me?"

He looks at me as though I'm speaking a foreign language; like he can't make out the words that are coming out of my mouth.

"Reid," I say softly. His expression softens just a bit as he ponders what I'm asking. Ever so slowly, I slide off the bed and kneel in front of him. He sits upright, almost as though he's afraid to have me so close. I work my way in between his thighs and place my hands on top of them. He is still. I move my hands gently up and down his thighs, feeling the taut muscles beneath the fabric of his pants. Just when I think I'm getting a reaction from him, he stiffens and grabs my hands.

"What are you doing?" He asks. His expression is a mix of confusion and anger.

"Tell me you don't find me attractive."

"Rose, I'm married."

"I realize that," I reply. It is then I notice that his hands still grip mine. I glance down at our entwined hands as he rips his hands from mine, leaving my hands free to resume their exploration of his thighs. "But I'm asking a very simple question. Are you attracted to me?"

He makes a funny, dismissive sound and rolls his eyes.

"It's all right," I say softly. "I think I already know the answer. And given the state of a certain part of your anatomy-" I glance down at the bulge in his crotch. "-I'd say I'm correct."

"Rose," he says tightly. "This can't happen. It doesn't matter if I'm attracted to you or not. I'm married."

"A-ha! So you are attracted to me."

He rolls his eyes. "A man would have to be dead to not be attracted to you. But that's not the point."

"Reid, please don't say it. I just can't bear it." Time to turn on the charm and show him my softer side. I think I might even be able to make a tear or two slide down my cheeks. "I know you're married; believe me, I know. I think about it every day." I've just about managed to get a tear to spill forth and when I finally succeed, I have to remind myself not to smile. I see the effect my tear has on him and the anger I saw earlier in his expression is gone and is replaced by concern.

"I can't help how I feel about you. Surely, you can tell how much I care." By now, the tears are coming pretty frequently and I have to admit that my performance may very well be Oscar worthy. Reid is leaning forward now and slowly, he wraps me in his arms and pulls me toward him. I sniffle for emphasis.

"Rose," he says. "It's okay. I'm flattered that you feel this way. I really am. But we can't ignore the fact that I'm married."

"Why not?" I ask, jutting out my lower lip. Pouty girl is making an entrance. I wonder what effect this will have on him. I glance up and see him grin. I cannot believe this is working! This is easier than I thought. He's falling for every trick in the book. Clearly, he's been married for too long. I sniffle again for effect and begin to rub my hands across his chest. He doesn't stop me. "Reid, I care about you so much. I just want to be with you...even if it's only for a little while."

He's looking at me with such concern on his face that I almost feel bad for him.

Almost.

Reid takes my hand from his chest and holds it still. The warmth of his hand on mine makes me realize that I desperately need to feel him naked on top of me, inside of me, underneath me.

It's time for desperation.

"Please stay with me," I whisper. "Just for a little while."

"Rose," he says. "I can't. I won't do this to Abbie...to my family."

But I hear the uncertainty in his voice and I know he's conflicted. He's torn between being faithful to his wife and succumbing to his desires. It's all the encouragement I need. I take his hand in mine and bring it to my mouth. Slowly, I take each finger and slide it past my lips, sucking gently. Reid closes his eyes and I know that he's thinking exactly what I am—what it would feel like to be inside of me.

I don't want to break the spell so I continue to suck on his finger while undoing the buttons on his shirt with my other hand. Once I reach bare skin, I hear him moan and I have to suppress a smile.

I will have him. Tonight.

I remove his finger from my mouth and look him in the eye. Slowly, I place his hand on the top button of my blouse. He knows what I am asking and begins to unbutton. He pushes it down over my shoulders and it falls to the floor in a heap. He reaches behind me and unclasps my bra to expose my breasts. He groans once again, then reaches to fondle them, dragging his thumbs over my nipples. I lean my head back, loving the feel of his hands on my body. I gasp when I feel his mouth close over my nipple. My hands reach around him and we stand together. He begins to kiss my chest and neck, making his way up my jawline until he finally claims my mouth. We stagger to the bed and collapse onto it. I am tearing at his shirt, desperately wanting his skin against mine. Reid is tugging at my skirt and I realize he's not going to be able to tug it off. I reach around and unzip it, then slide it down my legs. At the same time, Reid unbuckles his belt and removes his pants, kicking them to the floor.

He is touching every part of me but I want more. I feel his thigh between my legs but it's not enough. I want him inside of me. I've waited for so long for this moment and I'm desperate. His hips are moving against me and I know he wants the same. He repositions himself so that he's perched at my entrance and I widen my thighs so that he knows I want this. As he slides into me, I buck my hips toward him, unable to control myself. I reach around and grab his ass, pulling him deeper and deeper into me with each thrust. Our breathing is coming in short gasps and I feel my body climbing towards its release.

"Oh my GOD," I cry out, as my body is wracked with an orgasm more powerful than anything I've ever experienced in my life. Within moments, Reid thrusts deeply and comes inside of me, groaning as he does. He buries his face in the crook of my neck and I can feel the heat of his breath.

We lie there for several moments while our breathing returns to a somewhat normal rhythm.

"Reid?"

"Yeah?" His voice is muffled since his face is still buried in my neck.

"Stay with me?"

I hear a soft sigh but then he nods. He pulls out of me and together, we climb under the covers. I'm tucked underneath his arm with my head resting on his chest.

And I couldn't be happier.

Abbie

"Did you have a good trip?" I ask, as Reid enters the kitchen. He picks up the mail that has been tossed onto the counter and begins to rifle through it.

"Eh" he replies. "It was all right."

"How'd the Coke presentation go?"

"Fine. Just fine." Reid is slowly looking at each piece of mail, even opening up the flyer that comes every week with coupons for local restaurants.

"So...how do you think it went? Do you think they liked it?" I take a few steps over toward him and rest my palms on the counter. Instead of looking at me, his focus is on the flyer he has spread out in front of him. I watch as he peruses each page, then flips to the next.

"Reid?"

He looks up me almost as though I've startled him. It's as if he's forgotten I was even there. "What? Oh, the presentation." He shrugs. "It was ok. I'm not really sure what they thought of it." He looks at me and smiles but it's a smile that doesn't quite make it all the way up to his eyes. "We'll just have to wait and see."

I nod. I'm a little confused about why he's not talking about the presentation. Normally, he gives me a blow-by-blow of the entire meeting and then we analyze every statement. We worry until we hear the results but we worry together. I'm beginning to think, for whatever reason, the meeting went horribly wrong and he's either embarrassed or extremely worried about it. I want to probe him further about it but decide to let it go for the moment, figuring he'll tell me about it when he's ready.

"Well, I've got dinner in the over and I was just going to throw in a load of laundry. Where's your suitcase? I'll get your clothes out of it."

"Don't worry about it," he says. "I'll get it in a minute and start the laundry."

Now I'm thoroughly confused. Reid hasn't offered to do laundry since before the girls were born. When we were first married, he tried on more than one occasion to perform this task but for whatever reason, never quite got the hang of it, despite my numerous attempts to explain how it was done. Finally, after several wool sweaters were reduced to doll-sized and all of my whites had been converted to a shade of pink, we decided it was best that I take over that household chore.

"Umm…are you sure?"

"Yeah, why?"

I grin. "It's just that the last time you did laundry, I wound up with a bunch of pink bras."

"Abbie, I think I can handle a load of laundry," he huffs, then walks out of the room.

I stand there dumbfounded. My normally soft spoken, easy going husband just snapped at me over a load of laundry. By now, I'm figuring the presentation did not go well at all and he's just stressed about going into the office on Monday. I know Reid and I'm certain he views this as a personal failure and isn't looking forward to explaining it. I figure he needs a little space so I don't follow him into the bedroom. Instead, I choose to busy myself with prepping dinner and wiping down counters that don't really need to be cleaned. We'll eat dinner once he's had time to decompress.

I check the oven and see that the casserole is turning brown around the edges so I turn the oven off, figuring it can sit in the warm oven until we're ready. I grab the folded laundry I had piled on the stairs earlier and head up to the girls' rooms to see what sort of trouble they're causing. I'm shocked to find the two of them in the play room, together, in total collaboration and engrossed with their Monster High collection of dolls. I stand in the doorway for a few moments, relishing in the peace that has somehow entered my home. I slink away before I'm noticed, knowing that anything can upset the delicate balance I have just discovered.

After putting the girls' clothes away in their bedrooms, I wander back downstairs and find Reid in the laundry room staring at the machine.

"Where do I put the soap?" He asks.

I stifle a sigh and grin, knowing how much it must have frustrated him to realize he didn't even know how to work a washing machine we've had for nearly ten years. Stepping toward him, I reach out my hand to take the laundry detergent out of his hands. Then I reach out to the front of the washing machine and pull open the little drawer located on the top of it. I pour the correct amount of blue liquid into the container, then push it back into place.

"Now what?" He asks.

"Turn the knob to the type of wash you want," I say, pointing to a large colorful knob on the front of the machine.

"What kind of wash do I want?"

"Reid," I say, exasperated. "Why don't I just take care of this, all right?"

He runs his fingers through his hair, mussing it up in frustration, and then nods. As he steps behind me to leave the room, he wraps his arms around my waist and pulls me close.

"What would I do without you, Abs?"

"Well," I chuckle. "You certainly wouldn't have any clean clothes, that's for sure!"

He kisses my neck and holds me close for a few more moments, then turns to leave. I smile, knowing that whatever was bothering him earlier has magically disappeared.

My Reid is back.

As if they can sense a change in the atmosphere of the house, the girls come roaring down the steps clamoring for dinner. Reid jumps into their path and scoops them up into his arms, causing them to squeal with delight.

"Are you guys ready for dinner?"

"We're starving!" Cries Caroline. Hearing the tone of her voice, one might think she hadn't eaten in days instead of just an hour before when she inhaled a banana and a very large glass of milk.

"How 'bout we help mom set the table so we can eat? Hannah, you get the plates. Caroline, you can get the silverware."

The girls bustle about the kitchen, pleased to be helping out their father with what they perceive as a very important task. While Reid and the girls are setting out plates, I pull the casserole out of the oven and set it in the middle of the table. Within moments, we are all seated at the table, devouring the chicken casserole.

"So," Reid begins. "What do we have planned for this weekend?"

"Nothing really," I reply. "Caroline needs a new pair of sneakers and I need to pick up a few things at the grocery store but that's about it."

"Good," he says, then catches the girls' eyes. "Why don't we see a movie tomorrow?"

The girls cheer the idea and swiftly begin to plan which movie they want to see.

"If you like, I'll take them to the movie while you run your errands."

I smile, thinking of how easy a trip to the grocery store will be without two children begging me for everything they see. Every time I walk down the cereal aisle I silently curse the person who first put a cartoon character on horrible tasting cereal, thereby making the child want the cereal and the parent the bad guy because they know that there is no way on God's green earth their child is going to eat something that is shredded and wheat flavored, even if a Minion, Miss Piggy, or Pokemon is on the package. But there they sit, smiling at your children, begging to be purchased, all the while knowing that the box of cereal will sit on your pantry shelf until the expiration date has long passed.

"That'd be great," I reply.

Once we've eaten dinner, Reid takes the girls into the living room and sits between them on the couch while they watch yet another Spongebob Squarepants episode. I sneak a peek at them from the kitchen and see Caroline curled up facing Reid with her legs draped over her father. Hannah, being ten and "too old for such shows of affection" is sitting close to her father and has even allowed him to drape his arm around her. The fact that Hannah has allowed Reid to do this tells me just how much she misses him while he's away. It's still surprising to me how much Reid is missed when he's gone despite the fact that he has always traveled. The girls have never known a time when he was home each and every day. Reid's travel is not foreign to them yet they miss him terribly each and every time.

Foregoing the dishes, I instead opt to snuggle with my family on the couch. After the movie, Reid volunteers to put the girls to bed. Caroline climbs onto his back, piggy-back style and Hannah takes her father's hand as they walk upstairs. Though he has only been gone for two days, I'm exhausted. The toll of being the sole parent all day, every day wears me out. I muster up enough energy to heave myself off the couch and into our bedroom. It is only now that I realize just how tired I am and I walk directly to our bed, foregoing my nightly routine of washing my face and brushing my teeth. I pull the comforter back and crawl into bed. Within seconds, I feel the delicious pull of sleep and the last sounds I heard are my husband's footsteps from above my head as he tucks our two children into bed.

The next morning I wake earlier than usual. A quick glance to the clock on the nightstand tells me that it's just a bit after six. The light is just beginning to peek through the blinds, enabling me to see around me. I roll toward the center of the bed expecting to curl up beside Reid but am somewhat surprised to find his side of the bed empty. Not only that, it's clear by the absence of any wrinkles that it hasn't been slept in.

I climb out of bed and walk down the hall in search of my husband. Thinking he might have fallen asleep with one of the girls, I walk upstairs to check their room. As each door is opened I spy the angelic faces of my sleeping children and I can't help but smile. They may argue frequently, whine, cry, and make unreasonable demands, but while they are sleeping they are absolutely, deliciously perfect. I close each door and make my way downstairs, now assuming Reid has fallen asleep either in the living room or on the couch in our basement.

I spot him curled up on the sectional in the basement, a Yankees blanket wrapped tightly around him. Like our daughters, he looks peaceful while sleeping despite the stubble that has appeared over the past twenty four hours. Instead of waking him, I decide he's better of where he is and decide to leave him asleep. Knowing he will wake if he gets cold, I reach for the Giants blanket that is draped over the back of the sectional and cover him up with it, hopefully doubling his warmth.

After my trek around the house in search of my husband, I realize I'm not going to be able to fall back to sleep. Rather than lie in bed trying to force another hour of sleep to come, I decide to brew some coffee and watch the news. A silent house is just too appealing to turn away and I can't remember the last time I was able to watch something on television without the sound of arguing in the background.

Once the coffee is brewed, I curl up on the couch and settle in. It is nearly an hour before my eldest comes downstairs and snuggles up beside me. She takes a corner of my blanket and slides beneath it, molding her body to mine. I relish this, knowing it won't be long before she will shy away from my touch, even when we are in the privacy of our own home. I wrap my arm around her and pull her close.

Within moments, I hear the sound of footsteps coming from the basement. Reid opens up the door to the basement and walks into the room. Seeing Hannah and I curled up on the couch, he smiles.

"You're up early," he says to me as he sits down next to Hannah. He rubs the top of head gently, then leans in to give her a kiss on her forehead.

"Yeah," I reply. "When I woke up and saw you hadn't been to bed yet, I went looking for you. After that, I couldn't go back to sleep."

He rubs his face with his hands. "Sorry. I went downstairs to watch TV and I guess I just fell asleep."

"You want some coffee?" I ask. "There's a full pot in the kitchen."

"That'd be great," he replies. He stands up slowly, stretches, then makes his way into the kitchen.

I hear him opening cabinets in search of a coffee cup and then the sound of the fridge open and close. He comes back after a few moments and resumes his spot, placing the cup on the table in front of him.

"You still want to see a movie Hannah?"

She nods, still sleepy.

"Caroline still asleep?"

I nod. "What time are you planning on heading to the movie?"

"I don't know...1-ish?"

"Perfect. I'll head to the grocery store and run a few errands while you guys do that. Pizza for dinner?"

"Oooh, yeah!" Hannah sits up quickly as pizza is one of her favorites.

I chuckle. "Pizza it is."

The rest of our day is relatively normal. Because I have an abundance of free time, I decide to make a quick run-through the house I'm working on. I figure both Carol and Rose would like to see it as well and text them to meet me there. We catch up for a few minutes while tourning the work I've gotten done on the house, then I head to the store for some much needed groceries.

Reid takes the girls to the movies and they come home hopped up on sugar and soda. I'd be cross with Reid for allowing the girls to eat all that crap but it happens so infrequently that I can't begrudge them this treat. Besides, they'll wear it off by bedtime.

We stuff ourselves full of pizza that night and then the four of us curl up to watch Brave, the latest Disney movie. Caroline immediately becomes obsessed with Meridon, the princess who stars in the movie and begins to talk about all things Meridon for Christmas. I squelch a sigh knowing that I will hear nothing but Christmas wishes for the next eight weeks.

Once again, the girls are carried to bed by Reid but unlike last night, I vow to stay awake until he comes back down. He does, but only pops his head in for a moment, telling me he needs to go a bit of work but that he'll come to bed soon. I try to hide my disappointment but honestly, it stings a little bit.

The next morning, it stings just a bit more when, once again, I see his side of the bed has not been slept in. Reid has always been someone who prefers to sleep in his own bed as opposed to any place else. Though we vacation at least once each year, he makes a big production about returning home to his bed. When he first began traveling, I worried about him sleeping in all those foreign places with all the strange noises. I worried that he wouldn't sleep as well as he might've at home and that any lack of sleep might make him less efficient at work—something he'd never be able to tolerate.

The simple fact that Reid has not slept in his own bed for two nights has me terribly worried. Now it seems obvious that the Coke presentation did not go well at all and he is worried sick about it. So worried, in fact, that he can't fall asleep and instead chooses to watch TV in our basement until he manages to catch an hour or two.

He's got so much pressure on him that I worry it might be too much. Tossing back the covers, I climb out of bed in search of my husband. Today, however, I immediately head to the basement where I find him, once again, sleeping on the couch, his Yankees blanket covering the bottom half of his body. I sit down beside him and nudge him gently. When he doesn't stir, I shake his shoulders a bit, trying to rouse him.

"Reid," I whisper, trying to ease him out his slumber. "Wake up, babe."

He stretches slowly and I know he's coming to. He looks around as though confused and then his eyes find mine.

"Wh..what is it? Are the girls okay?"

He looks groggy still but a look of panic has crossed his face so I quickly shake my head.

"No, honey. They're fine. But I'm worried about you."

He sits up and faces me. "Worried about me? Why?"

"You've slept down here for two nights now and I know you." I point to him. "I know you'd rather sleep in your own bed than anywhere else. So, come on. Fess up. I'm pretty sure I know what's going on but I'd like to hear it from you."

A look of sheer panic crosses his face but within an instant, it's gone. It vanishes so quickly that it almost makes me wonder if it was ever there at all. But now I'm really beginning to panic. What is he so stressed about? Good lord, has he lost his job?

Instantly, I become angry. Reid has been with K&M for nearly twenty years. He's brought more money into that company than any other person, than any other *group* of people. They'd never let him go. Besides, if they did, it would take weeks to hammer out the non-compete agreement I'm sure they'd make him sign. His clients love him and if he were to leave, most of them would follow him wherever he went.

Reid takes in a deep breath, then exhales slowly. "Look Abbie. Don't worry. I'm fine. Really I am. I was a bit jet-lagged and came down here to watch some TV so I wouldn't disturb you. I guess I fell asleep without even realizing it." He pats my hand. "Really. Don't worry about me. I'm fine."

"What about the coke presentation? Are you worried about it at all?"

He shrugs. "I mean, a bit. But I did the best I could. No sense worrying about it now. If they want my campaign, they'll call us. If not? Well, you win some, you lose some."

I stare at him for several moments. I'm still worried but when I look at the earnest expression on his face, I immediately feel better. I know this man. If something were really bothering him, he'd tell me.

"Okay," I say, standing up. The anger I felt only moments ago has left me. "Let's go get some coffee before the kids wake up."

And for a moment, I feel a sense of normalcy.

Rose

This was the longest weekend of my life. I kept thinking about Reid and what happened in my hotel room. I so wish I could have called him, spoken to him or something.

I'm so worried about him. I'm sure he feels guilty and I just want to be able to tell him that it's normal. It's normal for him to feel remorse over what is happening between us. Yes, it's going to be hard for him but I've got to tell him that it will all be worth it. He and I are meant to be together. What we shared the other night is something I've never experienced with anyone before.

But now is comes the hardest part; the waiting. Waiting for Reid to come to grips with his feelings, waiting for him to see what's right in front of his eyes, and waiting for him to figure out just how we can be together. There is one thing I can cling to, however. One thing that is certain. Reid is most definitely attracted to me. He cares. It's something. It's a place to start. What we feel for each other can only grow from this point.

Because I had nothing but time on my hands this weekend, I met Abbie at her house. Not the one she lives in, of course. That'd just be crazy. I went to see the one she's flipping. I had nothing to do so when Abbie texted Carol and I to see if we wanted to meet at the house, I figured, "What the heck?"

Now, I know what you're thinking. I should stay away from her. It's bitchy of me to still be her friend, particularly given the events of my last business trip. But look at it from my point of view. She's research. My goal in the end is to be with Reid, not Abbie. She's really just another avenue for me to gather information and like they say…all's fair in love and war. And this most definitely is war. She just better stay out of the line of fire or she's going to end up being collateral damage.

97

Besides, if she happens to consider me a friend, even better. Maybe she'll confide in me....

Imagine that! Abbie talking to me about her marital worries; Why Reid isn't as attentive as he used to be or why they seem to be growing apart.... I'm really going to have to work on my poker face.

Anyway, Carol and I met Abbie at the house she's flipping and I have to admit, she's done wonders with it. I've seen pictures on Facebook but honestly, they don't do it justice. She's pretty much completed one of the rooms and it looks unbelievable! If she's able to do what she did with that room to the rest of the house, she'll have no problem making money off the house. And hey, it might even turn into a bit of income for her. I mean, she's going to have to get used to working. Reid's not going to be there forever to take care of her.

Viewing Abbie's house took less than an hour so that left me with the rest of the weekend to analyze and worry about everything I might have said or done wrong while I was with Reid. And, of course, a good part of the weekend was spent imagining Reid with his wife and children. Did he kiss her hello when he got home? Do they embrace when they pass in the hall? Do they curl up beside one another while they sleep? Did he make love to her this weekend? God, the thought of Reid actually having sex with that woman makes me sick to my stomach. I can barely stand the thought of it.

This may have been the only time in my life that I was glad the weekend was only two days. I simply couldn't wait to get back to work and see Reid again.

Finally, Monday morning rolled around. I got to work early so that I could get a few things done before he came in. Obviously, I'm going to spend a good portion of the morning in Reid's office.

Glancing at the clock, I see that it's nearly nine. I can't help but wonder where he is since he's normally in his office by eight. I turn back to my computer and try to busy myself checking emails but I'm almost immediately distracted when I hear the sound of his voice, which elicits a reaction deep in my belly. The hairs on the back of my neck stand up just knowing that he is close by. I wheel my chair around to see him walking toward me. He glances at me and I see an expression on his face that I've never seen before. He looks…distraught.

My hear thuds in my chest and I stand up. Reid walks up to me and nods. I notice he looks tired. There are the beginnings of dark circles under his eyes and he looks a bit pale. His tie is slightly crooked and the front of his shirt is wrinkled, almost as though he'd slept face down while wearing it. He's completely disheveled, which is completely out of character for him. But yet he somehow manages to look absolutely adorable.

"Rosemary," he says, a bit too formally for my liking.

"Reid," I reply, trying to put a bit of warmth in my tone but instead of sounding relaxed, my greeting sounds forced and almost formal. It's as though the closeness we had last week has evaporated into this air. The comfort and tenderness we showed each other is gone and this has me terrified.

"When you get a minute, step into my office."

"Sure," I reply softly. Partly because I'm dying to talk to him and partly because I'm worried about what he has to say, I immediately follow him into his office and take my usual seat at his table.

"What's up?" I ask, trying my best to appear calm and relaxed.

He sighs heavily and tosses his briefcase onto his desk. "I think you know why I need to speak with you."

Of course I do. But I'm not letting him off that easy. "Ummm…I'm not sure…"

"Rose," he says, clearly becoming exasperated. "Our trip last week…the hotel…you and me…" His voice drops to a stage whisper at the mention of the hotel. He glances at the open door, then quickly stands, walks over to it and gently closes it.

As I watch him move about his office, memories of the two of us together swirl around me. I feel a warmth begin to spread through my body and a slow smile spread across my face. But my smile is erased the moment I look at Reid and see the expression of sheer torment on his face.

"Reid," I say, leaning forward. "What is it? You seem…upset, or worried."

He sighs heavily. "Of course I'm upset!" His voice rises but then he glances around as though someone might hear him. He takes a deep breath and when he speaks again, his sounds much more calm. "Rose," he begins. "What happened last week was…a mistake. Surely you know that."

"I disagree."

He looks up at me, shocked. "What do you mean, 'you disagree?' How can you think what happened between us is anything but a mistake."

"I'm sorry. But I can't agree with you and say that it was a mistake. What I'm feeling isn't a mistake."

"What you're feeling? Rose, you shouldn't feel anything for me other that the mutual respect that we have for one another because of our work situation."

I shake my head.

"Don't shake your head at me," he scolds and I bristle. He's talking to me as if I am a child instead of the woman he made love to only 72 hours prior. He's acting like I'm *just* his employee when both of us know that is just not the case.

"Look," I say. "I realize that you're probably feeling a bit guilty-"

"A bit guilty?" He interjects. "Is that what you think? That I'm feeling 'a bit guilty?' You have no idea what I'm feeling. I could've ruined my marriage and my career in one fell swoop! I have no idea what the hell I was thinking but I'm telling you right now, nothing like that can ever happen again."

"But-"

"No buts. Never again," he says. "I'm terribly, terribly

sorry if I did anything to lead you to thinking there might be…" His voice trails off. "But there isn't. I love my wife. I'm sorry, Rose but I'm committed to my family."

I sit there quietly, waiting for him to finish speaking. I'm trying to figure out how to handle this situation. Of course, I anticipated this. I knew he'd feel guilty about our little discretion. Honestly, I'd be worried if he didn't feel some sort of remorse. But now that I'm faced with the amount of guilt he's carrying, I'm not sure what to do.

The thing is, he sounds so certain it will never happen again; that he and I will never be together, it scares me. I'm truly worried that he doesn't see how special he is to me and despite my vow to be a strong, independent woman, I find myself welling up with tears. Before I realize it, there are tears streaming down my face. Real tears. Not the fake ones that I used when I told Reid about my 'breakup.' These are the real deal and the emotions behind the tears are real as well.

But here's the thing: I'm not a pretty crier. In fact, I'm one of those women who, once the first tear falls, my eyes get all red and puffy and my cheeks become all splotchy. My nose begins to run and no matter what I do, I can't stop it. In short, I'm a mess. A hideous, sobbing mess.

In fact, I'm sobbing so hard that I don't even notice Reid get up out of his chair and and sit at the table beside me. In fact, it isn't until he takes my hand in his own and I feel the warmth of his skin on mine that I even realize he's right in front of me. We are seated so close together that our knees are almost touching.

And that's when I begin to practically hyperventilate because I've been crying so hard. By now, I can only imagine what I look like. I'm sure I've got snot running out of my nose and my face is one big, round splotchy mess.

And Reid is a foot from me, able to inspect every last ugly inch of me. My makeup is ruined, I have no mascara left and I'm sure the hair around my face is matted to my head because of the tears and sweat. Oh yeah, I also sweat profusely when I cry. Awesome.

Reid's free hand reaches in front of me and I see that it's holding a tissue, which I use to wipe my face. Seeing that one tissue isn't nearly enough to absorb the wetness on my face, Reid hands me the box of tissue. I pull several out of the box and blow my nose and wipe the tears from under my eyes and cheeks. After several moments, I look up to find Reid looking at me, concern etched into his features.

It's then that I realize that without even trying or planning, or conniving, I've elicited a response from him that give me hope. If he's concerned about me and the fact that I'm crying, he must care. Even if it's a little bit, it's something. Something I can work with.

Slowly, I lift my head to meet his gaze.

"Are you okay?" He asks softly.

I shrug. "I'm not sure."

"Rose, I'm sorry if I hurt you. That wasn't my intention."

"I know," I reply. "But it still hurts."

He looks down at this lap and I can tell he feels guilty, not about what happened between us, but about the fact that he hurt me! Now this I can work with.

"I'm so sorry, Rose."

"I…I just don't understand how you could make love to me and not feel anything," I allow my voice to break slightly on the last word for effect and it does just what I thought it might. When Reid hears the tremor in my voice, he flinches as though he's been slapped.

"I don't have an answer for you. I…guess I just got caught up in the moment." His voice sounds so uncertain, as if he's grasping for any answer that will pacify me.

"But Reid," I whisper softly, "you came back. You came back to my room after I…" My voice trails off, which leads him to believe I can't even utter the words blow job to him. I'm playing the innocent victim here magnificently. Someone needs to give me an Oscar for this performance. But let's be honest. It's not all an act. I really am upset Reid is telling me this is a mistake. I'm just whatever I need to do to make sure he realizes that the mistake wasn't making love to me; the mistake is thinking it will never happen again.

He's a man for God's sakes. Putty in my hands…as long as I figure out what makes him tick. And based on his reaction to my tears that he assumes are the result of his rejection, he can't handle feeling guilty.

He places his head in his hands. "I know," he cries. "I'm so sorry! Honestly, I came back because I wanted to clear the air. I didn't want you think….Christ, I have no idea what the hell I was thinking. I never should have gone to your room. It was completely inappropriate of me to do that. I'm so sorry, Rose. I'm sorry this happened but most of all, I'm sorry to have hurt you."

I begin to cry again, this time even more softly. And then another brilliant idea hits me.

"I just don't know what's wrong with me! Why does this always happen to me? I meet someone and things are going great for a week or two and then I get dumped! What is wrong with me? Am I hideous? Too fat? What?"

"Oh my God, Rose. No! Nothing like that! Any man who doesn't want to be with you has to have something wrong with him. His head's not screwed on right."

I look at him pointedly.

"You know what I mean. I'm not 'dumping' you. It's just that I'm married." He takes my hand in his once again and holds it tightly. "You are a beautiful, intelligent woman. Any man would be lucky to have you."

I sniffle just a bit for effect, then look up at him hopefully. "Do you really mean that?"

He nods. "Of course I do. That guy that dumped you? Well, there's something wrong with him."

"I just don't know why it happens over and over again! It's

gotten to be so expected that I can almost predict when I'm going to be dumped."

"You just haven't met the wrong guy yet," he says.

"What if I have but he didn't want me?" I ask.

He seems to understand what I'm asking and ponders it for a moment. "I'm sure he did want you, Rose. But there could be any number of things that are going on in his life. Maybe it just wasn't the right time. You know what they say: timing is everything."

In my opinion, Reid is taking this much better than he should be. After all, he has broken my heart. Time to step up my game and give him a bit more to be guilty about. I stand up slowly and take a deep breath.

"Look," I say, "I'm not handling this well right now. Would it be all right if I took the rest of the day off?"

"Of course," he replies immediately.

"Thanks. I just need to process all of this."

Reid looks at me as though inspecting me, pausing before he speaks. "You going to be okay?" He asks.

I shrug halfheartedly. "I just need a bit of time," I reply.

"Okay," he says. "Take as much time as you need."

Slowly, I open the door to his office and walk out. I neither turn to look back at him or pause in the slightest. I want to give him the impression I will be fine.

Then he'll never see the curveball coming.

Abbie

Finally, after months of humidity and temperatures over ninety degrees, we're firmly into fall weather. And that means the girls can play outside without being overcome with heat exhaustion. Finley and I have resumed our daily runs and occasionally, the girls hop on their bikes and come with me.

This is my favorite time of year but it is quite fleeting. There's really only a few weeks in North Carolina where you're able to have both the air conditioning and the heat off. It seems like we normally just switch the controller on the HVAC unit from A/C to heat but this year, I'm thrilled to be able to open windows and allow the fresh air inside. The days seem to be just warm enough where a ceiling fan keeps the air inside the house cool and the nights tend to be the perfect temperature to sleep with a light blanket on and be quite comfortable.

After months of non-stop humidity, and the tense moods that go along with never being able to quite cool yourself down, it's nice to see my family returning to their sunny dispositions—that is, except for the fighting between the two girls. But even that doesn't seem so bad when it's not ninety percent humidity outside.

The girls have just gotten home from school and they're badgering me to take them shopping for their Halloween costumes. This makes me smile because it seems as though each year, we do this earlier and earlier in the season. And each year, I hope the weather holds because I know the girls hate it when I bundle them up in overcoats and hats if it's cold. They'd rather brave the elements than hide their costumes.

Normally, the shopping for the Halloween costumes would be something Reid and I would do together. Reid has always been "that" dad who wants to make sure that his daughters don't select a costume that would indicate they are older than they actually are. He likes for them to stick to princesses or ghosts—anything that covers up most of their bodies. He's particularly cautious with Hannah, who has begun to show signs of puberty…and Reid really isn't ready for that.

Last Saturday, we were going to head out to the temporary costume store that magically appears just in time for the costume-buying season, but Reid was so exhausted and had so much work to do that he slept in, then spent the remainder of the day in our home office. While the girls always prefer for their father to join us on any outing, I figure this is on he can skip out on. Besides, if I can take care of this task one day after school, it's one less thing for him to worry about.

The girls arrive home at the usual time the following Tuesday. Like most days, Hannah barges in the front door, leaving her baby sister to play catch up. Today, Caroline has nearly caught up, only to have the front door practically hit her in the face.

"Mo-om!" She cries. "HANNAH SLAMMED THE DOOR IN MY FACE!"

I sigh heavily as I give Hannah the glare that tells her I saw exactly what she did. "Hannah," I say, "your sister was right behind you. Would it kill you to wait for her so that you don't slam the door in her face?"

"Yes," she replies, causing me to groan. I have no idea what I'm going to do when she's fifteen and hates the world. At least now she's manageable.

Well, somewhat.

"I HATE YOU!" Screams Caroline, as a few tears work their way down her chubby cheeks.

As I pull her into a hug, out of the corner of my eye I see Hannah make a face at her sister that tells her she hates her too. "Hannah!" I scold. "I saw that! Knock it off!" I squish Caroline close to me knowing that nothing I say will make her feel better. She and her sister have a love/hate relationship that most siblings share and this is just one of those days where there is more hate than love. I've seen this a thousand times. Later on in the evening, the two of them will be sitting on the couch side-by-side, snuggling under their blankets and watching a movie that the two of them agreed upon. All I can do at the moment is hug Caroline until the hurt goes away.

"Hey," I say to Caroline, "Do you want to go and look for your costume?"

She sniffs just a bit but I see the beginnings of a smile and I know that the hurt has nearly passed. "Okay," she says. She takes the back of her hand and wipes her nose, then reverses it to wipe the tears from her cheeks. "Can I have a snack first?"

"Of course you can," I reply. I glance at Hannah, who is standing near us trying to pretend not to hear the conversation. "Would you like a snack too?"

She nods.

"Do you think you can manage to sit at the kitchen table without making your sister cry?"

She shrugs. "I don't know." She glances at her sister out of the corner of her eye. "Caroline, you're such a baby."

"MOM!" Caroline screams.

"Hannah," I say, growing weary of these exchanges, "if you can't behave, you can stay here while I take your sister to get her Halloween costume. Jennifer is just a phone call away."

I was lucky enough to find the best sitter in the world several years ago. The girls love her and are always willing to have her over so that their father and I can go out alone together for our regular date nights. Luckily, Jennifer lives close to us and because she's a college student, her schedule is pretty flexible. Most nights that she watches the girls are easy for her. Once they're in bed, she can study or do homework. At this point, I really just need someone in the house to make sure the girls don't kill themselves or set the house on fire and Jennifer is just the ticket. But while Hannah loves her, I doubt very much she'd choose spending time with her over selecting her Halloween costume.

"No," Hannah replies. "I want to come."

"Then behave. I don't want the two of you fighting while we're looking for costumes. Got it?"

She nods and for just moment, looks properly chastised.

"Now sit down and try to act like you love each other. Quit pushing your sister's buttons. You're just getting her upset on purpose and I'm asking you to stop."

"Okaaay," she replies and slowly trudges to the table, pulls out a chair and plops down into it.

"Sorry, Caroline," she says, causing me to raise my eyebrows in shock. Did I just hear Hannah apologize to her sister without being prompted? Whoa....

"It's okay," Caroline replies, which makes me smile. That daughter of mine would forgive anyone anything. It seems her brain is able to forget the pain she experienced only moments ago, which makes my life all that much easier.

I rifle through the pantry and pull out some graham crackers, which is one of the girls' favorites. I pour two glasses of milk and set them down in front of them and then pull out a chair so that I can sit with them for a few moments before we head out.

"How was school today?"

"Good," replies Hannah.

"What was your special today?" I ask Caroline.

"Library." Already, her face bears a milk moustache and there are graham cracker crumbs down the front of her shirt. I can't help but smile.

"Did you get a book?" I ask.

"I got three of them," she says excitedly. "One of the books is about bugs, one is about Africa and I got the Percy Jackson book!"

"That's great!" I reply, knowing that Caroline has been waiting for several weeks to read the first book in the Rick Riordan series. I'm worried that it might be just a bit above her reading level but I figure we can read a bit of it together each night and I can help her understand it all. "How 'bout we start reading it when we get back?"

"Okay."

"Is dad coming?" Hannah asks, chewing on her graham cracker.

"No," I reply. "He's working so it'll just be the three of us."

"Aww, man! Why does he have to work so much?"

"Hannah, your father works very hard so that you and your sister can have all the stuff you need, like your hairbows and all your scarves. Try showing a little appreciation instead of so many complaints, all right?"

"All right," she mumbles.

I feel a twinge in my chest upon hearing Hannah's words because she has a valid point. Reid has been working a ton lately and he's been missing out on family activities here and there. Nothing major—a dinner here, a bedtime there—but it's clear to me that the girls notice these things, regardless of how minor they are. This just goes to show you that while you think something is small and insignificant, it really does mean something to a child.

I see Hannah's point but at the same time, she's got to realize that her father is currently the only person in this household who actually brings home a paycheck. I don't expect a ten year old to understand all the workings of a marriage but I think it's perfectly reasonable to expect her to cut her father a little slack.

The girls finish their snacks and I let Finley out for one last potty run before we leave. Once he's comfortably settled on the couch, I lead the girls out to the minivan. We pile in and head to the costume store. Once there, we find ourselves overwhelmed. The store, while not extremely large, is housed in a warehouse-type building where the ceilings are at least twenty feet tall. The walls display pictures of the costumes available with a number listed beside each one. As if figuring out which costume you want wasn't enough of a challenge, once you make your decision, you are then forced to search the store for the number that corresponds to the costume you've selected. I tend to forget about this process each year and when I enter the store, it all comes rushing back to me.

I let the girls wander up and down the aisle, reviewing all the pictures on the wall. It's actually quite funny to watch. There are dozens of little girls and boys wandering up and down a narrow aisle looking up at the costume selections. The parents are all standing off to the side out of the way, watching their little darlings try to decide what they want to be this year. Since all the kids are staring upwards and none of them are looking where they're going, there is a collision about once every three seconds. I giggle as I watch several collisions, then feel badly for doing so. Until, that is, I spy the rest of the parents giggling as well.

After several moments, Hannah comes to me and tells me she's decided on a costume.

"Okay," I say. "Show me which one."

She takes my hand and leads me to a far point on the wall that is so close to the adult costumes that I begin to get a bad feeling in the pit of my stomach. Sure enough, we reach the end of the aisle and she points to a picture of slender woman wearing what I'm certain is not a regulation nurses uniform.

I shake my head. "Absolutely not."

"What?" She says. "Why not?"

"Hannah, you and I both know your father would die before he let you out of the house wearing that."

"It's just a nurses uniform!"

"Find something else," I say. "Something your father would approve of. You know the rules."

"Fine," she huffs.

I stroll back to my spot near the opposite end of the aisle and watch as Caroline walks back and forth between two spots. Because I know my daughter so well, I'm certain she's deciding between a little red riding hood costume (complete with a long cape that covers most of her body) and a "Winter Princess" costume (With yet another long cape). Both of her selections will be 'father-approved' so I'm not worried in the slightest about her selection. I watch as she stops one final time in front of the Little Red Riding Hood costume and stares it for several moments. She places her hands on her hips and tilts her head to one side. I imagine she's trying to picture herself wearing the costume. Sure enough, after a few moments she is at my side telling me she has decided on a costume. Like her older sister, she takes my hand and pulls me toward a spot that is directly in front of Little Red. I smile since it is the one I'd hoped she'd choose.

"This one," she says, pointing up at the wall.

"Okay," I say, nodding. "Let's see if we can find it."

She tells me the number of the costume and we begin our search, scouring through shelves on the other side of the aisle. Thankfully, the costume comes complete with a picnic basket so we won't need to purchase any accessories. That's always been a pet peeve of mine. You purchase a costume, only to find that the key accessory that makes the costume believable isn't included.

Once we have the costume in our possession, Caroline holds it tightly in her hands since she's not letting it out of her sight, I focus my attention on Hannah, who is still pacing the aisle, trying to determine which costume to choose. Because Caroline has now made her selection, her attention span has reached its limit. She sighs heavily, then plops down onto the concrete floor to wait for her sister to make up her mind.

"Stay right here," I say to her and I walk over to Hannah, hoping to push her along in her decision making process. "Whaddya think?"

"I'm not sure," she replies while continuing to scan the pictures in front of her. "I like that one," she says, pointing to a 1950's pink lady costume. This makes sense since Grease has been on the television recently and Hannah has been glued to the screen watching what seems like a foreign world to her. "But I also like that one."

I glance up and see she's pointing to something that is the the 'I'm not sure it's father approved' zone. Recently, the girls have become obsessed with Monsters High dolls. It's based on a TV show where the characters are the children of famous monsters like Frankenstein and Dracula. Unfortunately, the characters all have unbelievably long legs and a girly figures that rival Jessica Rabbit. The costume is definitely borderline, but only because Hannah doesn't possess the accoutrements to fill out the costume properly. There is still the problem with the socks that go up to her thighs—a la Britney Spears, Hit Me Baby, One More Time. I'm just not feeling that Reid is going to go for that. I have to tread carefully, though. If Hannah gets one whiff of the fact that I don't approve of the Monster High costume, she'll veer right for it and nothing short of a screaming match will deter her. And I hate to pull out the 'because I'm your mother' speech while they select their costumes. I've always felt it's so important for them to have some choice in the matter, even if I have to nudge them a certain way.

"I love the jacket on that one," I say, pointing to the Monster High costume. "It would look adorable on you."

Hannah gives me a look that tells me 'adorable' is not a word I should be using to describe anything she wears.

"I want the Pink Lady one. Like in Grease."

"Hmmm…" I say, acting as though I'm not quite sure I agree with her decision. "Are you sure about that one?"

"Mo-om! Come on!"

I have to suppress a smirk. Kids are so easy to work with…most of the time. "All right," I say. "As long as you're sure."

"Yay!" She whoops.

We get the number from the picture and locate the costume.

Each girl is holding their costume tightly to their chest as we walk toward the cashier and I wonder if they're going to let them out of their grasp in order for her to scan it. They do, and a few minutes later, we're on our way home.

Glancing at my cell, I notice that it's nearly six-thirty. I'm shocked. We spent nearly two hours in the store. Reid is probably home by now and wondering where we are. Normally, I'd shoot him a text but since I'm driving and have a child who will be driving in five short years, I opt to phone him instead. He picks up on the third ring.

"Hello?"

"Hey, honey. I'm sorry we're late. The girls and I were out getting Halloween costumes and lost track of time. We'll be home in just a few."

"Don't worry about it," he says. "I'm not even home yet."

"Geez! Late day for you. Everything ok?"

"Yeah," he replies. "Just tying up some loose ends. I should be home in an hour or so."

"Okay, babe. See you then. Love you."

"I'll see you at home," he says, then ends the call. Weird, I think. He skipped the usual 'love you more' response that has become our thing. I quickly brush it off, assuming he's got someone in his office and doesn't want any co-workers to hear him talking mushy to his wife. I still find it amusing after all this time that he's embarrassed by it.

As if the people he works with don't know that loves his wife.

Rose

"Loose ends?"

Reid looks at me guiltily, then sighs heavily. "What was I supposed to say?"

I soften. "I don't know. But 'loose ends' sounds so...impersonal."

"I know it does," he replies. "And I'm sorry."

"It's okay," I reply, snuggling up beside him. I'm not sure if I'll ever get used to the him being in my apartment, sitting on my couch, making love to me in my bed, in the shower, on my couch...pretty much on any surface in my apartment.

By now, I'm sure you're wondering just what the hell is going on since Reid was so adamant about not seeing me...um, on a personal level. And he meant it. He really did. But like most men, when they see something they want, they have to have it. They just need to come to the decision on their own. They don't want to be pushed, prodded, or cajoled into anything. So I did just that. I did nothing to push, prod, or cajole him into coming to my place.

I did, however, do everything in my power to entice, arouse and lure him back into my life.

I made a point of being competent and efficient in the office and not once, did I stray into any sort of conversation that would lead us down a path of anything sexual. I was friendly without being overtly so while still maintaining a working knowledge of all of our mutual interests. Basically, I showed him I was just fine without him, thank you very much, but that I was still the same person he was attracted to.

I will admit that it took Reid longer than I thought it would - nearly a month. He did all the right things to prevent anything from happening between us. He made a point of not traveling with me, instead opting to have Brian, the dorky new guy, travel with him if it was needed. If we met in his office, Reid either made sure someone else from the team was there or simply left the office door completely open.

I admire his will.

It just wasn't strong enough. I feel certain he struggled with his decision and unless I'm completely off-base, he's going to continue to struggle with the guilt he feels about cheating on his wife. And that's okay. Together, we can work through it.

So how did we go from Reid refusing to see me to him sitting on my couch? I'll tell you.

Once day, a few weeks after our little conversation in his office, (and a few weeks after I'd had enough of waiting around for him to come to his senses), I had the brilliant idea to take a file that I knew Reid would be looking for. He had no choice but to come to my apartment; no choice, that is, if he wanted to get any work done. And I, of course, would have him all to myself to plead my case and there would be no interruptions.

When he showed up at my place that night, we went back and forth for the better part of two hours—him telling me how much he loves his wife and how the two of us couldn't be together and me nodding in understanding.

During the first portion of his "why I won't have an affair" speech, I sat on the other end of the couch and patiently listened to him, nodding at appropriate intervals. As the speech dragged on, I began to move closer to him by shifting my position. He was so engrossed in convincing me that we couldn't be together, he barely noticed my movements until I was practically in his lap.

Once he'd finished his "good guy" speech and I felt he'd spent enough time convincing himself that he'd done everything possible to push me away, I swooped in for the kill. And like most men, when it comes to sex, they suddenly become quite pliable.

I leaned forward slowly, then placed a soft kiss on his neck.

When I heard his sharp intake of breath, I knew I'd won the battle.

Of course, that was the easy part. Everyone knows that getting a man to have sex with you when he's aroused isn't much of a challenge.

In order to win the war, I needed to get him to think of me all the time, to want me when I wasn't around, and then finally, to want to be with me and only me.

That first night was only the step one. And with Reid, I knew I'd have to tread slowly. For now, there would be no pressure, no pushing, not even the tiniest of hints at where our future might be going. One thing I've learned about men is that they need to come up with the really big ideas all on their own. After we women plant the seed, of course.

As we sat there on my couch that night, I planted soft kisses all over his neck. My hands, seeming to have a mind of their own, traveled across his chest and down to his pants. When I felt his straining erection and he pushed his hips forward against my hand, I knew I would have him. I make quick work of his belt buckle and zipper and took him into my mouth before he even knew what was happening. I heard him moan in pleasure, then he dug his hands into my hair while I teased him with my mouth, taking in the full length of him, then nibbling and kissing the top of his erect penis.

What is it about men? The minute you're on your knees in front of them, they become mounds of clay—completely pliable. Reid especially. That man loves a good blow job and I'm more than happy to sink to my knees and perform that little service for him.

Reid came quickly that night, thrusting his hips forward while holding my head pressed against him. Just knowing that I had that power over him made me want him all over again.

Once the throbbing in his penis subsided, I pulled away and looked up at him. His head was thrown back onto the couch and his eyes were closed. His hands rubbed my scalp while his breathing slowed to a more normal rhythm.

"God, that was incredible," he said. He lifted his head off the back of the couch and looked down at me. "You're incredible."

I smiled at him, then curled up beside him, resting my hand on his chest and my head on my shoulder.

Our bodies fit together perfectly.

Tonight, we sit in much the same position we did that first night. Only now,there is a bit more comfort between us. We've talked to death about his feelings of guilt why we can't be together and while I've listened to him discuss the topic endlessly, he hasn't brought it up in more than a week. I think he's finally realized he can't ignore his feelings for me. He may still feel guilty, but we just don't talk about it anymore.

Tonight, it's quiet in the apartment and all I can hear is the sound of Reid breathing. He is relaxed and comfortable here, which is all I could ever ask for. Well, for now, that is. Reid is still skittish if I even hint at the future or moving our relationship forward. He's just not ready…yet.

The thing is, like most men, he's always ready for sex, Luckily, so am I. Even with him only sitting beside me sipping on a beer, I feel the familiar stirring between my legs. Slowly, I run my hand across his chest and the up towards his neck, massaging the skin there. After a few moments, I feel his muscles relax.

I let my hand trail a path from his neck, across his chest, down to the crotch, which is now becoming strained beneath the fabric of his pants.

I smile at him, holding his gaze in mine, then lean in to give him a kiss. I press my lips to his and place my hands on his cheeks, holding him close to me. He begins to kiss me passionately, sliding his tongue into my mouth. A moan escapes me as his tongue caresses mine. Reid understands me as no man has ever before. He quickly rids me of my clothing and when he pushes into me, he releases a moan of pleasure. I lift my hips up to meet him; encouraging him to quicken his pace. Our lovemaking is quick and frantic, almost as if we're desperate for each other, which of course, we are. When he finishes, he collapses on top of me and his heavy breathing warms my neck. We stay there for a few moments until his breathing slows. He kisses the side of my neck, pulls out of me, then slowly sits up and puts on his pants.

"I hate to do this, but-"

"You really need to head home," I finish for him.

He nods. "You'll be in work tomorrow?"

Now, it's my turn to nod. "As long as you'll be there."

He grins at me. "Why don't I pick us up some coffee?"

"Perfect," I say. He stands up and gathers the rest of his clothes. While he gets dressed, I grab my shirt, putting it on without a bra and only buttoning one button. He glances at me and I see him look at the expanse of skin I've left open. He reaches into the bottom half of my shirt and reaches his arm around to my lower back, pulling me toward him. He kisses me passionately.

"I'll see you in the morning," he says.

"Okay," I reply. As he turns to leave my apartment, I give him a quick smack on the ass. He turns back to me, laughing.

"Rose!" He says. "I am your boss," he says, chastising me.

"Didn't seem to matter a few minutes ago." I allow my gaze to drift toward the couch. As I meet his gaze once more, we both laugh out loud. "Now get out of here," I say. "I've got stuff to do."

I watch him walk out of my apartment and as the door shuts softly behind him, a feeling of sadness comes over me. It isn't entirely unexpected but still, it pinches a bit. I'm bound to feel a bit of jealousy knowing he's going to home to his wife to do God-only-knows what with her. Let's just hope I've worn him out enough.

Abbie

When Reid and I were first married, we were broke. Truth be told, we got married earlier than we'd planned. We always knew we'd end up together, but things have a funny way of working themselves out.

We'd only been together for about a year—long enough to know we wanted to be together forever, but not long enough to have a plan for it—when our relationship was thrust forward in a way that both of us were ill-prepared for.

I found out I was pregnant.

The unplanned pregnancy was both an embarrassment and a disappointment for us simply because we considered ourselves two intelligent, competent individuals. Things like this just didn't happen to people like us. How could two people who were college educated fail at Birth Control 101? Somehow, despite my being meticulous to the point of OCD at taking my birth control pill at the exact same time each and every day, we managed to conceive a child.

Our disappointment quickly turned to excitement as we realized this was something we both wanted, despite it happening a few years too early for us. We told our parents and quickly got married, foregoing the large, expensive wedding I'd always dreamed of for something much, much smaller—an intimate ceremony with only the two of us and our parents gathered around a courthouse in downtown Winston Salem. Oddly enough, I was able to brush aside my desire for a large elaborate wedding, telling myself that it was simply a waste of money and that those brides who chose to spend their money in such a frivolous way were only being silly. After all, Reid and I had much more important things to plan for besides a wedding. We were going to have a baby—a child of our own and I couldn't have been happier.

Here's the thing about being too happy: you get comfortable with it. You go about your day forgetting that such happiness can be ripped away from you in an instant.

Which is exactly what happened to us.

Barely two weeks after I became Mrs. Reid Hamilton, I miscarried.

It was during the time immediately after the miscarriage that Reid and I got closer than I ever thought possible. He was so attentive to my every need, wanting to make sure I was healing and that I was dealing with our loss completely. We both took a week off from work and spent most of that time snuggling in our bed and talking, not only about the loss of our child, but the hopes we had for our future children. During that week, it seemed as though there wasn't a subject we didn't discuss and by the end of our time together, I felt as though I knew my husband better than most women who'd been married for years.

For the better part of a week, we'd neglected all other parts of our lives and spent most of our time in bed, watching reruns of Gilligan's Island and old black and white movies. We'd doze throughout the day, my back pressed up against his chest with his arms wrapped around me, pulling the two of us closer with each breath.

The apartment we'd moved into less than a month before was still littered with unopened boxes, piles of crinkled newspaper and enough Styrofoam peanuts to fill the bathtub. Still, we barely left the bedroom, only coming out to answer the door when the pizza or Chinese food was delivered.

I often think back to that time and wish we could have it back. Not that I want to feel the sadness I felt then, but to have that time alone with Reid, without all the interruptions of daily life. Instead of having a week of time given to us, we have to seek out time to spend with each other wherever we can. Admittedly, there are days—weeks even—when this is an impossibility. And lately, it seems as though it's becoming more and more difficult. Between Reid's travel and the girls, it's hard for the two of us to spend quality time with one another. And honestly, I'd be lying if I didn't say it has me a bit worried.

Luckily, Reid will be home tonight and there's no travel scheduled for the next week or so. While I will have to share him with Hannah and Caroline, as long as I'm in the mix, I'm happy.

The girls and I are in the middle of bath time when I hear the sound of the garage door opening, telling me that Reid is finally home. A quick glance to the clock on the wall tells me it's nearly eight o'clock. Poor guy, I think. Wonder what problems he ran into today.

Hannah, who has professed she is too old for baths, is using our shower. I find I need to be close by or else she'll be in there for an hour, thereby using all the hot water in the house. Caroline, who still relishes being the baby of the family, sits contentedly in the tub while I rinse out her hair. I've found that if I bathe Caroline while Hannah is showering, it doesn't look so much like I'm monitoring her. I fill the tub for Caroline, then let Hannah begin her shower. This way, if she showers too long, she's he only one affected by any extensive hot water consumption.

There is always a method to my madness.

I hear Reid coming up the stairs from the basement and within moments, he's in the bathroom with all of us.

"Daddy!" Caroline screams.

"Hey, babe," I say, as he walks into the closet to change. "Long day, huh?"

"Yeah," comes the reply. When he finally emerges from the closet, he looks much more relaxed; baseball hat on, t-shirt and khaki shorts. Of course, both his shirt and hat display Yankees insignia.

"There's lasagna for you in the oven. I'm sure it's still

warm. Sorry we didn't wait for you but the girls were acting as though they hadn't been fed in a week. You know how that goes."

"Don't worry about it," he says. "I'm not hungry right now but I'll grab something later. Okay if it stays in the oven?"

Caroline has informed she is done with her bath by getting out of the tub and standing in front of me dripping wet. I take a towel and wrap it around her, rubbing her head to get rid of some of the moisture.

"It should be fine," I tell him. "You may have to nuke it just a bit if you wait awhile."

"I think I can handle it, Abbie," he retorts. His tone a bit snarky and honestly, very unlike him. For a moment, I'm taken aback.

I'm wondering just what sort of day he had to make him come home grumpy. Normally the sight of his kids is enough to cheer him up but tonight he barely even acknowledged Caroline. Honestly, I'm beginning to worry that his job is starting to affect him. But I brush it aside, figuring he's just had a bad day. Hey, we're all entitled to one now and again.

"I know you can," I say quietly. "Just want you to have a decent dinner."

He sighs heavily. "I'm sorry. I guess this day was just longer than I thought. I'm going to head to the office and check on a few things."

"Are you sure?" I ask. "You just got home. "

He shakes his head. "No. Unfortunately, there's a ton of work I still need to do. I'll be up in awhile, okay?"

"All right. Just don't be too long. The girls are going to bed soon. School night."

"Okay," he replies, as he walks out of the bedroom.

Focusing my attention back to my daughter, I take the towel and wrap it tightly around her, then wrap my arms around her. Her tiny body is warm from being in the tub for so long and I can't help but nuzzle her tightly to me. She begins to squirm and reluctantly, I release her.

"Okay," I say, "get dressed, then comb your hair."

She grabs her clothes from the counter, drops her towel, then runs naked out of the room.

"Hannah!" I yell toward the shower stall. "Are you about done in there?"

"What?"

"I said, ARE YOU DONE IN THE SHOWER?"

The water turns off and my eldest steps out of the shower delicately onto the floor mat. She takes one towel and wraps it around her torso, then takes another and flips her hair over and wraps her head in the towel.

I have to chuckle. She is such a diva.

Once the girls have put on their jammies and Hannah has spent an appropriate amount of time combing her hair, we settle on the couch to watch a little TV before it's time for them to go to bed. I can't help but glance at the clock every now and then and wonder when Reid will come upstairs. Since coming home nearly an hour ago, I haven't heard a sound out of him since he's been tucked away in the office. I wonder if he's stressed at work or has fallen behind because of his travel schedule.

The girls distract me from my thoughts by repeating each word of the Spongebob episode we are watching, which makes me realize once again that the two of them watch entirely too much television. Bedtime soon arrives and much to my shock, neither child argues when I usher them off to bed. As they walk to the steps to head upstairs to their bedrooms, I walk toward in the opposite direction and open the door to the basement to call to Reid.

"Reid?"

"Yeah?" Comes the reply.

"I'm putting the girls to bed. Come up and say good night."

"Be there in a minute!"

I close the door and walk upstairs to tuck the girls into bed, taking extra time because I know that once the lights are out, the two of them will fall asleep almost immediately and I want them to be awake with Reid comes up to say goodnight. Unfortunately, I can only drag out the process for so long or I'll have to deal with two cranky girls in the morning. I shut each door and slowly creep downstairs, intent on pouring myself a glass of wine in the hope that Reid will join me on the couch after he says goodnight to the girls. My earlier concerns return to the forefront of my mind and I make a mental note to check on my husband and make sure things are going well for him at work. Every so often, even if he's not demonstrating an increased level of stress, I worry that he's pushing himself too hard. I mean, I get it. Reid is one of those guys that is pretty much defined by how successful he is at the office. And of course, I'm grateful for how hard he works but at the same time, I want to tell him we can get by with much less.

As it turns out, I'm not able to address my worries with him. I sat on the couch for a while, drinking my glass of wine and flipping through the latest Redbook.

I wake up with a start at midnight to find my magazine crumpled on my chest and I'm still in my clothes. Half awake, I strip off my jeans and pull my bra through my shirtsleeves and climb into bed wearing only my underwear and my t-shirt. My final thought before falling asleep is that once again, I'm lying in bed alone.

Rose

The next day, as promised, Reid delivers a steaming cup of coffee to me. I'm not exactly sure how but he knows exactly how I take it—extra cream, no sweetener—but perhaps the best surprise of the day is that my coffee is delivered in a Starbucks location mug. Of course, it's a location mug with the words "New York, New York" printed on it. I'm not really sure how he managed to find this mug in North Carolina but I don't question it. I act appropriately thrilled and immediately take a picture of it and post it to my Facebook page. As I'm typing the caption to go along with the photo, it occurs to me that I don't really want to put out there for the world to see that Reid has purchased this mug for me so I decide to alter my post just a bit.

So glad I purchased this Starbucks location mug for myself!!!

There, I think. Now if anyone were to see my post, they wouldn't think anything of it. I just happened to purchase a mug from a town that I really, really like. It doesn't matter that I like the town that Reid just so happens to like as well. Purely coincidental.

As I sip my coffee, I can't help but smile. All the effort I put into this relationship with Reid is paying off. I've shown an interest in pretty much everything Reid has an interest in. We have tons of stuff to talk about, from television shows to sports and of course, we work together all day, every day. All in all, I would bet that not only do I have more in common with him than his wife but I also spend more time with him than her.

This is all working out very nicely.

I take another sip of coffee and think that this is perhaps the most delicious cup of coffee I have ever had. And let me tell you, I drink tons of coffee. I've become, admittedly, a bit of a coffee snob. I brew my own at home now that I've purchased one of those Keurig k-cup contraptions and on most mornings I empty more than one of those little plastic doo-hicky's. And while the invention of a machine is a huge advancement for mankind, the problem is that I can no longer bear to even smell the sludge we brew at the office. Coffee has now become a bit of an issue for me. There are several restaurants I won't even go into because their coffee is so horrendous—nothing more than brown sludge. No amount of cream or sugar will change the taste of that liquid poison.

All that being said, the coffee I am holding in my hand is not even close to delicious. Still, though it may be the best coffee I have ever had. Why, you ask? The answer is simple: over the past several months, Reid has paid attention to how I like my coffee. Not only that, but he thought of me this morning, which prompted the coffee I am how holding.

Those facts make this the best damn cup of coffee ever.

I take the last swig of coffee from 'the mug that bought for myself,' (Wink, wink.) and then reach into my top drawer for a mint. Now that Reid and I have reached this new level of intimacy, I know that we'll be sitting closer when I'm with him in his office and I certainly don't want him to smell coffee on my breath. I suck on the mint for several moments, then toss it into the trash as I run my tongue over my teeth to wipe off any remaining coffee residue. I stand up, smooth my skirt down, then stroll into Reid's office. He looks up at me and then smiles. For the first time, I notice that his smile is different than it's been in the past. It's no longer the friendly 'how are you today, Rose?' smile that he's used in the past. Now, his smile is indicative of something else… a deeper layer of intimacy and a knowledge that there is something between us. I feel a flutter deep in my belly and return the smile as I step into his office, closing the door behind me.

"Thanks for the coffee," I say, sitting down across from

him. "And the mug. I love it."

"I thought you might."

"Where'd you find it? I wouldn't think they'd have New York stuff around here."

"They don't," he replies. "I bought it last time I was up there and hadn't used it yet. I found it still in the bag in my closet this morning and thought you might like to have it."

"Well," I reply, smiling, "you thought right."

We sit in silence for a few moments and I can't help but wonder if he's thinking about his time at my place the night before. I know I've spent a good deal of time reviewing it. As is reading my thoughts, he says, "Last night was..."

"Yeah...it was..."

Then his expression changes and a knot begins to form in the pit of my stomach. Instead of the smile he gave me earlier, his expression is now one of worry and concern.

"Rose," he begins.

"I know." I have to interrupt him because I simply cannot go through this again. He cannot tell me that he doesn't care for me or that he can't see me anymore. I've worked too hard for this and by now, I care too much. Before I even know what's happening, the words tumble out of me and I find myself powerless to stop it.

"Look," I begin. "I get it. You feel guilty. You don't want to hurt your wife. You've got a family and you love them. But Reid, you've got feelings for me, too! You can't just ignore them. I'm not asking for anything from you. I just want to spend some time with you! Please! Can you give us a little time to see what this is?"

Reid looks at me expressionless for several moments and then leans back in his chair. I'm waiting for him to say something, anything. The moments drag on and on and I feel like I'm about to burst. Why doesn't he say anything? Did I show too much emotion? Was it too soon? Have I turned him off? Of course I did. A woman should never show so much emotion when a relationship is still at the delicate and fragile early stages. What the hell was I thinking? I'm silently berating myself for several moments. I'm lost in thought and thinking I've ruined everything between the two of us when I hear Reid sigh.

"Rose," he says softly. "Surely you know how wrong this is? We both know it. And you're exactly right. I don't want to hurt Abbie."

I cringe when he speaks her name.

He continues. "This would kill her. I never wanted this to happen. I'm not *that guy*."

"What do you mean, 'that guy'?" I ask.

"The guy who cheats on his wife. That's just not me!"

And that's when I feel my chest tighten and I think I might really love this man. Not love him like 'I want him' but love him as in *I love him.*

Fuck.

He's really a good guy. And I was right. He does love his wife. I can see that he's wracked with guilt over this and is beginning to see our relationship as something dirty or something to be kept hidden. And for now, that's just fine. I need to be patient and let him work through whatever stuff he's got to work through. I've been patient so far. What's a bit more time? Besides, when he's with me, there won't be any of the help-me-with-the-kids crap that I'm sure he's dealing with at home. When he's with me, it will be all carefree and fun. No stress. I'll show him what it can be like; what it should be like. Then slowly, he'll come to the realization that he should be with me all the time.

But for now…patience.

"I know it's not you. I can see you struggling with this and I'm so sorry about that. I know you'd never hurt Abbie-" I can barely say her name without cringing again. "or your girls. Believe me, I'd never want you to do that. But this…whatever this is between us…well, I'm not ready to let go of it just yet."

"Oh, Rose," he says, "why is it so hard to stay away from you?"

When I hear that, I want to tell him. It's because we're meant to be together. He married the wrong woman. He should be with me and leave her. He'll be happier with me than he ever could be with *her*.

But I don't say any of those things. Instead, I sit in front of him and lift my shoulders up an inch or so, not really answering his question but hoping he'll keep feeling the way he does right now.

"This sucks," he says, sighing heavily. "I would never, ever hurt Abbie and the girls but I just can't get you out of my system."

"Look," I say, "we'll just take things day by day, all right? No pressure to do anything. No time restrictions or limits. If you want to see me, stop by. If you don't, that's fine too."

Reid raises his eyebrows at me questioningly. I'm quick to respond. "Of course, I *want* to see you but I'm not going to put any pressure on you. This," I point my finger between the two of us. "-whatever we have between us…well, it is what it is, all right?" I nearly cringe as I utter the words. Not only do I hate the statement, 'it is what it is,' but I'm lying my ass off. My relationship with Reid is anything but casual, despite what I'm telling him. I'm in this for the long haul. I just need to wait for Reid's emotions to catch up to mine.

He looks at me for several moments before he speaks. "That's just not fair to you. You shouldn't have to sit around your apartment waiting for me to find time to see you. You deserve better than someone who has to sneak around to see you." He shakes his head. "As much I enjoy being with you, I can't do it. It's just not right. I love my wife."

I'd like to say I was shocked at hearing Reid's words but I'm not. There's not a doubt in my mind that he loves Abbie. It's part of the reason I fell so hard for him. He is a decent and good man. He's going to feel horribly guilty until he comes to terms with his feelings for me. And I can handle it. He wouldn't be the Reid I know and love if he was able to carelessly toss aside his marriage. Waiting for Reid is all part of wanting him. And I'm perfectly willing to wait for him….as long as it takes.

"Just think about what I said, all right? I mean it. If you want to see me or stop by, even for a minute, I want to see you as well."

Reid meets my gaze for several moments, then nods. "You're really great, you know that, right?"

"Of course I know that," I reply, tossing my hair back playfully.

"And I hope you understand where I'm coming from."

"I do." I stand up and point in the general direction of my cubicle. "I guess I'd better head back to work."

As I leave Reid's office, I'm smiling. Most women would be devastated with the conversation they'd just had. But not me. I know better. The conversation I just had was merely one step in a long journey. A journey that will have its missteps along the way but will be complete when Reid is mine and mine alone.

After all, both Reid and I know he can't stay away from me for very long.

Abbie

Reid has been on the road all week but somehow managed to arrive home a bit after noon today. Once he dumped emptied his suitcase, he was able to nap for a couple of hours, waking up just before the girls came home from school. When he offered to take them to see the movie Frozen, I knew my night would be free. Luckily Nora, one of my dearest friends, was free as well and we decided to spend some time together. I immediately put a bottle of wine in the freezer and grabbed the book I'd been reading. I figured I'd at least get a chapter done before her arrival.

As it turned out, I was able to read the better part of three chapters before I heard her knock at the front door.

"Hey," I said, grinning at her. "Come sit down. You want a glass of wine?"

"Need you even ask?"

I chuckled.

Nora is perhaps the most striking woman I know. Despite being nearly forty, she still looks much the same as she did when she was twenty. Really the only difference is that her hair is now shorter than it was. She looks so young, in fact, that it's almost a certainty that she will be carded each time she makes a wine purchase. I however, never have that problem. While I look good for my age, I certainly don't look anywhere near twenty-one.

I pour Nora a healthy glass of chardonnay, then put the bottle on the table between us, knowing that it wouldn't get warm by the time one of us needed a refill. Actually, the more I thought about it, the more I thought I should probably go ahead and put another bottle in the fridge. Surely we'd go through at least this one.

"How was your week?" I ask.

She shrugs. "Ugh…Paul is being a douche again. I tell you, Abbie, I don't know how much more of this I can take."

Nora's husband, or ex-husband, I should say has been being a bit of an ass, if I do say so myself. I leaned forward, not wanting to miss the latest in what would surely be another good story.

"What'd he do now?"

She sighed. "I texted him today to ask him if he could pick up Jessie from soccer practice Monday night. I can drop her off - no problem - but I'm getting my hair cut that night and it might run long. You know how busy Shannon is."

She looked at me pointedly and I nodded. Her hairdresser, Shannon Willoughby, was the busiest hair stylist around. So busy, in fact, that she was frequently late. Because she was so skilled, anyone who went to her was absolutely willing to put up with this little inconvenience simply because they looked so fabulous once she was done with them. I went to her as well and had learned to make my next appointment as I was leaving the salon after my own appointment. Shannon's slots filled up quickly, there were never any cancellations, and if you didn't schedule as you were leaving, you might not be able to get an appointment for months.

"So Paul texts me back and says, 'I'll try.' Really? He'll try? What the hell is that? Why does he only have to 'try' to be there for his children? Why does it all fall on my shoulders?" Nora took a large sip from her glass and put it back down before continuing. "I just don't get it, Abbie. They're his kids too! Why does he get the option of whether or not he has to take care of his kids? Why is he the only one that gets to parent when it's convenient?"

"I don't know," I reply softly, fingering the rim of my glass. "Maybe it's because they never carried them? Maybe they don't feel the level of responsibility we do?"

"What's this 'we' shit? I know for a fact you don't have

these issues with Reid. Take tonight, for example. The man traveled all week, right?"

I nod.

"See? And now he's out with his children so you can have a break and enjoy some girl-time with a friend. Why can't Paul ever think like that? He's so fucking selfish." She lifts up her glass and drains it, then slams it back down onto the table, making me flinch at the sound of the glass hitting the table-top.

"I'm sorry, Nora. I wish I could say that it will get better."

"But it won't," she says, finishing my sentence for me. "It's like the minute he moved out, he checked out of the kids' lives. I just don't understand. I've told him he can take the kids whenever he wants—dinner, movies, the park—whatever. But do you think he ever does that? Nope. The shithead can't be bothered to spend any time with his kids."

"What's he got going on?"

Nora's lips pursed into a thin line. "I have no idea. All he ever says are that his plans are 'uncancellable,' whatever the hell that means." She made quotes in the air with her fingers. "I mean, come on! When you're a parent, the only plans that are uncancellable are the ones with your kids....or surgery. If he's having surgery, I'll let him off the hook."

"Is there a chance he is?"

"Ha!" She replied. "Not a snowball's chance in hell. That man probably has an appointment with his personal trainer."

I nodded. Once Paul and Nora had separated, Paul began to focus much of his energy into transforming his body and 'getting healthy' as he referred to it. The only problem was, instead of actually doing the exercising, Paul had spent a good deal of money on equipment for his home, a gym membership, and countless hours of personal training sessions. I kept looking for a change in him but honestly, he looked the same to me—maybe even a bit heavier. Surely cancelling one session with his personal trainer wouldn't cause much damage to his 'physique.'

"I can pick up Jessie from soccer Monday night, if you like."

Nora puts her hand on top of mine and pats it. "I hate to ask you to do that."

I smile back at her and lift my shoulders an inch or so. "You didn't ask. I offered."

She nods knowingly. "I know you did. And actually that'd be great. If for some unknown reason her father decides to rearrange whatever important plans he has in order to spend time with his daughter, I'll let you know. But just knowing that you'll be there for me is great. I really appreciate it."

"Of course," I reply.

I hear the front door open and then the sound of someone calling my name. "I wonder who that is?"

Just then, Carol enters the kitchen carrying a bottle of wine in each hand. Rose is behind her and her hands are also laden down with bottles. I laugh out loud.

"What are the two of you up to?" I ask, grinning.

Carol lifts up the two bottles. "We were going to head out for some Mexican food but thought we'd swing by here instead." She looks pointedly at the half-empty bottle on the table. "I see we got here in the nick of time." She glanced back over her shoulder at Rose. "Grab a seat, Rosie. There's wine that needs to be consumed."

I chuckle once again and slide my chair back so that I can grab a couple of wine glasses from the kitchen. Carol puts a hand on my shoulder to stop me.

"You sit," she says. "I know where the glasses are."

As I sit back down, I reach over and pull out a chair from the table. "Have a seat," I say to Rose. "Join the party." Carol returns with two glasses in her hands.

"I put the wine in the fridge," she says.

I nod. "Perfect. Nora" I say, glancing around the table. "This is Carol and Rose. Rose works at K&M and so does Carol's husband."

"Really?" Nora replies. "Small world, huh?"

"I know, right?" Rose chimes in. Steve has been there for a few years but I've been there less than a year."

"What do you do there," Nora asks.

"I work for Reid in the products division."

"Reid…you mean Abbie's husband?" Nora asks.

"Yep," Rose replies. "I spend my days keeping him in line."

I laugh at that one, knowing that there just might be days when Rose is required to do just that.

"Where is that boss of mine, anyway?" Rose asks.

"He took Hannah and Caroline to see Frozen," I reply. "So I get to have a girl's night at long last. And I need it. This has been a long week."

"Oh, right," Rose says, nodding. "Reid was traveling this week. I'm sure it was a rough week for him…and for you," she adds quickly. "Let's see…Monday was Phoenix, then Tuesday it was Michigan for a couple of days, then he finished the week in Santa Fe. That's a lot of time zones!"

I take a sip from my glass and nod. "I'm not sure how he does it. If I had a week like that, I'd come home and spend the weekend catching up on my sleep. But Reid took a nap earlier, then decided he'd take the girls to see a movie."

"That's incredible. He's such a great dad," Rose says.

From beside me, I hear Nora mutter something but I can't quite make out the words. When I glance over at her and raise my eyebrows, she just gives me a look that I can't quite read. I shake my head and flash her an expression that tells her I have no idea what she is talking about. In return, she shakes her head dismissively, then takes a sip from her glass. She places it back down onto the table and turns her attention to Carol.

"So," Nora begins, looking at Carol. "Your husband works at K&M? What does he do there?"

"He's in graphic design. Does all the print work for the presentations and designs the logos and whatever else is needed

135

once K&M signs a new customer."

"Ah," Nora says. She takes another sip from her glass then tilts it toward Rose. "What about you, Rose? You work for Reid, you said? What's he like as a boss."

"Oh, My. God!" She replies, grinning. "He's the best. Just the best. He really knows his stuff and he's so creative. I'm so lucky to be working for him."

"Really," Nora replies tartly. "How nice." When she speaks, I pick up a little something in her tone that tells me she doesn't think it's nice at all. I glance at her as I take another sip of wine and she raises an eyebrow at me. I look back at her with an expression that says, "what?" She just shakes her head and turns back to Rose.

"And you said you've been working there for how long?" Nora asks.

"Almost a year," Rose replies. She takes a sip from her glass, then turns to speak to Carol. "How long has Steve been there?"

"God," Carol replies, pondering the question. "I really have no idea. Six? Seven years?"

"Wow," Rose says. "That's a long time."

"Not so long," Nora jumps in. "Course, when you're as young as you are, I'm sure it *seems* like a long time. How old are you, by the way?"

I nearly gasp, so blown away am I by the boldness of Nora's question but when I look at Rose, she's smiling and doesn't seem the least bit bothered by it. I have to assume that in our youth, we don't mind so much telling our age. Plus, had I not known Nora so well, I would have thought her question was purely innocent, but knowing her as I do, I can tell there's more to it than meets the eye.

"I'm twenty-five," Rose replies. "I'll be twenty six in March."

"Wow," Nora says. "Twenty-five. So you've been able to legally drink for, what? Four years now?"

Carol, oblivious to the sarcasm Nora is spewing, grins and nods her head. "I know! She's just a baby. Graduated from college, what? Four years ago?" She looks toward Rose for confirmation. When Rose nods, Carol continues. "Where did you work before K&M? I know you've told me this but I can't remember."

"I worked in that doctor's office, remember? I was their customer liaison?"

Carol nods. "Oh, right, right…"

"And I hated it," Rose says. She takes a large sip from her glass before continuing. "The job sounded so glamorous but all I did every day was call patients and remind them of their appointments. It was tedious and boring."

"Unlike where you are now," Nora says. "Where your days are filled with excitement."

I can hear the sarcasm dripping off Nora's words but it seems everyone else is oblivious to it. I begin to wonder what has gotten her so irritated. Clearly, her venom is directed at Rose but I can't figure out what she might have done. The woman brought wine for us. Surely, Nora thinks that was a nice gesture. Could she be upset that our little party was interrupted by these two? Perhaps, but then I wonder why her animosity is only directed to Rose and not Carol.

Rose laughs. "Oh, I don't know if I'd say my days are exciting but it's certainly better than calling people all day long."

"I'll bet it is," Nora mumbles.

I stare pointedly at Nora but she avoids my gaze. Had I not been the hostess of this little get-together, the entire scene would have been hilarious. Between Nora's blatant animosity, Rose's complete obliviousness, and my discomfort, this is swiftly turning into a Seinfeld episode.

As the night progresses, the four of us drink a healthy amount of wine and consume pretty much all the food in the house that was able to be eaten without turning on the oven. As a result, there are no crackers left, no cheese, and all the snacks for the girls lunches have mysteriously disappeared. Carol, knowing she had to drive, only had a glass or two, which unfortunately meant that Nora, Rose and I consumed most of the wine. Once Carol decided it was time to head out, Rose followed, giving me a hug before she left. Once I walked the two of them out, I returned to the kitchen and sat down with Nora.

As I lifted my glass, Nora fixed a steely gaze on me.

"What?"

"What do you mean, 'what'," she replied. "Rose."

"What about her?" Nora looks at me as though I've lost my mind. "What's your problem with her? She was nice to you."

"Oh sure, she's nice. As long as she's getting what she wants. But the minute she doesn't? Look out."

"What the hell are you talking about?"

"I got a funny vibe from her, that's all. All that talk about her job and Reid and…well, she's just so young! Her outlook on things is so warped, probably from lack of experience."

I chuckled. "She is young, I'll give you that. But from what Reid tells me, she's a hard worker and a quick learner."

"And what about her enthusiasm? Did he mention that as well?"

Once again, I hear the disdain dripping from her words. "What is with you? Why are you hating on Rose?"

"I'm not hating!"

I fix her a pointed look.

"Okay," she says, acquiescing. "Maybe I'm hating a little bit. But can you blame me? What with all that fake cheer and 'happy to be at work' bullshit? Come on. Does anyone really like to be at work?"

I shrug. "Maybe she does. Maybe she really likes what she does. But anyway, who cares? Don't worry about her. It's not like you're going to start hanging out with her. She's never even stopped by here before. She only probably came over because she was with Carol and Steve is out of town."

"No," Nora mumbles. "I don't have to worry about her. But what about you?"

"What about me?"

Nora leans forward, opened her mouth, then shut it. She waved her hand around dismissively. "You know what? Forget I said anything. I'm probably all wound up because of Paul. Anyone could have stopped by tonight and I wouldn't have liked them. I'm sorry I was so bitchy."

"Don't worry about it," I say, grasping her forearm. "You're just going through a really tough time. You're practically a single parent which means you've got a ton of stress. You're bound to lash out at someone."

Having known Nora for quite some time, I begin to realize that her behavior tonight was actually quite tame given the fact that her reputation for having a sharp tongue and a quick mind is legendary. She has, on numerous occasions, put people in their place with a single comment—one that both chastises them and at the same time, makes them regret they ever crossed paths with her. Her snarky comments and biting wit are things I've always envied. While I can come up with the perfect comeback to almost any situation, it normally takes me a day or two, which is well past the time it would have had any effect on the situation.

"You're probably right. But even so, I want to go on record as saying that something about that woman doesn't sit right with me. She's hidden her bitch deep inside of her but you and I both know, we all have one inside of us."

Now, I had to laugh. "Come on. Rose doesn't have a mean bone in her body."

"She's a woman," Nora said, peering at me from over her wine glass. "We all have a mean bone somewhere."

It isn't until much later when I'm cleaning up our mess that I think back to Nora's words of warning about Rose. It is then that I recall the first evening I met Rose and how I felt for just an instant, there might have been something amiss. I smile, remembering how foolish I felt for even thinking such a thing, even more so now since Rose has been nothing but kind and genuine to me.

I quickly dismiss Nora's words of warning, then creep upstairs to check on the girls before I head to bed. They are both sound asleep, which is to be expected, given the late hour. I adjust the covers over each of them before going back downstairs to crawl into bed with Reid, who is also sound asleep and snoring slightly. I pull off my jeans, somehow managing to do it without falling over, which is quite a feat considering the amount of alcohol I have consumed. I pull back the covers on my side of the bed and crawl in, slowly working over to Reid's side of the bed where he had graciously and unknowingly warmed up the bed for me. In seconds, I am fast asleep, my body molded against my husband's.

Rose

Just before five, I poke my head into Reid's office and stage whisper to him. "See you in a bit?"

He looks up from his computer screen and nods, then looks at his watch. "I'll be there in a half an hour."

Karma must be with me as I drive home because I manage to hit every single light green on the way to my place and make it there in a record twelve minutes, which gives me just enough time to brush my teeth, fluff my hair, and remove all my dirty clothes from the living room. (I'm quite the slob and if I didn't occasionally have company, I've never clean.) After tossing several armfuls of clothing into my spare bedroom and closing the door, I hear a soft knock on my door. After a quick glance in the mirror, I open the door to find Reid standing there, looking absolutely delicious.

"Come on in," I say, tugging the sleeve of his shirt. Despite after the countless times he's been to my place, each time he enters he looks as though he's about to run off. It's almost as though as he crossed the threshold into my apartment, he relives all his guilt about what he knows is going to happen once the door closes. I quickly guide him to the couch and sit down beside him. "Want something to drink?"

He nods. "Sure. I'll have a beer if you've got one."

If I've got one? Does he actually think I'd have him to my place without making sure the fridge is stocked with any beer he's mentioned in the past several months? Come on. What is this, amateur hour? I'm playing for keeps here. There will be no mistakes. I saunter over to the kitchen and pull out one of his favorites—Michelob Ultra. I also have a selection of Sam Adams, Killian's red and several dark beers if he ever has a hankering for those.

I crack open the beer and walk back into the living room. After handing him the open beer, I curl up beside him, angling my body toward his. Almost automatically, his left arm reaches around me and rests gently on my shoulders, his fingers barely touching my collar bone. After he takes a few sips of his beer, he pulls me toward him and gives me a kiss. As he pulls back, he looks at me for just a moment and once again, I feel anxiety welling up in the pit of my stomach. This man is like skittish kitten. I can't move too fast or he'll run away terrified.

For several moments, he sits still, just looking at me and I can tell he's got something on his mind.

"Reid," I say, "what is it? What's wrong?"

He sighs heavily. "I just can't help feeling so guilty for being here. This isn't right. I shouldn't be doing this."

I nod, wanting to be sympathetic but honestly, I'm a bit exhausted with this conversation. I mean, really? He shows up at my place and then expresses his guilt? Why doesn't his guilt drive him home?

Why, you ask? Because he doesn't want to be at home. He wants to be here with me; he just doesn't like the way he feels about it.

Look, we both know he wants to be here but we need to do this little dance where expresses his guilt before he fucks me in order to alleviate some of his anxiety. Is it some sort of penance before he commits the sin? Whatever it is, I'm tired of it. But I can't let him now this. I've got to be supportive and understanding. "I know it's a horrible position to be in and I know you must feel awful about all of this, but surely we can't help how we feel?"

He shrugs halfheartedly. "Still…"

"Look," I say softly, "I know how difficult this is for you. But I just want to spend some time with you. Why does it have to be right or wrong? Why can't it just be?"

Slowly, I climb into his lap, straddling him. He places his hands on the side of my hips and leans his head back against the couch and looks up at me. I can see he's torn. He wants to be here with me but he also feels terribly guilty about the fact that he's cheating on his wife. I've gotten so far with him and I'm so afraid to lose him that I realize I simply cannot let it happen. I lean forward, place my hands on the sides of his face and kiss him deeply. When he responds, I have to suppress a smile. Slowly, I pull back and begin to kiss his neck, opening up the collar of his shirt so that I can reach more of his skin. Before he even realizes what I'm doing, I've slid down the length of his body and unzipped his pants.

When I finally take him in my mouth and feel him shudder, I have to suppress a smile. Slowly, I caress up and down the length of him with my mouth. I tease him mercilessly, nibbling on the tip of his penis, then rubbing my lips down the underside of him. After several moments, I stand up in front of him and remove my skirt and panties, keeping my gaze locked on his. I straddle him, slowly easing down onto his penis. He groans as he slides into me and grabs my hips in order to push in deeper. I begin to move slowly up and down the length of him until I can no longer stand it and I begin to move my hips faster, urging my body toward release. I cry out as an orgasm rips through me and moments later, Reid's fingers dig into my hips, holding me in place as he throbs inside of me. Completely spent, I collapse on top of him, still breathing hard.

"You are fucking incredible," Reid whispers.

All I can do is smile. It doesn't matter that he leaves. He'll always come back.

Abbie

Each year, I play a game with myself and the heat in the house. I try to see how long into October or November I can go before turning on the heat. This drives Reid absolutely crazy. He is someone who believes that the heat and air conditioning is meant to be used whereas I want to use the weather outside as much as possible so that we can reduce our heating costs. Admittedly, I've taken this little game of mine to extremes and this year is no different. We've been sleeping with the windows open a teeny bit each evening because it's been relatively mild. Up until only recently, that is. Mother Nature, it seemed, was tired of my little game and brought in a cold snap which meant I had to admit defeat and turn the heat on. I managed to make it to November first this year, which was when I woke to find the house a balmy sixty two degrees and my girls quite unwilling to get out of their warm beds.

Reid was only too happy to flip the switch for me.

Ever since the girls have been in school, it seems like the days, weeks, and months just fly by too quickly. The girls always tend to be counting down the days until the next vacation, day off, or break. And thanksgiving week is no exception. This is one of the few weeks during the year that both girls get up out of bed and are ready on time to go to school. Probably because they only have to do it twice. Both today and yesterday, I was able to drop off the girls and actually stop for a cup of coffee before heading off to do the countless errands that always seem to fill my day.

Tonight, the girls are in a wonderful mood. They are out of school for the next five days and will get to see my father when he arrives for Thanksgiving tomorrow night. By then, I'll have most of the prep work done for our thanksgiving dinner.

Tomorrow, most of the day will be spent making pies, prepping the stuffing and making sure the turkey is fully thawed. Tonight, however, Reid and I are meeting some of his co-workers for dinner, which means I get the night off. Perfect, since I'll be doing nothing but cooking for the next two days.

After Reid gets home from work and changes into jeans and a t-shirt, the four of us pile into the minivan and head out to dinner. We're headed to this hole-in-the-wall restaurant that Reid keeps hearing about so we decided to try it and see what the fuss is all about. Apparently, this place has the best pizza around. Since the girls will eat any type of pizza and I'm not the one cooking it, it's a win-win.

We pull up to a dimly lit, dilapidated old building and for a moment, I wonder if coming to this place was a mistake. Hopefully, they've spent money on the food they're serving instead of the appearance of the building. Then it occurs to me that Reid might have gotten the address wrong. As I turn to ask him if he's sure we're in the right place, I see Steve and Carol pull into the parking space beside us. Carol leans forward and waves to me excitedly. I wave, then step out of the car and open the back door so that the girls can climb out.

"Hey!" Carol says, embracing me. "How are you? How's the house coming?"

She is such a warm person and since I'm sort of sequestered due to my stay-at-home-mom status, I'm once again thankful that Reid had the forethought to introduce us. "Hey, Carol," I say, returning her hug. "We're all good! And the house is great! I've gotten both of the bedrooms done and now I'm working on the dining room. You and Rose need to come back for another visit!"

She smiles. "Absolutely!"

We begin to walk across the parking lot toward the entrance. "Are you all set for Thanksgiving?"

She nods. "There will be no cooking for me this year. Steve and I have decided to eat out."

I stop abruptly, nearly causing Hannah to run into me. "What?" I say, aghast. "Don't you have any family coming to town?"

"No," she says as the smile leaves her face. "I thought my parents were going to drive here but my dad's arthritis has been so bad lately that they don't think he'll be able to manage. And my mom has never been a good driver to begin with so it's not as if she can take over."

"Gosh, Carol. I'm so sorry. I hope he's all right."

"He will be. I just hate that I won't get to see them this year. Maybe for Christmas, though."

We walk into the restaurant and locate our seats. There are several tables pushed together and I assume someone called ahead to let them know we were a large party. I see that Rose has already arrived and is seated at the empty tables by herself. I wave to her and she grins back at me and then motions to the empty seats around her as is to say, "See? I'm sitting here with all my friends."

I chuckle, then turn to help the girls with their coats. Once we are all seated, Reid and Steve walk over and sit at the opposite end of the table. They are engrossed in conversation and I assume it will be like this most of the night since the two of them work so closely together.

I settle the girls into their chairs and take my seat between them. I direct my attention to Rose and ask, "So how are things with you? I haven't spoken to you in what? Two weeks?"

She nods, then takes a sip from the glass of water in front of her. "I'm good, but busy. I've started Christmas shopping for my family," she looks at the shocked expression on my face and chuckles. "I've got to start early so my credit card doesn't melt from overuse. I've got three brothers and a sister who, between all of them, have nine kids."

"Good lord!"

Rose's smile reaches up to her eyes as she talks about her family. "They're all just so great. I know I don't have to buy something for all of them but I want to. I want them to have something special from me. My family does the whole 'pull names' thing for gifts but I still get something for the kids – even if it's something little."

"Wow," I say, glancing at Carol. "Did you hear this?"

She nods. "I know. She's nuts."

Rose laughs. "Well, I don't have any kids so really, there's no one else to buy presents for. Might as well make it all about the little ones, you know?"

And I do know. When Reid and I first had Caroline, we decided that gifts for each other weren't really necessary. While we were able to live a decent lifestyle, we weren't without our financial challenges. Any 'extra' money - if that's even a real term—we came across during the months leading up to Christmas, was set aside so that we could focus on making the holiday magical for the kids. And mostly, that meant lots of presents.

Of course, both Reid and I have always managed to find even more of this 'extra money' so that we could purchase even a little something special for each other. One year, I managed to squirrel away enough money for a leather briefcase I knew Reid has been eyeing for some time. Other years, the presents weren't anything as luxurious; a cashmere scarf for me, a new name plate for Reid or even more frequently, we'd give each other gift certificates to restaurants which would guarantee us a night out.

"That may be the nicest thing I've heard all week," I said. "Kids are little for such a short amount of time and before long, the magic goes away." I leaned in and whispered. "Santa…."

"Oh, yes," she replied. "One of my nephews has-" she glanced at Caroline and Hannah to make sure they weren't paying attention- "lost the magic, so to speak. My brother told him if he said anything to his baby sisters, he'd never see his Playstation, Phone, or Ipad again!"

"I wish those electronics were around when my boys were

young," Carol said. "When Ryan was…oh, I don't know. Ten, maybe? He 'lost the magic' when he found our stash of presents while looking for an eight track tape for his father." She paused to give Steve the stink- eye but he was too engrossed in his conversation with Reid to notice. "In any event, he found the tape and a whole lot more. When Steve went outside to put the tape in his car, Ryan grabbed his younger brother and brought him to the stash." She chucked. "God, when I think about how mad I was? I couldn't even speak!"

I glance down at Hannah and Caroline, who are engrossed in coloring the menu. "I don't know what I'm going to do when those two figure it all out. It's so much fun doing all the prep work. Reid and I are up til God-only-knows how late wrapping and setting up. We finally crash after it's all arranged and then it feels like a second later, the girls are poking us and trying to get us out of bed. It's exhausting, but it's all worth it."

The waitress comes over and takes our drink order, then leaves so that we have time to look over the menu. When she returns, we place our food order and discussions around the table resume.

Rose looks at Carol. "Are we still on for Thursday?"

"Sure," Carol replies. "Want to meet at my house around two? Steve wants to watch the parade and then the dog show." She rolls her eyes.

"Sounds perfect."

I lean over toward the two women as it dawns on me that these people I consider friends don't have family coming in for thanksgiving and are most likely going to eat out someplace. "Wait a minute. Are you guys all going out to dinner on thanksgiving?"

Carol and Rose nod in unison. "We're going to head to Annabelle's," Carol says. "See if it's any good." She turns to Rose. "I heard they're steaks are unbelievable."

Rose grins back at her. "I heard their martinis are

unbelievable!"

"I really can't believe you're not cooking this year." The thanksgiving production at Carol and Steve's house each year is nothing short of amazing. There is, of course, a turkey and all the sides, but Carol also cooks a ham, a prime rib, and an entire assortment of gooey, delicious desserts that would rival any bakery in town.

Carol shrugs. "With no one coming into town this year, I thought I'd skip it. Don't get me wrong, I love to cook all that stuff. I'm on Pinterest for days searching for new things to try, but with no one to eat it but me and Steve….my waistline can't afford it. So short of sitting at home eating sandwiches or something, we decided to try Annabelle's. And since Rose isn't flying home this year, we thought she might like to go too. Though I will admit, I'm going to miss all that turkey."

I heard the sadness in her tone and knew that going out to a restaurant on Thanksgiving was probably on her top ten list of things she did not want to do. The thought formed in my mind almost immediately. "Why don't you come to our house? I've got plenty of food and we'd love to you have you!"

Carol purses her lips as though in thought. "Oh…I don't know, Abbie. I hate to impose. We're fine going out to dinner."

"Really," I reply. "It's not an imposition at all. You have no idea how much food I have at the house. And there's only going to be my dad and Reid's sister. Trust me, I have enough food to feed an army."

Carol glances at Rose, then looks back at me. "Tell you what. Let me talk to Steve and if he's okay with it, we'll join you. You're sure it's not an imposition?"

"Not at all," I reply, shaking my head. "We'd be glad to have you, right girls?" I poke Hannah and Caroline to get their attention. "Wouldn't you like if Carol, Steve and Rose came to our house for Thanksgiving?"

"Sure," says Hannah.

Caroline smiles but is engrossed in coloring her place mat. I make a mental note to tell Reid that I've invited his co-workers to our home for Thanksgiving. I probably should have mentioned it to him before offering up our home but I'm sure he'll be fine with it. We've been out with this group on several occasions and both Reid and I get along with everyone. Besides, I wasn't kidding. I have a ton of food and if we don't have people over to eat it, Reid will be eating turkey sandwiches, turkey soup, and turkey pot pie for a month. I'm certain he'd appreciate a little help eating the thirty pound turkey that is currently thawing in our fridge.

After we eat our dinner, we head home. The girls are chatting animatedly in the back seat and are practically bouncing out of their seats. A direct result, I am certain, of the inhuman amounts of soda they consumed during dinner. It is a rare treat I allow them and since there is no school the next day, I figure they'll go to bed late and sleep late in the morning. At least that's what I'm hoping they'll do. God knows I could use a morning when I'm not woken up by a small face breathing into mine as soon as the sunlight breaks through my window.

I reach across the center console and place my hand on Reid's thigh. "That was fun," I say. "I'm completely stuffed now. Pizza was a great idea considering we'll all be eating nothing but leftover turkey for the next week."

He laughs. "So what were you and the ladies talking about all night? It seemed like you were having a pretty intense conversation down there."

I think back to the earlier conversation I had with Rose and Carol about Christmas and the loss of magic and realize I can't share it with him because there are bionic ears in the back seat.

"Nothing much," I reply. "Though Carol did tell me that they're all going to Annabelle's for Thanksgiving dinner."

"She's not cooking?"

"Nope. She doesn't have any family coming in and Rose is staying in town for the holiday. When I realized what they were planning, I told them all to come to our place."

"What? Why would you do that?"

Even in the dim light I can see that Reid has gone pale. The sharpness of his tone surprises me and I flinch. For a moment, I feel a bit defensive. It's almost as though he's questioning me inviting someone to our home. Then I realize how much he's been working and traveling and realize he probably just has a lot on his mind and I choose to let his tone not bother me.

"Carol clearly didn't seem thrilled with going out to dinner and we just have so much food! It's only the four of us, your sister, and my father. We're going to have leftovers for days."

"Then why did you buy a thirty pound turkey? Jesus, Abbie. What were you thinking? And then you invite people over without even asking me? It's like you're trying to justify the fact that you bought a turkey that would feed a small country. "

Again, I flinch as though I've been slapped. "Reid, what the hell is the matter with you," I hiss, aware of the fact that the girls will zone on the conversation in the front seat the minute they detect even the slightest hint of animosity between their father and I. When I speak again, my voice has dropped to barely more than a whisper. "You know that every year I buy a very large turkey because you and the girls love turkey sandwiches as well as all the other leftovers. Do you all of a sudden have a problem with the size of turkey I bought or are you upset that I invited someone to our house? Honestly, it's like you're saying I need to ask your permission before inviting someone to our home or check with you before making a turkey purchase. Besides, it doesn't affect you at all. It's not like you're the one doing the cooking."

"Mommy?"

I cringe as I realize that not only has the sound of my voice risen, but the back seat is so silent, you can practically hear the crickets.

"What Munchkin?" I reply, trying to make my voice sound light and cheery, despite my anger at my husband who has apparently stepped back into 1950.

"Are you and daddy fighting?" Hannah asks.

"We're just having a discussion," Reid replies. "That's was grownups do. They discuss things and sometimes their voices get loud because they want to get their point across."

We drove the rest of the way home in silence and I couldn't help but wonder what I'd done wrong. Reid remained stoic and distant for the rest of the night, only coming upstairs to say goodnight to the girls. I wound up going to bed early, anticipating a long day of food prep.

By the middle of the next day, the tension in my home dissipated and Reid seemed to be back to his former self, chatting and joking with me while he chopped onions and celery for the stuffing. Later that night, I received a call from Carol telling me that she and Steve had decided to go ahead with their initial plans for Thanksgiving so the Hamilton's ended up having a small, intimate dinner with just the four of us, my father and Reid's sister. As I figured we would, there was enough turkey leftover to feed a small country. We made sandwiches and soup and then I froze the rest, figuring at some point in January, my family would be ready for more turkey.

Despite the pleasantness of our holiday, I couldn't help but feel a bit of tension between Reid and I. Of course, no one else would notice, but he seemed a bit distant during the holiday weekend, almost as though his thoughts were elsewhere. I quickly brushed them aside however, knowing that if something were wrong, Reid would come to me to unload as he'd done so many times during the course of our marriage. I just needed to wait for him to work it out in his mind and then come to the conclusion that talking about it always made him feel better.

Still, though. There was this nagging feeling in the back of my mind that something was just a bit off with my husband. This was one of those times when I wished men were a bit more transparent.

Rose

The five days during Thanksgiving were excruciating. Initially, I thought things were looking up, what with Reid's invitation to dinner. And then, Abbie invites me to their house? Jackpot! For a while there, I was on cloud nine, thinking I'd get to see his home, play with his kids, and really work my way into his life. I had a fantasy that Reid would see how well his children and I got along and then he would see that I'm a perfect fit for him. His girls would tell their father how much they loved me and Reid would realize that his children would be fine with me as the new woman in their father's life.

That all ended rather abruptly when my phone rang about an hour after I got home from our dinner.

I'd barely walked into my apartment when I saw Reid's face pop up on my phone. Smiling, I answered, expecting…well, I don't know what, but certainly not him screaming at me and practically foaming at the mouth.

"WHAT THE HELL ARE YOU THINKING?" His voice boomed through the speaker of my phone and I had to pull it away from my ear in order to avoid losing a good portion of my hearing.

"What are you talking about?"

"Are you crazy or something?"

"Reid, calm down and tell me why you're so upset."

I hear him take several deep breaths. When he finally speaks, his voice is much softer but it has a tension I can hear clearly through the phone. It sounds as though his teeth are clenched tightly together. "Abbie told me she invited you, Carol and Steve to come to the house for Thanksgiving. You're not actually going to come, are you?"

So that's what this is all about. I wait several moments

before replying. "I hadn't thought about it, actually. Carol was going to check with Steve and then call me later. Why? Would you mind if I came?"

"Mind? Are you out of your fucking mind? Do you really think it's a good idea for you to be in the same room as my wife and children? What the hell, Rose?"

"What is it about this that bothers you? I mean, I've been out with Abbie before. We've gone shopping and she's shown me the house she's working on."

Through the phone I hear him exhale heavily. "I don't know. It's just...you...her...the kids..."

I think I know what he's getting at. It would be weird for him to have me in the house he shares with his family. While I've been there, I've not been there while he has been home. And if we were going to sit and have a meal together? All of us? That just might throw him over the edge. Besides, the minute Abbie were to see Reid and I together, she'd know. She'd know we have this connection that can't be denied. He's protecting her, of course.

"I won't go."

"What?" He sounds like he's choking on his tongue. "You won't go? Just like that?"

I smile. Men are so naïve. "Of course I won't. If it upsets you, I won't go. Your feelings are what matter to me. I can eat dinner with Carol and Steve like we originally planned. Don't worry about it."

"Oh. Okay," he says softly. "Ummm, thanks."

"Reid, the last thing I want to do is cause you any stress. If you don't want me there, it's fine. As long as you still want me, we're good."

"Rose..." His tone tells me he is not amused by my joke but he doesn't deny that he wants me.

"-Bye, Reid," I reply. I don't demand an answer. I don't push. "Have a good Thanksgiving. I'll see you Monday."

"-Bye," he says.

As I end the call, I can't help but smile. Reid still wants me. He's just not ready to let the world know…yet.

Did I want to see him on Thanksgiving? Of course I did. But giving in to this one tiny thing now will provide a tremendous return at a later point. Plus, it's sealing Reid's affection for me. What man doesn't like to know that if he's upset about something, the woman in his life will do whatever she can do to fix it?

And that's me. I'm the woman in his life now.

Given the somewhat tense phone call I'd just had with Reid, I felt like I needed a bit of a release. I needed to go out and have a little fun. Plus, I hadn't seen some of my friends in what seemed like an eternity. I dug my phone out of my pocketbook and quickly sent out a group text to Rachel and Ava, my two closest friends from college asking them if they wanted to head out for a movie or something.

I roomed with Rachel my freshman year and we'd become pretty close. She was, without question, the funniest person I had ever met. Our sophomore year, she somehow managed to secure a room in the most popular dormitory—one that only held single rooms. Although she wanted to continue to live with me, she simply couldn't turn down the possibility of privacy when there was so little to be had in our current dorm.

I'd met Ava in a Psychology class freshman year. She and I hit it off rather quickly since we discovered a mutual love for fashion and a general dislike for those who neglected all of its rules. Admittedly, Rachel was one of those people but we chose to ignore her lack of fashion sense and general clumsiness when it came to dressing herself in a style that suited her body type because we quickly determined that she served another, more important mission.

It happened innocently enough. The three us were headed to a party off campus, hosted by one of the commuters. Ava and I chose our outfits carefully, wanting to look casual but not sloppy. Rachel, on the other hand, pulled a pair of

Zubaz pants from the back of her closet and pulled them up the length of her more than generously sized thighs. When she snapped the elastic waist in place, I nearly shouted my dismay. First of all, the pants went out sometime in the early-nineties, which told me that Rachel has probably gotten the pants from the Goodwill or Salvation Army. Clearly, someone with a bit of fashion sense was getting rid of the pants so that poor fashion choices could be spread among the poverty stricken in our little college town. Why Rachel, who came from quite a bit of money, shopped at the Salvation Army boggled my mind. Then again, someone her size probably had a tough time finding clothes to fit her.

Anyway, the three of us trudged across campus to go to this party. Ava and I dressed neatly in crisp jeans and flowing, feminine tops while Rachel, wearing those stupid pants and a t-shirt, trailed behind us, breathing heavily as though the walk was too strenuous for her.

It probably was, now that I think about it.

When we finally arrived at the party, it was in full swing. Rachel led the way into the house, since she knew the guy hosting the party. She led us into the kitchen where she poured us each a beer that was sitting on the linoleum floor, then led us into the living room where we sat together on some folding chairs that had been put out.

That's when I noticed something. The guys would survey the room and since Rachel was seated facing the door, they would spot her first. I would watch their expression change from curiosity to distaste when their gaze fell on Rachel. Their lips would pinch together and they would crinkle their noses as if they'd smelled something foul. Then, they would rip their gaze from her and they would locate the person sitting beside of her, which was, of course, either Ava or me. We would get a smile, a wink, and if the guy had consumed enough alcohol to give him a little extra courage, he'd saunter over and strike up a conversation. I watched this happen all night to Ava, only distracted by the occasional guy striking up a conversation with me.

I didn't think anything of it, really, until the next morning when Ava showed up at my dorm. Rachel had gone to the library to study so the two of us were free to gossip.

"I'm not sure how to ask this," Ava began. She sat down on my bed and curled her legs underneath her.

She sounded worried so I sat down on the other side of the bed. "Just spit it out."

"Last night when we were at that party…ummm…did you notice anything?"

"Like what," I asked.

"Well, the guys were sort of acting weird. Like, they'd see our little group and…well…I noticed some weird expressions."

By this time, I thought I knew exactly where Ava was referring. "I think I know where you're going with this."

She nodded. "None of the guys approached Rachel."

"I know," I replied. "I felt sort of bad for her but then again, she didn't seem bothered by it. She seemed like she had a good time."

"Did you think that we….I don't know…got a lot more…." She looked up at the ceiling as though trying to find the right words. "Traffic? I mean, it's like sitting next to Rachel…God! I don't even want to say this because I LOVE Rachel!"

I was nodding enthusiastically. "I know! I love her too! She's great. But I know what you're talking about. We got a lot more 'traffic'—I like that word, by the way—but do you think it's because…"

It was as if neither one of us wanted to say it out loud. We stared at each other, waiting for the other to be the one to say it.

"Do you think we have…"

"Is it possible Rachel is our…"

We were both grinning and nodding our heads. When we realized we had both realized the same thing, we shouted in unison, "A DUF!!!"

Ava fell back against the pillows and tossed her arm over her face. "I can't believe it. I really cannot believe it! We have our very own Designated Ugly Friend!"

I was still grinning. "I know! Now, don't get me wrong," I said, my voice turning serious. "I love Rachel. I do. It's just that she-"

"-doesn't give a shit about her looks," Ava said, completing my sentence for me.

"Right."

Ever since that day, the three of us would go out together to parties, concerts, and pretty much any event where either Ava or I were hoping to hook up with someone. Rachel never failed us. Her poor hygiene and lack of style were a gold mine to those of us that stood by her. You couldn't help but look good when you were standing beside someone who clearly cared so little about herself that she barely combed her hair most days.

Rachel never disappointed. As I expected, Rachel showed up wearing pants that were too tight on her, only accentuating the mounds of thighs she tried to hide. I nearly sighed out loud. Why was it that she insisted on wearing clothes that were too small for her? Just because you can get into it, doesn't mean you ought to wear it. But then again, dressing as she does continues to cement her role as my DUF. Everyone needs one of these. The Designated Ugly Friend. Someone who, when you sit beside them, only enhances your beauty even if you're having an off day. Rachel was key to my success when meeting people. Strategically placing her in the visual line of the entrance of any establishment made me look that much more attractive. Once they saw her, they'd quickly look for something better.

And I'd be right beside her just waiting for their gaze to land on me.

Abbie

I feel like I haven't seen my husband in weeks.

His travel schedule has picked up tenfold. Reid does his best, though, by calling when each day before the kids go to bed and by chatting with them about their day. It may not be much but that daily phone call is enough to ge the girls through just one more day. And it has to be enough. Reid just can't decide one day that he doesn't want to travel. It's all part of the job.

When he calls, he and I will chat for a minute or two. It seems we only have just that minute or so before the girls begin to clamor to speak to their father. What's been happening lately is that Reid and I are only able to discuss housekeeping types of issues—what should we get the girls for Christmas? What time is Hannah's play? Can Caroline attend a sleepover? When we do manage to find a few minutes together, Reid seems to be a bit…well, cranky, if I were being honest. Just the other day, he opened the fridge for a snack and when he didn't find anything, mumbled, "Plenty of stuff in the fridge to eat, just nothing for the guy that pays for it all." It was all I could do to stifle a gasp. Comments like that are so unlike him that by the time the anger seeped in and I was going to say something snarky in return, he'd already left the kitchen.

Not only have his trips been more frequent, but they tend to last longer now. Whereas before, he'd be gone from say, a Tuesday to a Thursday, now his trips tend to have him leaving on a Sunday and returning Friday, often times after the girls have already gone to bed. Trying to keep them awake for their father's return at ten or even eleven o'clock at night has failed on more than one occasion.

I know the travel has got to be wearing on him. Besides the

fact that he's away from all of us sleeping in a bed that's not his, he sees families on his flights with children that are the same ages as our girls. When Hannah and Caroline were still in diapers, he would come home from a trip and tell me in great detail about the little girl on his flight or the family in the lobby of the hotel he'd stayed in. I could hear the anguish in his voice. It always made me love him that much more, knowing that he missed his children so much that he saw them in others. It would be the hair color of one child, or another child holding the same toy one of our children had. During those times, even if the kids were asleep, Reid's first stop would be to their room to simply look at them as if to make sure they still existed or that they hadn't somehow magically disappeared during his absence. Only after checking on the girls was he able to settle down and relax with me on the couch.

I've always loved that about him. It's so true what people say; you can love someone an incredible amount but when you see them holding the child the two of you made, suddenly you love them all that much more. The love a woman feels for the man who holds her child knows no bounds.

But besides his travel, lately I've gotten the feeling that there's something more to his distance. Of course, this tends to be the busiest time of the year for both of us. Reid is at work trying to get everything in by year end so that K&M can show the largest profit yet. And I'm at home trying to shop for the girls for Christmas, which involved not only the shopping but the wrapping of the presents and then the hiding them where little eyes won't think to look. Each year, my task becomes just a bit more challenging. Hannah, I feel certain, is fully aware of the fact that her parents are the ones keeping up with the whole Santa charade. I'm just lucky that she's a good kid and so far, has kept her mouth shut and not said anything to Caroline. I know it's silly but I really want Caroline to believe for just another year or so. Christmas is so magical when you've got to sneak around and wait for the kids to be fast asleep before putting out the presents. Once they know it's you doing all the work, you might as well forego the wrapping and just shove the presents under the tree as you buy them.

So maybe I'm just being a bit paranoid when I worry about Reid. I keep trying to think of past years during this time and all I can recall is a flurry of activity. Reid would take the kids out for a movie or the park while I'd frantically wrap presents, always listening for the sound of his car in the driveway. Each year, it seems, despite my endless wrapping, I always end up on Christmas Eve wrapping until the wee hours of the morning.

Now that I think about it, I'm sure it's just the time of year. We're both so busy that the time just slips away from us. Luckily, I know he'll have a few days off around Christmas so we can just relax and be with each other. Once we're able to do that, I'm sure I'll stop my needless worrying.

Rose

"You okay in there?"

I glance over the counter into my living room to see Reid sitting on my couch looking quite relaxed. And why wouldn't he? He's now been here several times and with each visit, he becomes more relaxed and comfortable. Though wouldn't any man if any time they entered an apartment they were guaranteed a blow job followed up by some incredible sex? Of course.

At first, I wondered how we'd get to see each other. Even though we work together, he travels so much that I don't really get to see him all that often. Particularly since our traveling together didn't work out as I'd hoped it would. Reid got a little freaked out about the fact that I wanted to travel with him all the time. Thought it'd look odd if all of a sudden I went with him every time he needed to visit a client. As much as I hate to admit it, he was right. That being said, I'm extremely grateful for getting to see the sights of the Greater Atlanta area on our only trip together…well, at least the inside of a hotel room. Atlanta, I think, will always be one of my most favorite cities—after New York, of course—since it's the place Reid and I first…well, you know.

Reid is particularly busy during the months of November and December. It seems like everyone at K&M becomes consumed with finishing all their projects so they can show completion and therefore, revenue, by the end of the year. There's such a flurry of activity around me that I can barely find time to have a moment alone with Reid.

Anyway, Reid's travel picked up marginally so I wasn't able to see him as much as I would have liked. I wondered if I'd get to see him at all and since he would normally go home to his family after a business trip, I worried that if he spent more time with his wife than with me, I'd begin to fade from his mind.

And that is not an option.

So a solution came to mind.

A week or so after Thanksgiving, Reid somehow managed to find time to come to my apartment. I guess Abbie took the girls to a movie or something. (I'm not sure since as soon as he mentions her name, I tune him out.) Anyway, he had some free time so he came over to my place. We chatted for a bit and then he broke the news to me. Instead of heading back to work on Monday as he thought, he was instead leaving first early that morning to head to Michigan. He'd be gone until Wednesday night, which meant I wouldn't be able to see him until Thursday when he came into the office.

I'm not sure exactly how the idea came to mind. We were sitting on the couch holding hands and all I could think about was that he was leaving my place on Saturday and I wouldn't see him until Thursday.

"Michigan," I cried. "It's in an entirely different time zone!"

Reid smiled at me. "It's only an hour earlier than it is here. I'll call you. I promise."

"It's not the same," I replied, pouting just a bit. And then the words tumbled out of me and I knew it was the perfect solution. I was thinking about the days (and the nights) that I'd be away from him and before the thought had entirely made its way into my brain, I blurted it out.

"Why don't you just sleep here Sunday night? I mean, you 're leaving early Monday morning anyway?" The minute the words were out of my mouth, I smiled. I knew it was an absolute perfect idea.

"I can't sleep here, Rose."

"Why not?" I asked. Now that the idea was out there, there was no way I was letting go of it. "Just say that you're flight got changed, or the meeting got changed and you need to be there first thing in the morning so you got a flight out Sunday night. It's not like she's going to know what your schedule is." I'd recently discovered that I couldn't even mention her name. Instead, I'd taken up calling his wife 'she' or 'her.'

I do have to admit that the first few times Reid came over, I worried that it would be the last time he ever visited my place. Now don't get me wrong, we've had incredible sex each and every time he's entered my apartment but those first few times, I could tell he was still adjusting to this new world he found himself in. I hated every minute of it for him. He was so wracked with guilt and focusing the fact that he was committing adultery that it seemed like he wasn't able to enjoy the time we spent together. We'd have sex, then it seemed as though he'd close himself off, frequently lying in my bed silently, almost as though he was waiting for the right amount of time to pass so he could leave.

Then slowly, he seemed overcome his hurdle. Each time he came here he seemed a bit more relaxed. It was little things that I'd notice. He'd simply go into the fridge to get a beer if he wanted one, or grab something to eat if he was hungry. Then, he began to leave a personal item or two at my place. I found several of those little hotel shampoo bottles on my bathroom counter and even found his brand of soap in the shower. After that, it was only a natural progression for me to make some room in the closet for him so that he could hang his coat up and even some of his shirts. I made room in my underwear drawer so he could leave some of his socks and boxers there. I have to admit that every morning when I open the drawer and see his undergarments next to mine, I get a little thrill.

Though we've only been *involved* for a few months, things seem to be moving along quickly. It's like once Reid admitted to himself that he had feeling for me, it was a natural progression to simply let them out and explore them. For the most part now, he begins his business trips with a night at my place and then ends them once again by spending the night with me. Sure, he still goes home to *her,* but he spends less and less nights there, which means there are fewer chances for him to anything at home but sleep.

My friendship (if we're still calling it that) with Abbie is still continuing. I really don't see the point in ending things with her. I actually do enjoy the occasional lunch with her or shopping trip with her and Carol. They're a nice diversion from missing Reid when he's not with me. And as much as I hate to admit it, she's actually quite a nice person. Plus, Abbie just might give me some insight into how her relationship is with her husband. If she does that, I can, like any friend would do, counsel her on how quickly she should leave him. So far, she hasn't mentioned Reid at all so I'm going to assume she's not noticed anything different at home with him. Either that, or things are different and she just chooses not to mention it.

I do have to wonder how he acts when he's at home. Is he different now that he's spending so much time with me? Does he come home and greet her with a hug and a kiss? Are they still having sex? It is more or less frequent than it once was? And of course, the ultimate question: Will he ever leave her?

Surely, at some point he's got to, right? But the thing is…and this one of the things that's so attractive about Reid— he loves his children. I mean really loves them. As in, spends all his free time with them. I can't help but think about the future and wonder if they'll like me. Will they compare me to their mother? Will I simply be the "fun" parent in their lives? Of course, it may be a bit too early for me to be wondering about all of this but it's certainly nice to think of all the possibilities.

Though Reid hasn't mentioned anything about leaving his wife or even hinted at any sort of future with me but that doesn't mean he hasn't thought about it. And if he has, I need to make sure he knows I'm on the same page as him.

But not just yet. He still has the tendency to be the tiniest bit skittish so I need to bide my time and only nudge him when the time is right.

Abbie

I miss my husband.

It seems like he's away more than he's home and honestly? It's starting to bother me. While I'm fine being by myself and actually sometimes enjoy it, I'm smart enough to realize I didn't get married so that I could be by myself—not all the time anyways. I got married so that I could share my life with someone and lately? Well, that's just not been the case.

The girls and I speak to Reid every night and so far, that seems to pacify them. Kids are easy. They can bounce back from just about anything and seem to accept everything at face value, even if it's painful. My children are no exception. They seem to accept Reid's travel as though it's simply a part of their daily life, which of course, it really is. Ever since they were little, their father has traveled. So for them, this year is no different.

So then, why, I have to wonder, does this year seem to be so much more different?

I've tried to figure out why this year's travel schedule is hitting me so hard and for the life of me, I can't figure it out. Like the kids, I talk to Reid every night. He's always available by text so if there's a question about something that I can't answer, I can just text him and he'll let me know what to do. Last week, we blew a fuse in the house, apparently because we had too many electronics plugged into the same breaker. When the lights in the living room went out, I just sort of sat there, unsure of what to do. I'm embarrassed to say I didn't even know where the breaker box was. Luckily, I texted Reid to tell him what had happened and he was able to tell me where the breaker box was. (On the wall in the garage, in case you were wondering.) Disaster averted. I shudder to think of what might happen if Hannah and Caroline weren't able to get their daily dose of Wizards of Waverly Place or SpongeBob Squarepants.

Each night, when I put the girls to bed and kiss them once extra because their father isn't there, I head back into the living room and try to distract myself from the silence that fills the house. Sometimes, I'll attempt to read a book. Other times, I'll see if there's a movie on TV that might distract me for a couple of hours.

I've not had much luck.

What normally happens is I fidget on the couch for an hour or so, then crawl into bed with the girls and the dog and spend the next couple of hours tossing and turning until I finally fall into a fitful sleep. I wake up a few hours later and prepare to do it all the next day.

You'd think that when Reid was home for the weekends, I'd feel a sense of normalcy return. But the feeling of normalcy in my home has somehow escaped me. I know he's busy at work and probably stressed beyond belief but I can't help but feel that we're growing apart. I only hope that once Christmas rolls around, we're able to spend some time together and reconnect.

Christmas at our house has always been just the four of us. Reid and I will be up until the wee hours of the morning wrapping presents. We'll wait until the darkest part of the night when the house is at its most silent, then fill the living room with presents and sneak into our bedroom for an hour or so of sleep before the girls clamor down the steps around four am and demand to open their presents. This entire process was excruciating when the girls had no idea just how early they were waking their parents. Now, however, since they can both read the digital clocks beside their beds, we've told them they are not allowed to wake us up until six am. They're allowed to come downstairs and view the presents under the tree but their father and I get to sleep until six. We'll see how that works out this year.

The thing is, Reid and I haven't spent much time talking over the past few weeks. It's been a rush of packing and unpacking, saying hello and goodbye and a flurry of text messages. I can feel the beginnings of something I don't want to put a name to but it feels like the beginning of us not being the close couple we once were. It's something that happens gradually, so gradually in fact, that you don't notice it until you've not spoken in weeks. By then, the bridge between the two of you is so great that neither one can cross. Once you've lost the intimacy, it's hard to get it back.

I don't want to say I see this happening to us but I can see how it might. With Reid gone all the time, we're not able to spend as much time with each other as we'd like. I just hope that this year is like all the others and I'm worrying for nothing.

Reid will be home Friday night and he's off for the next week. We'll spend some time together and things will soon be back to normal. I may even get a sitter so we can go out to dinner and a movie one night.

Before long, things will be back to normal and this tension I'm feeling with be a distant memory.

I'm sure of it.

Rose

"I really wish you could stay."

I'm standing in my living room wrapped in the sheet from my bed watching Reid gather up his clothes that I ripped off him last night when he arrived. It had been four days since I'd seen him and you can only imagine how hungry I was for him. I watch as he bends over to find his sock that somehow made its way underneath the couch. When he pulls it out, he looks up at me as if to say, "Really?" I just shrug. What can I say? I wanted him naked and his clothes were in the way.

"I've got to go home at some point," he says. "Abbie says that Hannah and Caroline really miss me."

"But I miss you too!" I can't help it but when I speak, my voice comes out sounding just the tiniest bit whiny. "Can you come back later?"

He shakes his head. "I wish I could but Abbie made plans for us to go out to dinner. I can't just cancel."

"What if your flight got delayed? That wouldn't be cancelling, right? I mean, it's not like it'd be your fault."

Reid stops and looks at me. "Rose, I've got to go home. I miss the girls. Surely you can understand that. If I can figure something out, I'll come back, all right?"

I don't need to look in the mirror to know that I'm pouting. "Oh, all right," I reply.

He chuckles, then wraps me in his arms. "Now don't be all pouty," he says, teasing me. "I promise I'll try to come back and see you this week."

"You promise?"

He nods. "I'll do my best," he says, taking three fingers and holding them up, Boy Scout style.

"Well, if you can manage to get away, I'll be waiting right

here for you…just like this." I unwrap myself from the sheet and let it fall to the floor in a puddle at my feet. Reid inhales sharply and I grin. He quickly steps toward me, envelopes me in his arms and kisses me passionately.

"I'll never leave if you keep this up," he says.

"All part of the plan," I reply.

His hands trace a path down my back until he is cupping my buttocks in his hands. He pulls me toward him and I can feel his erection through his pants. He moans as I thrust my hips against him and he begins to nibble his way down my neck and onto my chest until he takes one nipple into his mouth and gently tugs on it. I reach between us to unzip his pants and then reach inside to stroke his penis. He urges me back toward the couch, kicking off his shoes and pants as I push them down over his hips. I feel the back of the couch behind me knees and fall backward so that I'm sitting on the edge of it, pulling Reid with me. In an instant, he is moving inside of me and I can feel an orgasm building within. Our breathing is ragged and I know we are both close to climax. With one last thrust, Reid plunges deep inside of me and as I come, I shout his name and pull his hips toward me so that I can feel every throbbing inch of him. Seconds later, he collapses on top of me, breathing heavily.

I look over his shoulder and see my living room littered with his clothing and the sheet I was wearing up until only moments ago. Though I try to suppress a giggle, I fail miserably.

"What?" he says, as he lifts his head off my shoulder.

"I like the look of my living room with your clothes scattered all over it."

He sits up and glances over his shoulder at his shoes, pants and my sheet scattered all over the floor and shakes his head. "All part of your plan, huh?"

He slowly stands up and pulls on his pants, then grabs his shoes from across the room. He sits down beside me and pulls them on. Then he turns to me and places his hand on my thigh.

"I'm sorry," he says, "but I really have to go."

"I know you do," I reply.

We both stand up and walk toward the door. Reid waits until I once again wrap myself in the sheet, then kisses me goodbye before grabbing his suitcase and heading out the door. Once the door clicks shut behind him, my smile fades. I know that it won't return until he is back in my apartment. What makes this even harder is that I really can't call or text him. It would be completely out of the ordinary for one of his employee's to call him at home while he's on vacation, which he is next week for Christmas. I can hardly bear the thought of not seeing him for an entire week.

But given the frequency he has been coming to my place, I find it hard to believe that he won't be back before the week is up.

Abbie

"Do you want a glass of wine?"

I'm standing in the kitchen pouring myself a glass when Reid walks in, scanning something on his phone.

"Nah," he says. "I think I'll just grab a beer." He puts his phone down onto the counter and opens up the fridge, surveying the contents inside. He finally makes his selection - not that there's much to choose from as there's only a six pack in there- and then pulls out a bottle. "The girls just about ready for bed?"

I nod. "They're going to finish watching *The Santa Claus* then head up to bed." I point toward the stove where a few dozen cookies are cooling on wire racks. "The cookies have been baked, I have the special tray for Santa, and Caroline has placed a bowl of carrots outside for the reindeer."

Reid chuckles. "Hannah still hasn't said anything?"

"Nope." I reply. "She's being great about keeping the secret from her sister."

It was only a week ago during a trip to Target that Hannah whispered to me that she knew about the whole 'Santa thing' as she referred to it. The girls and I were stopping to get a snack from the counter and she pulled me off to the side to tell me. Why she felt the snack counter at Target was the appropriate place, I have no idea. I begged her not to say anything to her baby sister and she agreed, not wanting to spoil the magic for Caroline. After she broke the news to me that she no longer believed in the fat guy in the red suit, she further informed me that she'd known since last Christmas. Apparently, the 'Santa wrapping paper' had been seen prior to Christmas morning. When Hannah came downstairs to see all the presents from Santa wrapped in the paper she'd seen the week before, she put two and two together.

Poof! Magic gone.

I still can't believe she waited nearly a year to tell me. I could have put her to work wrapping presents instead of creeping around and doing it myself whenever she and Caroline were asleep!

When I came home that day, I told Reid how Hannah knew there wasn't a Santa. He looked absolutely heartbroken and then mentioned how 'the magic was gone for Hannah.' It took some effort but I was finally able to convince him that Caroline didn't know and that the magic was still there for her. It took some convincing given that Reid felt certain Hannah would tell her sister, if only to hurt her. And while I would normally agree with his assessment, Santa is such a huge thing to a kid and I can't think of anyone who would purposely destroy someone's childhood by revealing the best kept secret in all of childhood. Not even an older sister who claims to hate her sister most of the time.

So…Reid and I are going through all the motions of past Christmas'. There will be half-eaten carrots left outside, an empty plate of cookies, and a signature from the big guy in the red suit. (Both Hannah and Caroline have a bit of skepticism in them and since the time they could write, have asked for 'proof' that Santa actually came into the house by asking for his signature on a sheet of paper. Once they received said signature, neither one noticed the similarity between Santa's handwriting and their father's.)

Once we put the girls to bed, I'll wrap the final few presents we purchased over the past few days. Despite planning our Christmas budget for months, we tend to make several purchases the few days prior to Christmas always thinking we haven't gotten enough for the kids. As a result of these last-minute purchases, our budget gets blown year after year.

Reid takes his beer and takes a seat at the bar. "Any chance of snow tonight? I didn't catch the news earlier."

"You know? I'm not sure," I reply. "Lemme check." I glance around the kitchen looking for my phone, intending to use it to check the weather but since I can't locate it, I grab Reid's off the counter. I swipe the phone to unlock it but find that it's passcode protected. "What's your code?"

"What?" He says, getting up. He walks over to me and takes the phone out of my hand, then taps the screen a few times.

"Since when do you lock your phone?"

"I put a code on it because I've got our banking information and some of the credit cards numbers on here."

"Oh. Okay," I reply. "Well, check the weather and see if there's any chance of snow. I'd love for the girls to wake up to a winter wonderland. I can't remember the last time we've had snow on Christmas."

Hannah rounds the corner and wraps her arms around me. "Can we go to bed now?"

I glance at Reid and grin. "Only on Christmas Eve do I hear that from one of our children. Is the movie over?" I ask, looking back down at Hannah.

She nods.

"Well then, let's get you girls off to bed. You know Santa won't come if you're awake."

"Mom," she says, rolling her eyes.

Reid follows me out of the kitchen and coaxes Caroline off the couch. Together we walk upstairs and supervise teeth brushing, then tuck the girls into bed. After giving them both a final warning about not coming downstairs until six am, we close their bedroom doors tightly and head back downstairs.

"How much wrapping do you still have to do?"

I groan as I think about the pile of stocking stuffers shoved in the bottom of my closet and the unwrapped presents hidden in the garage. "Tons," I say. "I'll bet I'll be wrapping for at least an hour."

"Let's give them time to fall asleep before we get started,

all right?"

"Sure," I reply as I sit down onto the couch. Reid walks into the kitchen and I remember that I have a glass of wine in there. "Will you bring me my glass of wine?"

Moments later, Reid places the glass beside me on the table. He walks through the living room and opens up the door to the basement. I look at him, confused. "Don't you want to watch a movie or something?"

"I'll be back up in a minute," he says. "Just gotta check a few things."

"But it's Christmas Eve. Can't it wait?"

"Abbie, I'll be right back." I can hear the irritation in his voice and wonder what could possibly be so important that he needs to review it on a holiday. And Christmas Eve, no less. But I decide to let it go, figuring he's probably just stressed about work and probably needs to make sure someone received a proposal or something.

As I wait for him to return, I sip my glass of wine and flip through the television channels. After trolling through twenty or so channels, I find Shawshank Redemption on one of the HBO channels. It's just started so I put the remote down and focus on the show. Before I realize it, my glass is empty and Andy Dufresne has dug a hole all the way through the walls of the prison. I'm so engrossed in the movie that I don't realize nearly an hour has passed. By now, I'm wondering what is keeping Reid so busy in the basement.

I traipse down the steps and find him in the office. Just as I enter the room, he tucks his phone into his pocket and looks up at me. "I was just coming upstairs," he says. "You ready to wrap?"

"Yup," I say nodding. "Let's get to work. It's going to be a late night."

For more than an hour, I wrap and Reid stacks the presents in a pile for each girl. Occasionally, we hear a sound that makes us stop in our tracks and glance toward the stairs as though we're robbers about to be caught by the homeowner. There are many quick trips up the flight of steps to make sure there are no little girls wandering around the living room or sneaking down the steps. Finally, at nearly midnight, I have finished wrapping, Reid has done a count of the presents to make sure there are an equal number of presents for each child, and we are ready to put the presents under the tree.

Now comes the tricky part.

Reid and I both know that our girls develop bionic hearing on this night so we are extra cautious when carrying the presents up the stairs. After several trips, the living room is full of presents and we dive into our bedroom so as not to get caught in the act of delivering the gifts. It is now well past one am and I'm utterly exhausted. I climb under the covers after stripping off my jeans and pulling my bra out of the sleeves of my t-shirt. Within moments, I am asleep. And it is only moments later that I am woken up by the feeling that there are two faces mere inches from mine. I open my eyes with a start to see my two children standing over me.

"Aaah!" I shout. "Why can't the two of you go to your father's side of the bed?"

Reid rolls over and wraps an arm around me. "Because I've trained them."

"Ha, ha," I reply, nudging his arm off of me and getting out of bed. I throw on some pajama pants and trudge into the living room, the girls close behind. When I don't stop but instead walk into the kitchen, I hear the two of them cry out.

"MOM! Where are you going?"

"Coffee," I reply.

Thankfully, I had the forethought to prepare the coffee for this morning and I only need to push the button for it to begin to brew. Within moments, the rich aroma of Arabica beans fills the kitchen. I fill my cup before the coffee maker stops brewing, then fill a cup for Reid and join him in the living room. The girls are seated on the floor on either side of the tree waiting for a nod from one of us telling them that they can begin. Reid knows this, of course, and begins to chat with me about nothing in particular.

"This coffee is really good, Abs," he says in a cheery voice meant to frustrate our children.

"Well, thank you," I reply in the same cheery voice. "I prepared it myself."

"I think I'd like to sit here and just sip on my coffee for awhile and then perhaps I'll read the paper-"

"DAD!"

Caroline looks as though she's about to burst. She's got a very large present situated on her lap and her hands are poised on either side of it. She's clearly prepped and ready to tear open the present.

"Can we open our presents now?" She asks, looking at me.

"Oh, I don't know," I reply. "Honey, what do you think?"

Reid glances at the invisible watch on his arm. "Hmmm… maybe in an hour or so?"

"Come on," Hannah cries. "You said six o clock and it's six-ten!"

I hear the desperation in Hannah's voice and give Reid a look that tells him now is not the time for us to be joking with the girls. If they don't get to open their presents soon, they might explode.

"All right, all right," Reid says. "I'm just kidding. Go ahead and start."

The girls squeal with delight and then each tear into a present. Caroline's present is a large stuffed minion from the Despicable Me movie. I still can't believe I found it. She loves the movie and has been obsessed with those little yellow guys since she first watched it. Hannah, always the calmer of the two, opens a smaller present that reveals a necklace with a tiny locket on it. It's something she pointed out to me over the summer while we were at the mall. I went back the very next day and purchased it, knowing it would be special to her. Once

I had it, I found a picture of Reid and I and another of Caroline and cut them to fit inside the locket. I watch now as she opens the locket and sees the pictures inside.

"Oh!" She says as sees the rest of her family looking at her from inside the locket. "I love it!" She squeals. Then for good measure, she says, "Thank you, Santa," while looking up at the ceiling.

We spend the next hour or so watching the girls open their presents. Each year we try to make them slow down so they can appreciate what they receive and each year it's an epic failure. The girls barely acknowledge one present before they are reaching for the next. Then, once all the presents are opened, the two of them will do an inventory of their gifts while I try to take a short nap. Reid is usually forced to stay awake and put things together, open packages and fill toys with batteries.

As I watch him open the seemingly endless presents and put them together, rip them out of the packages and fill them with batteries, I realize something.

Reid is different now.

To anyone else, it would be imperceptible, but not to me. I have lived with this man for nearly fifteen years. There's nothing that gets by me.

And as sure as I'm looking at my husband, I can feel that something is different; just a bit off with him.

Because I've always been the one he turned to when things happened in his life. I was the one he'd come to when something was going well or something didn't turn out the way he'd intended. Honestly, I can't remember the last time we sat on the couch together and talked about our day. I'm not sure if it's intentional or if there is really something wrong with him and he's simply afraid to tell me. Could he be sick? I begin to recall the past month or so and search for any time when Reid might have gone to the doctors. Were there any co-pay charges that I overlooked? But nothing comes to mind.

Whatever it is, we will work through it, just like we've done for so many years now. Whatever it is he's going through, we can handle it, as long as we're together.

Partners.

Rose

"When are you going to leave her?"

"What?!" Reid was looking at me with a look of sheer terror on his face. The bottle of beer he'd been drinking was not frozen about six inches from his mouth. Slowly, he lowered it back down to the table beside him and turned to look at me. "Leave Abbie?"

Christmas week was sheer hell. Because Reid was on vacation, there were no travel plans, meaning there was no way he could come to my place either at the end or at the beginning of his trip. It was torture. I thought about him all the time and wondered what he was doing. Was he kissing *her?* Holding *her?* Making love to *her?* It wasn't anything I wanted to think about but somehow, those thoughts wouldn't leave me. By the end of an entire week of not seeing Reid, my mind was made up.

I decided I wasn't waiting any longer.

At seeing the shock register on his face, I couldn't help but roll my eyes. Did he actually think this day would never come? "Yes, Reid. Leave Abbie. Who do you think I mean? Do you have another wife somewhere that I don't know about?"

"That's not what I meant," he says, shaking his head. "Why are you bringing this up now? I thought you were happy?"

"Oh, come on Reid. Do you honestly think any woman can be happy with only seeing the man she loves when he can fit her into his schedule? A schedule, I might add, that includes a wife."

"Rose," he says carefully. "Where is this coming from? You knew I was married and we've never discussed me leaving my family."

"What did you think was going to happen? That I was

going to be fine with the way things are forever?"

"Huh…I guess I hadn't really thought about it."

"Of course you hadn't," I reply tartly. I hear the bitchiness in my tone and make a conscious effort to tone it back a bit. This is not the right way to handle this. "Look," I say, snuggling closer to him, "don't you want to be with me? All the time, I mean?"

"Well, sure I do. But-"

"-but you don't want to hurt Abbie."

He nods. "I just don't see why we can't just go on as we have? Haven't you been happy?"

"Of course I have. But that's the problem. You make me so happy that I just want you more and more. And I want you all the time; not just when you can squeeze me in."

"It's not like that and you know it. My life is just….complicated."

"Then make it *un*-complicated." I sat up and looked him in the eye. "Look," I say, taking his hands in his. "I know this isn't going to be easy but it's got to be done. Don't you want to be with me?"

He nods. "Of course I do!"

"Then you've got to take care of things at home."

"I will. Soon. I promise."

I'm sure he means it but I just can't do it. So many women have heard it all before. 'I'll leave her. I promise. Just give me some time.' Well, not me. I'm not falling for it. This relationship is going to move forward on my time—not his and most definitely, not Abbie's.

"I know it will be soon. And I'll be waiting right her for you."

He relaxes visibly, which tells me he doesn't fully grasp what I'm saying.

"So come back here once you've got everything worked out."

Reid looks at me and I watch him ponder what I've just

said. After only a few seconds his eyebrows raise and I can tell her understands what I've just said. "You mean…"

I nod. "I want you Reid. Forever. But I can't keep going on like this. I want you all the time and I want you to be only mine. It's not fair to me to have to share you."

I realize I'm taking a huge risk but I'm also supremely confident that Reid will make the only choice possible. He simply can't stay away from me and if he wants to be with me, he's got to make the choice. Either me or his wife. He can no longer have both of us.

Reid stands up and reaches for his jacket. As he shoves his arms into the sleeves, I can tell he's angry. "I cannot believe you, of all people, are doing this to me! Rose, your timing couldn't be worse. It's two weeks after Christmas, for God's sakes!"

"I'm sorry about the timing, but you and I both know there will never be a perfect time for something like this. You've got to leave her so we can be together. I just can't go on like this indefinitely."

"Why can't you just give me a bit more time? Why all the pressure?"

"Look, I'm really not trying to pressure you but for once in my life, I've got to think of myself. I have to be selfish because I don't want to share you any longer. I've been very patient but it's nearly killed me to know you go home to *her* every night. It's more painful that I could've ever imagined! Surely you can understand that."

Reid sighed heavily. "I do understand."

"Then take care of this. Please!"

"It's just not that easy. I've got to consider how the girls are going to take this. How it's going to affect them. You've just got to give me some time to…figure all of this out."

But time was the one thing I wasn't willing to give. I had been patient. I had spent time in the shadows, played mistress and hidden girlfriend for long enough. There had been too many nights where I'd been home alone, just wondering what he and his wife were doing. I couldn't help but wonder how he'd handle it if the situation were reversed.

"You know what? Take all the time you need."

"What?" Reid looked at me with an expression of complete and utter astonishment. His eyebrows were raised, his eyes were wide open and his jaw hung loosely at the bottom of his face. I nearly laughed out loud.

I simply shrugged. "Look," I began, "I'm not going to push you into anything you're not ready for. If you want to stay in your loveless marriage, then so be it. When you're ready to leave your wife and be with me, let me know." I stood up to show him I was finished but also to show him it was time for him to leave.

"Thanks? I guess…" He ran his fingers through his hair, utterly confused as to what to say. "I know this is hard for you—the waiting and all—and I'm sorry about it. Like I said, I just need…some time. Surely you can understand that."

"Of course," I replied. I tossed my hand around dismissively, trying to be flippant.

Reid shoved his hands in the front pocket of his jeans and slowly walked to the front door. "I really hope you're okay about all of this. I mean, I know it's been hard on you, believe me I know. You've been so patient, waiting for me to take this huge leap and I can't tell you how much I appreciate that." He took a step back toward me and pulled me into his arms. "I promise you, we'll get through this."

I wrapped my arms around him and pressed my face into the curve of his neck, relishing his scent. As much as I hated to admit it, I was terrified. This was going to go one of two ways; he was either to take the bait hook, line and sinker, or he was going to run screaming in the opposite direction. I began to frantically pray that the latter didn't happen.

Reid pulled back and met my gaze. "I'll swing by tomorrow, all right?"

"That's not going to work. I won't be here," I replied.

Just as I'd hoped he would, Reid became utterly still and he stared at me, once again, mouth agape and wearing an expression of sheer astonishment.

Priceless.

It always amazes me how silly these men are when you wait around for them for only a few months. They begin to think you'll do it for the rest of your life. Still, stupid boys. And that's what they are. They're a bunch of stupid boys who want their cake and eat it too. Well, there wasn't going to be any more eating of this cake. (Pun intended) If he wasn't ready to commit, then neither was I.

"What do you mean, 'you won't be here.' Where will you be?"

I purposely avoided his gaze and began to inspect my fingernails thoroughly. "I'm not sure. Rachel texted me earlier about heading out to some new club in Greensboro. I might head out with her. And if she's driving, I may get blitzed. I've earned it, don't you think?"

"I don't know if I like the idea of you heading out to 'some new club' with a bunch of your single friends."

And there it was. It was fine for him to go home go his wife but it wasn't okay for me to go out with my friends. He was worried what might happen if I had a few drinks. Would I end up taking some strange man back to my place? Would I meet someone new? Doubtful. But I wasn't going to let him know that.

Then I allowed myself to meet his gaze, partly so I could see his expression when I said what I had to say, but partly so that he could see by my expression I meant business. "Look, if you're leaving this apartment and heading back to the home you share with your wife, you are not allowed to have any thought or opinion on what I do with my time when you are with *her.*" I practically spat the word at him. "If you think I am going to sit around and wait for you to make up your mind about whether or not you want to be with me, you are out of your mind. I refuse to be *that woman.*"

"What do you mean, 'that woman?' I have no idea what you're talking about."

I stepped closer to him. "Oh, I think you know exactly what I'm talking about. Somewhere in the back of your mind is a guy who is still stuck in 1962. And it's that guy that thinks he can go home and play happy family with his wife and kids while I sit here by the phone, hoping and praying that my lover will call, text, or stop by. I'm telling you right now, Reid Hamilton. I am not that woman. If you want to be with me, then be with me. But do not keep stringing me along with the whole 'I'm so confused. I need more time' speech."

"What the hell has gotten into you?"

"You have," I replied softly. "I love you….so much. And the thought of you going home to that woman every night kills a little bit of me each time you do. I just can't take it anymore. I'm sorry."

When I looked up at Reid, he looked utterly defeated. It was like it finally hit him; all that he'd asked me to do, all I'd given up for him. I was only asking him the same that he'd asked of me: Make me your number one. Be with me….forever.

"I'm so sorry, Rosemary." Slowly, he turned away from me and left the apartment, closing the door behind him with a soft click.

It was then that I was enveloped in fear. I worried that I'd pushed too hard, too fast and lost him forever.

But I was not one to sit around and wait for some guy to realize he wanted to be with me. I was most definitely not that kind of girl.

I grabbed my pocketbook and headed out the door, not even glancing back behind me.

Abbie

It's Friday, and I'm looking forward to Reid's arrival home. It's been a long week of travel for him. He left early Sunday afternoon and is only coming back now. I've made beef stroganoff, which is one of Reid's favorite. It's all part of buttering him up so he'll talk to me about what's bothering him. I'm determined to yank it out of him if need be.

When he arrives home, the girls are thrilled and run toward him and tackle him. It always surprises me that they have this reaction to his return. It's like they can't really adjust to the fact that he's gone. I know these longer trips really tend to get to him and by Wednesday or Thursday night, I tend to soothe their cries of "I miss daddy!" which breaks my heart.

Once the girls release him from their grasp, he leans over to me and places a chaste kiss on my cheek. I smile politely and feel a tiny piece of my heart chip away. I'm terribly worried now. It's obvious to me that there's something wrong. I'm not sure why now it's so obvious to me; things have been a bit off for some time now. I guess it's like when you come down with the flu. For days you feel a bit tired, maybe a little sore or out of sorts. You may cough or have an ache here or there, but it's not until you find it nearly impossible to get out of bed and do something productive that you're able to put together all those individual symptoms and realize they were an indication of something greater.

I've noticed all the individual symptoms over the past few months - the distance, the long work hours, the impossible travel schedule, and the short temper while Reid is home. It's just now that I've put all those little indicators together. Something is definitely wrong with my husband and I can't go on any longer without finding out what it is.

As has become the norm lately, Reid treks down to the basement after dinner while I clear the dishes and tidy up the kitchen. I supervise bath time, making sure Caroline washes all the soap from her hair. Once they are toweled off and dressed in their jammies, I shuffle them off to bed, hoping they don't notice that it's a few minutes before their nine pm bedtime. Luckily, they do not. I'm too on edge to handle arguing with two little girls about a bed time that is a mere ten minutes earlier than normal.

Once I tuck the girls in, I open a bottle of wine and grab two glasses. Opening the door to the basement, I slowly walk down the steps to find Reid staring at his laptop. He barely glances at me as I sit beside him. For a second, I think he visibly stiffens but the movement was so fleeting that I second guess myself and quickly rid the thought from my mind. The two glasses are held in place awkwardly by my fingers and keep clinking together so I place them on the coffee table before I shatter them. After pouring myself a glass, I turn to Reid, bottle poised in front of me. "You want some?" I ask.

"Nah," he replies, keeping his eyes glued to the screen.

I take a large sip from my glass, hoping it will somehow give me the courage to inch my way into this conversation.

"Reid?"

"Yeah?" His eyes remain fixed on the screen in front of him.

"What's been going on with you lately?"

At this, he looks up at me, almost as though he's seeing me for the first time. "What?"

I sigh. "I know there's something…off with you. I can feel it. You've been so distant lately and it's got me worried. Are you sick? Is there something going on that you need to tell me?"

He smiles, but it's not genuine, more of a nervous 'I can't tell you what I'm thinking' smile and I begin to feel the terror pulse through me.

"Reid," I say sternly. "Please tell me what's going on. I'm worried sick."

He closes his laptop and slides it off his thighs and onto the couch. Then he leans forward and pours himself a glass of wine. He lifts the nearly full glass to his lips and swallows several times, nearly emptying the glass. Now, I'm utterly terrified. What is this horrible news he's about to deliver? Is he sick? Good lord, does he have cancer? Is he dying? I reach over and grasp his hand.

"Reid," I say. "Whatever it is, we can work through it."

Slowly, he pulls his hand out of my grasp.

"I don't even know how to say this to you," he says, and I feel my stomach drop. It is then that I notice the expression on his face. It's not one I've seen before on my husband. He looks as though one might look when they've been told they have a terminal illness and only have weeks to live.

"Good lord. Did someone die?" I leap up out of my chair and take his hands in mine. When he avoids my gaze, I begin to feel a rather large sense of panic begin to wash over me. Our list of friends and family is running through my mind as I look at him and try to meet his eyes. The possibility of calamities are endless. Thankfully, I know that the girls are sound asleep and barring any midnight vomit session, we're in the clear to have a frank and open conversation without interruption.

"No one died," he says.

Yet. The thought enters my mind before he even completes his sentence. He's prepping me for some horrible illness. Oh. My God. He's really sick. There's some cancer inside of him, eating away at him. It's probably something incurable like pancreatic cancer. I think back to the pictures of Patrick Swayze right before he passed and imagine my Reid the living skeleton that Patrick became. The thought of my husband wasting away like that is something I simply cannot bear.

By now, I'm imagining countless hours spent in a sterile environment. I'm planning sitters for the girls while I sit beside

Reid as he receives chemo and radiation treatments. I feel my resolve stiffen and I'm overcome with the will to save my husband.

"I won't let you die!"

Reid has a funny look on his face. "Jesus, Abbie! What makes you think I'm dying? Why are you so morbid all of a sudden?"

I feel a wave of relief wash over me. "So you're not dying? Well, how bad is it? I mean, you are sick right? You're sick and you're afraid to tell me." I sit back down and scooch closer to him on the couch. "We can beat this, whatever it is. I know we can. We'll fight it every step of the way. There are new treatments coming out all the time!" I'm rambling but I can't stop myself. I'm on a roll now, spouting out every article I've read on cancer during my lifetime. I'm reaching into the recesses of my mind for any statistic that tells me the success rate of any procedure. Granted, I'm reaching here but I'm doing whatever I can to convince Reid that there is hope.

Several minutes into my speech, I notice Reid looking at me with a strained expression on his face. It's a cross between agony and disbelief.

"Oh my god," I cry. "I'm right, aren't I? It's pancreatic cancer, isn't it?"

"What in the hell…. Abbie, I don't have cancer, for Christ sakes!" He runs his hands through his hair in frustration and sighs heavily.

"You don't? Then what's been going on? You're always stressed, you're short with me and the girls, you're always distracted. Even when you're with us, you're not really "with" us. It's like you're a completely different person!"

Reid is silent. He looks down at the carpet between his legs and says nothing. He is so still I feel the urge to look at this chest to make sure he's breathing.

"Reid?"

For several moments he sits beside me, still. My hands are

clasped in my lap and I my mouth has gone dry. I'm really hoping Reid decides to say something because at this moment, I'm not sure my tongue will work.

"You're right. I am a different person."

"Okaaaay….but what exactly does that mean?"

He takes a deep breath, then slowly exhales. "It means I can't do this anymore."

Somewhere in the back of my mind, there is a spark of both fear and an inkling that my life is about to become very different. My throat becomes very dry and I find it difficult to form even a single word. I force myself to swallow, which gives me just enough vocal control to eek out one word. "What?" My voice is only slightly more than a whisper.

He sighs heavily and leans forward, resting his elbows on his knees. "I really didn't want to do this now…"

"Do what?" I barely recognize the sound that comes from my mouth. I don't sound like myself at all and I know exactly what it is. It's the sound of panic. Desperation. At this moment, I'm desperately trying to ignore the nagging feeling in the back of my mind but it's becoming more and more difficult to do so. Right now, it's just an inkling that something horrific is about to come out of my husband's mouth and I feel certain that with his next utterance, my world will come crashing down around me.

"What can't you do?" Though I utter the words, I'm desperate for him to leave the question unanswered. If he can just ignore the question, then I can go on with my ignorant bliss. But somehow, I know it's too late for that. I can see the resignation in Reid's eyes. He's got to get it out.

"This," he says, pointing a finger slowly toward me, and then back at himself. "The thing is…." He sighs slowly. "The thing is, things between us lately have been….well, difficult. I've been traveling so much and you've been busy with all you do. I guess we've just grown apart."

Grown apart? Did those words actually come out of my

husband's mouth? Is he actually going to use something so trite to end my marriage?

Bastard.

The word comes into my mind before I even realize it. But once it's there, I can't help but notice how perfectly it fits. Reid is a bastard. Grown apart. What a fucking cop-out. I can't help but wonder what it's code for; mid-life crisis? Tired of being married? Another woman?

God, he is pathetic. And I am suddenly extremely pissed off. I have given this man the best years of my life, two children and a beautiful home and he's going to end it all because we've 'grown apart?'

The anger has allowed me to find my voice. When I speak, it's clear and strong, and laden with sarcasm and disgust. "I can't believe you're doing this. Why would you do this? What about our children? Our home? This life we have together?"

He continues to stare at a spot somewhere on the carpet about a foot or so in front of him. "This...life we have just isn't working anymore. Can't you see that?"

"No," I say, shaking my head. "I can't see that. We're a team. We're supposed to work things out together. Not bail."

"I'm not bailing-"

"The hell you aren't," I retort.

He shakes his head slowly from side to side, almost as though he's pitying me, which only enrages me further. "I'm just smart enough to know when things aren't working. I'm trying to save our sanity here. The girls are going to realize something isn't right between us. Do you want them to grow up sensing their parents' indifference towards each other?"

"Is that what you're feeling? Indifference?" Reid's gaze finally locks on mine and I see it in his eyes. He's no longer looking at me like his wife, the woman he's supposed to care for. Right now, he's looking at me with impatience. As though he just wants this conversation to be over so he can move on. I've simply become something in his path. Something that is preventing him from getting where he needs to go. Reid has always been going in the same direction as me, but now? He's set on heading in the opposite direction.

I always thought that if something like this were to happen to me, I'd lose my mind. I'd turn into one of those women who completely loses it and falls to the ground in a heap. Perhaps have a screaming fit or pound their fists against their husband's chest, demanding an explanation. It seems, however, I am not one of those women. Inexplicably, I remain seated on the couch with all my faculties still working. For whatever reason, I remain eerily calm. I will not beg him to stay if he no longer wants to be with me. I will maintain at least a modicum of self-respect.

"I'm going to pack a few things," Reid says, shoving his hands into his pockets.

"So you're just going to leave tonight? Now?" My voice is rising and I feel my calm demeanor evaporating. "Where will you go? What are we going to tell the girls?"

He sighs heavily. "We don't have to tell them anything right now. They're used to me traveling so they won't question if I'm not around for a few days. Once we get things settled, we can sit them down and tell them."

The matter-of-fact way he answers my question makes me raise an eyebrow. Clearly, he has though this through. I'm dumbfounded that I didn't see it coming. How could I miss this? How could I not see this coming? These thoughts make me wonder just what I've been focused on during the past…weeks? Months? Who knows?

This it hits me. I didn't see anything because Reid didn't *want* me to see anything.

Still, though, there must have been signs, signals…something! Nothing comes to mind at the moment but honestly, it's not as though I'm thinking clearly at all at the moment. The one thought that does run through my mind however, is that I'm certain in the days and weeks to come, I'll recall things that given what I know now, will make me feel like an idiot for being so obtuse then.

Reid is standing in the middle of the room. He looks anxious, like a bird about to take flight if the slightest movement is made in his direction. I can see the tension written across his face, something that would be indiscernible to anyone else. To anyone who doesn't know him as well as I do. Then I wonder how well I really know my husband. If I had no idea he was about to leave his family, did I really know him at all? Have other women been in this place I now find myself? Were they just as shocked and surprised as I am at this moment? After a few moments, I begin to feel something else inside of me. The initial shock appears to be wearing off and is replaced with something much more venomous. I realize Reid has been planning this for some time. Planning and prepping to leave his family. I feel so utterly betrayed that he has his plans laid out for him and has chosen this path instead of keeping his family together and doing everything possible to work things out.

I'm pissed. The anger is running through my veins, propelled forward by the adrenaline rush I'm feeling.

"Well, it appears you've got it all worked out. But tell me, where will you be staying exactly? The girls may need to reach you. I may need to reach you. I think telling the mother of your children where you'll be staying is the least you can do."

"I haven't worked out all the details," he replies, clearly avoiding the question.

"Well," I say, crossing my arms over my chest. "Let's start with tonight. Where will you be tonight?"

He sighs heavily and I can tell by the sound of it that he's already tired of answering questions. "I just know I can't be here. Not anymore."

"Why won't you tell me where you're going?"

"Because it's not important, all right?" He snaps. "If you need to reach me, call my cell." He walks over to the stairs.

"I'll pack a few things and then I'll be gone. I'll come back in a few days for the rest of my stuff."

That stops me dead in my tracks. How has it come to this? Instead of having my husband with me day in and day out, instead of my girls getting to see their father nearly every day, we are now relegated to contacting him by cell phone? That just doesn't sit well with me. What if Hannah or Caroline want to see him? How is all of this going to work?

I look up at him and feel a tear slide slowly down my cheek, making me even angrier that I can't hold back the tears until Reid is at least out of my line of vision. "You're really going?"

He nods. "Yeah, I'm really going." He rubs his face with his hand and then manages to look me in the eye. "Look, Abbie. Things haven't been right between us for awhile now. I don't think they're going to get any better. Me leaving is for the best."

"The best for who?" I screech. "Who exactly is this good for? Because I know it's not the best thing for Hannah or Caroline! Having their father leave is not what's best for our children, Reid."

He sighs heavily, sounding exhausted and irritated at the same time. It's almost as if he's annoyed I'm asking these questions. What does he expect? That I'll just let him walk out of our lives without so much as a decent explanation? And one that doesn't involve "indifference". Everyone knows that's bullshit. It's simply code for "I don't want to be with you anymore."

He looks at me and shakes his head as though he pities me, which makes my stomach turn. I sit back down on the couch and listen to the sounds of his footsteps as he makes his way up the steps. They sound...normal, which surprises me. His footsteps sound like they did every other time they went up and down those steps. I'm not sure what I was thinking but the normalcy of that sound disturbs me. But then, what was I expecting? That his footsteps would somehow convey his sadness? Perhaps they'd be slower, heavier…something to indicate that he feels something other than the all-consuming desire to leave our home.

After the sound of the footsteps is gone, there is silence and I assume he's throwing a few things into a bag. I imagine him packing his Tumi bag—ironically, the one I purchased for him for our wedding—and filling it with items I purchased for him over the years; a Bobby Jones golf shirt, his favorite pair of jeans, a button down denim shirt from our most recent trip to the mountains, the deodorant I dutifully make sure he never runs out of and the razor blade refills I just picked up yesterday. The thought that I have cared for this man so tenderly for so long only to be discarded makes me ill. I'm completely dumbfounded as to how anyone can so carelessly toss aside a family they've spent years creating.

Then I realize, it's not our family he's tossing aside; it's me. Reid will always love our children, it's just me he no longer wants to be with.

The realization of this hits me like a ton of bricks and I feel my resolve weaken. The tears come, slowly at first. They slide down my face slowly because I am still trying to hold them back. After several moments, I completely give up and the tears begin streaming. The release I feel at allowing myself to sob is cathartic.

I sit there sobbing hysterically for what must have been the better part of an hour. It is the sound of garage door opening and closing that ends my pity party. From the distance, I can hear the sound of Reid's Accord driving him to God-only-knows where.

It takes me several minutes to muster up the strength to rise. Even then, standing is difficult and I sway back and forth, trying to get my bearings. Walking up the stairs seems to take forever; each step upward sapping my strength. Finally, I make it up to the top and manage to walk into the bedroom. I ease myself onto the bed, then fall backward as another wave of tears envelopes me. Before long, the sides of my face are wet and the tears have soaked into my hair. I feel certain my eyes are, by now, red and puffy and will remain that way all night and for most of tomorrow despite whatever remedies the internet might have. I'd take a look in the mirror to see just how bad I look but feel certain it won't be pretty. At this point, I decide self-preservation is best and make it my mission to avoid any glimpses of myself in the mirror.

Rolling onto my side, I instinctively curl up into the fetal position. Though I'm willing myself to move, I find my limbs will not listen to me. I glance around the room and can't help but notice that all everything is as it was. Reid neglected to take any of the pictures carefully placed on our bureau, or the pottery we'd purchased on a day trip to Sanford. The only evidence of his absence is an empty drawer and even then, I'd have to open it to see it.

My gaze finds the Ipod dock on my nightstand and with a jolt, I realize that it has been less than an hour since I first went downstairs to talk to Reid, which means it was less than sixty minutes ago that my husband told me he was leaving.

It seems to me it should take more than sixty minutes for your world to fall completely apart.

Rose

Reid shows up at my condo much later than I thought he would. Later in that it's nearly midnight and later in the fact that I'd been badgering him for months to leave his wife. I mean, how long does it take to leave someone you no longer love? Someone you no longer have anything in common with, other than your children? But as it turns out, what Reid actually needed was a gentle nudge from me. Apparently the thought that I would no longer wait around for him to call, text, or swing by whenever he had a moment shook him. Enough to make him quicken his journey and leave his wife.

I open the door and smile as I see him standing there with his suitcase. He looks weary and tired, as though he's had a rough time of it all. I know he needs comfort so I open my arms to him and he steps into them, pulling me close.

"It was awful," he says. "I just had to get out of there. Abbie was..."

"I'm just glad you're okay," I reply, unwilling to even acknowledge his now ex-wife. Even though he has left her, it's still tenuous. He could at any moment, decide he's made a mistake and want to return to the home he's known for the better part of fifteen years. Any mention of Abbie, whether positive or negative, will no doubt, stir up memories that are better left alone. Though he's mine now, I still need to tread lightly until this initial phase passes and he's comfortable here and comfortable with our live together.

"Come on," I say, leading him into my bedroom. "I've cleared out some space for you. Just go ahead and make yourself comfortable. After all, this is your home now too."

He glances at me, then places his suitcase on the bed and begins the task of unpacking. His movements are slow and I can sense his hesitancy as he hangs up several shirts in my closet. He pauses to look at them for a few moments, almost as though trying to determine whether or not they look as though they belong in the closet that is now ours; a closet he no longer shares with his wife. He dumps out the remainder of his suitcase—some socks, underwear, and some toiletry items— and puts them in their appropriate spots. He fills the drawer I've cleared out for him and then zips up his suitcase and tucks it underneath my skirts in the closet. The entire process takes less than five minutes and I realize how quickly he must have packed to come here. I know Reid. The amount of clothes that man has could put any woman's closet to shame. For him to leave with only the marginal amount of items he took tells me just how awful the situation was for him. Poor baby. I step toward him and embrace him.

"I'm so glad you're here," I say, nuzzling my face into his neck. "I've waited so long for you to be mine and now you finally are."

Though it's only a slight movement, I can feel him tense beneath me. He masks it well, though by smiling at me as he pulls away. "I need a drink," he says.

I nod. "Of course. I'm sure it's been a rough night for you." I walk the few steps out of the bedroom and into the kitchen where I grab a bottle of wine from the fridge. As I pour him a glass, I begin to wonder how he's actually going to feel living here. My apartment is nice but it's only a one bedroom and Reid is used to a much larger home. Granted, he shared it with three other people but I wonder if he's going to feel claustrophobic. Well, I feel certain it won't be long before move out of this place and purchase something that suits both of us.

I hand him the glass and watches as he takes several swallows. He puts the glass down on the tiny table I have against the wall, pulls the chair out, then sits down heavily.

"Reid," I say, sitting down across from him. "Baby, tell me

about it."

He shakes his head, sighs heavily, then takes another long sip from his glass. "It was awful," he says. "Abbie kept asking me where I was going and I just avoided the question. It was almost like she knew something was going on."

That piques my curiosity. "Do you think she knows about us?"

He pauses for a moment, then shakes his head. "I don't think so. Although the fact that I didn't tell her where I'm going might make her think something's up."

"You were right to do that. She doesn't need to know where you are at all times now. You're no longer her concern. You did the right thing, baby." I'm cautious with my words, only focusing on the fact that Reid did the right thing. I don't even respond to what Abbie may or may not think.

"Did I?" He looks at me with such an expression of anguish, I can't help but feel bad for him. I'm sure it was difficult to leave but it's for the best. Reid was living two lives, which was one more than he wanted. But right now, he doesn't need to hear that; all he needs to hear is that he did the right thing. I know it will get easier for him in the weeks and months to come, but right now he's in pain and just needs to know that I'm here for him.

"Reid," I reply. "You did the right thing. And I love you for it." My voice comes out sounding strong and confident and I can only hope it's enough for the both of us.

He doesn't answer me in kind, which concerns me just a bit but I figure he's working through his guilt. He'll get there, I tell myself, and before long, we'll be perfectly happy.

Besides, he has nothing to feel guilty about. Abbie should have taken better care of her man. If Reid was totally happy at home, he wouldn't have been so receptive to my advances.

Stupid woman. She didn't know what she had.

Abbie

I'm still not sure how I've managed to make it through the past few weeks. It must be the girls. Simply knowing that others are relying on me to care for them gives me the strength to get out of bed each morning. And I certainly don't want them to see me crying all the time. Quite frankly, it'd scare them. No, I keep my tears to late at night while alone in bed; a bed that is now much too big for me.

Though I hide my tears from the girls, Caroline sees my red eyes and blotchy cheeks each morning. No amount of cucumbers over my eyes or cold compresses will erase hours of crying in the time between the time the girls are put to bed and I finally fall asleep out of sheer exhaustion.

Besides, the evening hours are when I allow the pain to roll over me. It's when I release the tears I've held back each day. The sobbing, while wreaking havoc on my appearance, is giving me the outlet I need so that I can function each day so I've just learned to live with the evidence of each agonizing evening when I allow myself uninterrupted crying.

I thought the process would get easier with each passing day but I'm finding that not to be the case Reid has not only vanished from my life, but from the girls' lives as well. He has called them only once since leaving and has only contacted me by text. And even the texts were short and to the point; their intention was more information sharing than wondering how any of us were doing.

I've come to the conclusion that Reid is making every possible attempt to completely cut me out of his life. It's almost as if he's turned off a switch and no longer has any feelings for me whatsoever. I can handle that…well, someday I'll be able to handle it. But Reid has also, it seems, cut our children out of his life. His contact with the girls has diminished to a weekly phone call and maybe a text that I'm asked to show them. He even opted not to come to the house when we were supposed to talk to the girls about our separation. Instead, he texted me at the last minute telling me I should "go ahead and talk to the girls" without him because he was busy at work.

Honestly, that was the final straw for me and it just lit me on fire. I sat the girls down and mustered all the strength I could find and told them that while their father still loved them very much, he was not going to live with us anymore. Boy, that was a tough sentence to choke out, particularly since I was just about ready to choke Reid.

Both the girls took the news better than I anticipated. They cried for a bit and then went to their rooms. Caroline instructed me not to follow them because they needed time alone. God, she's getting to be so grown up!

After an hour or so, they came downstairs together and asked for something to eat. I made them some macaroni and cheese from a box and they inhaled it. Imagine that! Heartache makes my girls ravenous.

Since Reid has moved out, the only time I've left the house is to bring the girls to school. Today, however, I have decided to shower, blow-dry my hair, and actually apply some makeup so that I don't look like someone who has been locked in a closet for a month. I nearly gasped when I looked at myself in the mirror this morning. My skin was sallow and pasty and my hair hung limply around my face. My cheekbones were much more prominent than they'd ever been and I could tell instantly that I'd lost weight. Perhaps the only silver lining in this entire mess.

What can I say? At this point, I'm grasping at straws.

After showering and making a decent attempt to fix my hair and apply some makeup, I reached for a pair of jeans. They slid up over my hips with an ease I'd not felt in several years. When I buttoned them without having to suck anything in, I allowed myself a tiny smile. Though simply not eating wasn't the best way to lose weight, it was most surely the fastest method.

Walking into the kitchen I began to search the fridge and pantry, trying to make a mental list of items I'd need at the store. It didn't take me long to realize that a list wasn't needed. Based on the barren wasteland that was my pantry, I needed to pretty much restock my entire kitchen. Even the ten or so boxes of flavored rices and assorted dried pastas with seasonings had been eaten by the girls. And God only knew how long those had been sitting there.

Closing the pantry door softly, I grabbed my purse and headed to the grocery store. I pulled into a spot and checked my watch. It was only mid-morning. The girls wouldn't be home until nearly three o'clock so I had plenty of time to peruse the aisles and actually plan out some meals instead of rushing through the store, grabbing whatever interests me at the moment or anything with a BOGO sticker affixed to the shelf. Inevitably, the one thing I desperately needed to purchase is the one item I would forget, which meant yet another trip back to the store in between some of the other ninety seven tasks I needed to accomplish on a given day. Today, however, I only want to accomplish one—getting some food in the house.

During my time spent perusing the aisles, I begin to think about all that's happened over the past month or so. Things still don't make sense to me. I mean, I'm not completely naïve; I get that people divorce. It happens all the time. I guess I just figured that if it were to happen to me, there would be some sort of indication of things to come.

But I never saw it coming.

Abbie

"I think Reid might be seeing someone," I say, testing out the words on my tongue. They sound oddly foreign to me though the words have been turning around in my mind for the past few weeks. Today is the first time I've said them out loud and I say them to only person I trust with them.

"Of course he is."

The swiftness of Nora's response takes me by surprise and I gasp. "Why do you say it like that? You know, so matter-of-fact. Like you were expecting it or something."

"Expecting what? That Reid is seeing someone or that you'd actually come right out and say it."

"That Reid...that I... Oh, hell, I don't know." My gaze travels across the expanse of the crown molding in my kitchen as I think about my next question. "You really think he's seeing another woman?"

Nora looks at me with an expression that tells me I'm being stupid for even asking such an idiotic question.

"What?! You mean you're not even the least bit surprised?"

"Frankly, no."

"Jesus, Nora." I force a stiff laugh. "He's only been out of the house for a few weeks."

Nora raises an eyebrow at me. "Come on, really? It didn't occur to you that he'd begin seeing someone immediately? If he hadn't been seeing someone before he left, that is."

"Wait, what?! Are you suggesting that he was seeing someone before he left me? That he was having an affair?"

Nora sat very still and simply stared at me. After several moments, she raised her eyebrows in a 'don't you see' expression. Finally, the realization dawned on me and like a puzzle—a cheap, cliché of a puzzle—all the pieces clicked into place. I thought of the late nights, the constant travel, the evasiveness when I'd ask his schedule or hotel phone numbers. For the several months prior to our separation, Reid had been, for the most part, unavailable to me. Even when he was home, he wasn't really with us. Constantly distracted and working non-stop, though now I felt the need to put air quotes around the word 'working.' He had definitely changed over the past year. He'd gone from a loving, happy man to someone who was always stressed and on edge. Was it possible that his stress wasn't caused by his work as I'd initially thought but instead, caused by the stress of carrying on with another woman?

It all made sense. As I stood there, more memories came into focus. The cell phone that he'd recently put a passcode on, him 'forgetting' to give me the name of the hotels he was staying at or his flight schedules, the numerous times the girls or I would call and his cell phone would go to voice mail. It was so clear to me now that I wondered how I'd missed it before.

God, my life was one big, fucking cliché.

And I'd had no idea. And wasn't that the biggest cliché of them all—the wife is the last to know.

Nora got up from the table and stood in front of me, then wrapped her arms around me. "I'm so sorry, Abbie. I'm just so sorry."

"How could I have been so stupid?"

She pulled back and looked me in the eyes. "Now you listen to me. You weren't stupid; he was. He's the one who was out fucking around. Good lord, one day I just want to meet a man who can keep his dick in his pants."

Despite my pain, I smiled. "I just don't see how he can go from one relationship to the next. I mean, doesn't he need time to…I don't know, heal?"

Nora burst out laughing. Seeing my look of shock, she immediately pressed her lips together to stop laughing. "Oh, honey. I'm sorry," she said. "I don't mean to laugh about this because it is not funny. What I find funny is that men are all the same. When they're young, they don't want to get married—the old ball and chain, they always say. Then, they finally get married and realize it's a great situation for them to be in."

A look of confusion passes over my face.

Nora continues. "See, you were a stay at home mom for…What? Ten years?"

I nod.

"So Reid goes to work every day—and I'm not discounting the fact that he works very hard, mind you. But he goes to work, does this thing, has to travel a bit, do some work at home sometimes, blah, blah, blah. Meanwhile, you've been at home—your office, if you will—and you're taking care of everything. But the difference is, you don't get to take a break. Your office is with you all the time. The girls need something, they call you. The 'office' -" Nora makes little quotation marks in the air. "-needs something, you go out to get it. Married men get used to having all those little details done for them. And once they're married for any length of time, they just can't handle being alone. They'll marry the next woman who opens her legs for him without even thinking about whether or not she's right for him. Those fuckers are so hell-bent on getting married again, they don't even wonder what went wrong the first time around."

I shake my head. "I can't imagine Reid getting married again. Good lord, we're not even divorced! I still have some of his underwear in a drawer in the bedroom!"

"Abbie, think about it. You did everything for that man, like most women. He became completely dependent on you. It's like sending an animal out to the wild after they've been in captivity all their life. He's like the goddamn limping gazelle in the herd out there! Other women see how his clothes are pressed and cleaned, how he's been fed well all these years. Hell, I'll bet he even parades those two beautiful girls around—after you've gotten them bathed and dressed, of course. Right now, he looks like he's got it all together. And he does, for a bit of time. Women will flock to that well-kept appearance he's got going. But that won't last long. Before you know it, he'll have to figure out how to work the iron, cook for himself and he may even have to dress the girls one day. Imagine what that'll look like."

Nora grinned, lost in her imagination.

"I'm not following," I said.

"Abbie, Reid can't be by himself. He's been taken care of for too long. Like most men. You've done everything for the man but wipe his ass and now he's got to do it all: work, cook, clean, dress himself, take care of the girls. All of that takes effort; effort he's not going to have because he doesn't know how. Like most men who have been coddled—not meant as an insult, by the way—they are completely dependent on the women who have cared for them. The result is that these men can't function on their own. They're helpless."

"The limping gazelle in the herd?" I ask, repeating her earlier words.

"Exactly!" Nora replied, nodding. "Once they realize how much effort it takes to do all the stuff their wives have done for years, they realize they're helpless. Most of them just latch onto the next vagina they find."

"God, Nora," I said. "You make it sound crass."

She lifted up her glass to me in a toast. "I call 'em like I see 'em."

As I lift my glass to my lips, I can't help but hope Nora is dead wrong about Reid.

Rose

"Reid," I asked, somewhat exasperated. "When are you going to introduce me to the girls?"

He kept reading his paper as though I hadn't even spoken.

"Reid? REID!"

He looked up slowly, his gaze lingering on the page as if her were so engrossed in an article he couldn't bear to look away. "hmmm....?"

Men. They're all infuriating.

"When are you going to introduce me to the girls?"

He crinkled his forehead the way he does when he's confused. "What do you mean? You've already met the girls."

I sighed heavily, more for emphasis than anything else. "What I mean is, when are you going to introduce me to the girls as....your girlfriend?"

Reid looked at me with an expression I'd become all too familiar with over the past few weeks during the other forty times I'd broached the subject of introductions. His expression fell somewhere between irritation and fear. I think he knew I was becoming a bit frustrated with his avoidance of the subject and he also knew I was anxious to move forward with our relationship. His girls were a very large part of that. They needed to accept me as part of his world, and quickly. I no longer had any desire to hide in the shadows as we'd done for so long. Reid was free now and I wanted everyone to know I'd staked my claim.

"Rose," he began slowly. "We've been over this. I think we need to wait awhile before making any introductions. Let the girls get used to one change at a time, you know?"

"But when?" I couldn't help it, I was pouting. "I know they've been through a lot but they're kids. They're resilient.

They'll adjust fine to all of this. Besides, isn't it important for them to know that their father is happy?"

"I just think it's too soon."

"Too soon? How can you say that? We've been together for nearly a year!"

"Rose," he said stiffly. "While we may have been together for that long, to the girls - and everyone else for that matter—this is a new development."

"I know that," I replied. "It's just that I want the girls to know about me, about us."

"They will," he said. He stands up, walks over to me and takes my hands in his. "I just need to give the girls some time to adjust to all the changes before I toss something else their way. This is going to be a drastic change. They're used to seeing me with their mother. I think if they were to see me with another woman so soon, it would be jarring to them."

"I just don't see why we can't tell everyone. I've waited so long to be with you and I want everyone to know how I feel about you. Your kids are a big part of your life and it's important they know about me."

"They will," Reid nodded. "Don't worry, Rose. They will. I just want to be careful about how we do this. I mean, come on. No one is going to believe that within weeks after leaving my wife of fifteen years, I 'got lucky' and found a new relationship. And with one of my employees? Come on. Everyone will start to whisper the minute we go public."

"I know you're right. It's just hard waiting for our life to begin."

"I know," he replied. "But we need to do this the right way."

I nodded, but not because I agreed. I really just wanted the conversation to be over. I was sick of waiting. I wanted our life together to begin and that wasn't going to happen until I met the girls, not as Reid's employee but as a part of their father's future.

Besides, I was no longer Reid's employee. I'd managed to transfer to another department within the company without much trouble. I guess a glowing recommendation from your boss helps when you're interested in making a switch.

I'd done my part and switched jobs. It was now time for Reid to do his part and introduce me to his children as the woman in his life.

Abbie

The girls are finally asleep and as I trudge down the stairs, I picture myself curled up in bed with a book in my lap and a glass of wine beside me. The girls, oddly enough, have been sleeping in their beds, mostly because I've insisted upon it, but also because I think they realize that if they begin to sleep in my bed, it will become permanent. And even I know that's not the healthiest habit. As much as I want them to be beside me, I know it's best for them if they learn to sleep in their own beds. Finley, on the other hand, has taken over Reid's side of the bed as though it's his own. Though a part of me wonders if he thinks I'll slowly start to creep over to that side of the bed while I sleep and he's doing his part to prevent me from doing so.

As I approach my bedroom, I head a series of pings that tells me I'm receiving numerous texts. My phone is lying on the nightstand so I walk over to it, pick it up and see numerous texts from Nora. Each one of them is in all caps. As I'm holding the phone, two more texts come in.

ARE YOU HOME?

WHY ARE YOU NOT TEXTING ME BACK?

I sigh heavily, sit down on the bed and type a quick reply, explaining to her that I was putting the girls to bed. In mere seconds, I receive yet another text from her telling me she is on her way over and moments after that, there is a soft knock at the door.

"Good lord," I mutter. "What is so damn important that she is coming over here now?"

I swing open the door and see such a look of sheer disgust and anger on Nora's face that I step back. Nora doesn't say a word. Instead, she walks past me, staring at me the whole time, and walks into my kitchen. I watch her pull out two wine glasses from the cupboard, a bottle of wine from the fridge and then fill the glasses to the rim.

"Drink," she says.

"Nora, what the…"

"Drink," she repeats.

Obligingly, I take a tiny sip of wine. Before the glass is even below my chin, she reaches out with her hand and gently lifts it back up to my mouth.

"Go on," she says. "Take a gulp or two. You're gonna need it."

I'm eyeing her waringly but I do as she says and take a large swallow from my glass. Satisfied, she nods at me and I place the glass down onto the counter.

"Now, will you tell me what in the world is going on? And why do you look like that?" I wave my hand around her face. "You're scaring me. Did someone die?"

"Not yet," she mutters. She takes a large gulp from her glass and I hear her swallow hard.

"Nora. What is it?"

"I know who Reid is involved with."

Up until this moment, there was the tiniest bit of hope in the back of my mind that Nora had been wrong when she pretty much suggested that Reid had left me for another woman. Now, faced with the actual information about to be told to me, I feel the color drain from my face. Not knowing what to do, I lift my glass and take a large gulp from my glass. Nora reaches to the bottle between us on the counter and refills my glass to the rim.

"Who," I whisper.

"God, Abbie. I fucking hate this. I hate that I was right. You have no idea how I struggled with how to tell…"

"Nora! Just spit it out." My hands are gripping the edge of the countertops. I glance down and see that my knuckles are pale white.

She takes a deep breath, then slowly exhales. Her gaze remains locked on mine. "It's Rose."

"Rose who?" I ask, shaking my head confusion.

Nora reaches down and takes both my hands in hers. "Rose Fuller." My face must have not shown any hint of recognition because she continues. "Rosemary Goddam Fuller."

"Wait," I say, not really hearing her...or not wanting to hear her. "Reid's employee? That Rose?"

She nods. "Yes. That Rose."

As what Nora is telling me sinks in, I begin to recall her earlier warning and a cold chill runs through me. I think of all the time I've spent with Rose, all the times she's come to my house or met me for lunch, shopping...whatever. I can't believe it. Surely no woman would do this to a friend? Surely, I wasn't completely off-base with her.

But sadly, I was.

The realization dawns on me. My husband has been unfaithful to me with a woman that not only worked for him, but is much younger than me and was also someone I considered a dear friend. In a single instant, my life has turned into one giant, fucking cliché. And I've hit a tri-fecta.

How the hell did I not see this coming? I glance at Nora, suddenly realizing just how dead on her initial assessment of Rose. Why didn't I listen to her? Why didn't I pay closer attention to Reid? And especially, to Rose.

"My god, Nora," I mutter. "You were right. You were fucking right about her."

Slowly, she nods. "I am so sorry. Sometimes, I really hate being right all the time."

I know she's trying to make me smile, even if only for a second, but her effort seems to help and the edges of my lips lift slightly.

"How did you...ummm, find out about...?" I can barely finish the sentence as I'm not even sure I want to know the answer.

Nora is silent for several moments. I stare at her for several moments and I know she is avoiding my gaze. She is chewing on her lower lip and glancing a spot on my floor.

"Nora," I prompt. "Just spit it out."

She sighs heavily, then allows the words to tumble out of her mouth. "I saw the two of them at dinner earlier tonight. Paul and I were at The Bonefish Grill-"

"Wait. You met Paul for dinner?"

She puts her hand up to stop me. "I know...I know. We just met to discuss our summer vacation schedule. It's easier if we meet out somewhere without the kids. Believe me, the last thing I want is to have dinner with that asshole but I think of it as something I need to do for the kids. The man is a fucking four year old and it wouldn't even occur to him to take some time off during the summer to spend time with his kids unless I mark it on his calendar for him. Idiot..."

I nod and take another sip from my glass. It occurs to me that I may very well find myself in that same position—meeting my ex-husband out in public so we're able to decide on a schedule for our children. The thought saddens me.

I realize Nora has been speaking the entire time and I focus back on her.

"...so because it was so busy, we were having a drink at the bar, which you know as well as I do, that I need to have a very large glass of wine in order to be even civil to that man." Nora took a sip from her glass, then set it down in front of her. "After the first glass, I needed to pee so I got up and headed toward the restroom. I got about half way there when I spotted Reid and Rose in the corner, making out like a couple of teenagers. I think I may have actually thrown up in my mouth when I saw the two of them going at it. Fucking disgusting."

Despite Nora's eye for detail, I had to ask. "Are you sure it was them?"

She nodded. "Yep. Once I spotted them I just stood there waiting for one of them to see me. Of course, Rose never took her eyes off Reid. She was looking at him like she was some school girl who just spotted her first crush. Reid eventually looked away and saw me. I do have to admit, he had the decency to look embarrassed. And he should me. That man is making a total ass out of himself. Jesus Christ, he's still working, isn't he? Can't he afford to get a hotel room with that *child* so the rest of us don't have to watch her suck off his face?"

My stomach heaves and I feel as though I've been punched in the gut and am going to vomit the contents of my earlier dinner- a leftover chicken nugget and a few fries- onto my floor. I somehow manage to suppress the urge and look up at Nora.

"Really. Rose Fuller. His employee? My friend?"

"Former friend," Nora corrected.

I nod, properly chastised. No longer can I think of Rose as my friend. She is the woman who destroyed my marriage. Though, I have to wonder, did she? What if their relationship is new? What if it began after Reid moved out? Still, it's a pretty shitty thing to do to a friend. I mean, while I'm going through a horrific time, Rose should be making sure I'm all right instead of making out with my husband—*ex-husband,* I correct myself. I feel compelled to ask the question of Nora.

"It is….is it possible they've only started seeing each other? You know, like since we split?" Even as I'm asking the question, even before I see Nora shaking her head, I know the answer. The two of them were involved on some level way before he actually moved out of this house. Given the long work hours, the traveling, and all the other time spent with each other, I feel certain this whatever-it-is began long ago. Besides, knowing what I know now, there is no going back. The two of them have betrayed me in such a manner, I know I will never be able to forgive, let alone forget.

Oddly, I find my anger swaying between the two of them. While I'm absolutely pissed that my husband cheated and will make no excuses for his behavior, I find her behavior somehow more appalling. I honestly think I'd feel better if Reid has screwed some unknown face. The fact that this is a woman I've spent time with, invited to my home- our home!- is almost more than I can bear. This woman befriended me, spent time with my children…Good god! How will I explain this to the girls? And what the hell am I going to do if Reid wants to involve her in his life with the girls? They know her, for Christ sakes! They know Rose as mommy's friend and they're not going to forget that simply because she is now their father's girlfriend.

The more I think about this, the angrier I become. Unfortunately, I will have to deal with Reid for the rest of my life and I will find a way to do that with grace and dignity, despite the hurt and humiliation he has put me through.

But Rose? Something tells me my feelings of hatred toward that woman will reside with me for a very, very long time.

It is then that I recall my mother saying something when I was a little girl. I had been upstairs playing in my room when I heard sobbing downstairs. Slowly, I crept down the steps, afraid of what I was going to find. As I got closer, I could make out two voices, both that I was quite familiar with—my mother and her best friend Debbie. I crept into the kitchen but slid down beside the cupboard so that they couldn't see me. When I finally had the courage to peek around the edge of the cabinet, I saw the face of my mother's best friend looking completely torn apart. My mother held on tight to Debbie's hands and spoke clearly to her.

"Let me tell you something," she said. "That bitch will get what's due to her. After all, a woman can run faster with her skirt up, than a man can with his pants down."

At the time, I had no idea what she was talking about. In the weeks and months that followed, I learned that Debbie's husband had been having an affair with another neighbor and my mother firmly shifted the blame on that neighbor. It is only now I understand why.

Women should stick by one another. We owe it to each other. And to pursue another woman's husband is the lowest thing one woman can do to another. My mother was simply implying that we women need to be held to a higher standard. Of course, she was also implying that once a man has his pants down, he's completely helpless.

Fuckers. All of them.

Rose

Finally, finally, things are all falling into place.

Reid is living with me and he's agreed to introduce me to the girls, though it took some serious prodding on my part. I finally convinced him to introduce me because it was silly that he couldn't even bring the girls to the apartment when he spent time with them. His time with his daughters was spent going to the movies, Chuck E. Cheese or playing mini-golf. They couldn't sleep over because Reid felt it was too soon to have them sleep at another woman's house, even though their father lives there too.

But now, everything is moving along nicely. This past weekend, we began to look for a larger place to rent. We're not able to purchase anything just yet since Reid is still paying the mortgage on the house he owns with Abbie. For the time being, she's living there with the girls, which, while I have a huge issue with, I'm keeping quiet for right now. There will be plenty of time to make Reid understand that his ex-wife now needs to get a job and that it's not his responsibility to support her any more. The kids? Sure. But Abbie? No way. And once she gets a job, she can find a place for the three of them and they can sell the house. When that happens, Reid and I can buy a house of our own.

Today, we are looking at some two and three bedroom apartments so that at least the girls will have a place to stay over when they visit him. Come to think of it, he needs to work on that once we're settled. I really think he should get his children half of the time. After all, the amount of child support he has to pay is based on the number of nights spent with each parent. The more the kids are at our place, the less he'll have to pay *her*.

"You ready to head out?" Reid pops his head into the bathroom where I'm putting on the finishing touches of my makeup. I still pay close attention to how I look all the time. It's very important that Reid knows that I care about how I look. So before we head out, even if it's just to run to the grocery store, I do a cursory glance at myself and touch up anything that looks awry.

"I'm all set," I reply. I take a final look in the mirror and smile, pleased with who I see looking back at me—a very attractive woman who has the man of her dreams.

Reid is staring at his Iphone and swiping his finger across the screen. "We've got a few places to see today. There's one over on Lakefield that looks like it might be the best one for the girls. There's a pool, tennis courts, and a playground. I think they'd really like that."

"Then let's hit that one first."

He smiles. "Perfect, since that's the first appointment of the day."

We head out of the apartment, careful to secure the deadbolt as we leave. One of my neighbors had her place broken into recently so I've been particularly careful to lock the door when I leave. Of course, now that Reid is living with me, I feel even more secure.

The afternoon is spent driving around all of Winston Salem, looking at quite a wide variety of apartments. Some of them are immediately off the list because they aren't well kept, while others are crossed off because of their severe lack of any amenities. Reid insists on both a pool and a playground so that when the girls are with us, they won't be bored.

After several hours, I am sick to death of looking at apartments. Reid has discounted every single one we've seen for some reason or another; it's almost as though he's looking for reasons not to sign a lease. He actually dismissed one of the apartments because he didn't like the sink in the half bathroom. I had to roll my eyes at that one.

When I was just about to suggest we call it a day when Reid pulled into a rather nice apartment complex—and I say the word 'apartment' loosely. What I actually saw when I looked up from my phone were what appeared to be townhomes. I felt certain he'd driven here by mistake.

"Reid, babe, I don't think these are rentable?"

He grinned at me. "Rentable? Is that even a word?"

"Shut up," I replied, punching him in the shoulder. "Seriously, these are houses. And those are townhomes." I nodded to a row of homes out the right side of the car. "Look at the grassy areas. The landscaping."

"What? Why?" I couldn't for the life of me, understand why I was supposed to look at the shrubs, but I did it. "I don't get it. What am I supposed to be looking at?"

"They're all the same," he replied.

I sighed softly, still not understanding. "Okaaaayyyy….."

"All the houses and the townhomes-" He nodded toward the row of houses I'd spotted earlier. "-have the same landscaping. The same bushes in front of each house, the same amount of pine straw…almost as if one person took-"

"-care of all the yards!" I exclaimed, finishing his sentence. I finally understood what Reid was referring to and turned to look at the greenery we were driving past. Now it was clear; every house had identical landscaping—one tree off to the left, in front of a large window- and every townhouse had three green shrubs to the left of the front door. I started to notice other similarities as well. The townhouses alternated colors and exteriors—stone on the front with white siding, then a solid brick front. The individual houses at first glance appeared to be different from each other but on closer inspection, one could see the similar roof lines and window placement.

"Let me see if I can find an office somewhere," Reid said as he drove slowly through the curved street. After several moments, he parked in front of a house that looked remarkably similar to all the other houses but had a small, nearly undetectable sign in front with gray lettering that seemed to blend into the house itself. He put the car into park and turned off the engine. He peered through the windshield at the front door of the office. "I wonder if they have anything available…"

"Well, there's only one way to find out," I reply, opening up my door and climbing out. I bend over at the waist to grab my purse and look back at Reid. "You coming?"

"Yep," he replied, scrambling out of the car.

Together we walk into the office and it is only a few minutes before we find ourselves on a tour of one of the properties. We loved the unit we saw, though both of us tried to contain ourselves so as not to appear too eager. When we returned to the office and were told the rental amount, I nearly gasped. Reid, however, didn't even blink. He simply reached for the rental contract and signed his name, then motioned for me to do the same.

I was completely blown away. The place was absolutely gorgeous and much more than I'd ever hoped for. This was something I could never do on my own. My entire salary would cover the rent and not much more.

We drive home in silence with Reid holding my hand tightly the entire way. Every few seconds or so, he would take his eyes off the road and glance at me, grinning from ear to ear. He was thrilled with the house we'd found and I was thrilled for him. Nothing made me happier than knowing he was happy with his decision.

That night, our lovemaking was more intense that it had ever been. Feral almost. Reid ripped my bra from my body and took claim of my nipples with his mouth so forcefully, I nearly cried out. His hands roamed all over my body and clung to every inch of skin he could. He seemed almost desperate. When at last he plunged into me, he did so with such force and determination, I felt as though he were staking his claim on me. He drove deeper and deeper into me until I cried out as an orgasm ripped through me. I clung to his back as he continued to thrust in and out of me, quickening his pace as he got closer and closer to his release. When he came, he grabbed the back of my head, holding me still while he cried out with his release. Once the throbbing subsided, he collapsed on top of me, breathing heavily. I can't be sure, but I think I heard him whisper, "You are mine."

As if he had to say it out loud. I'd been his since the first moment I'd laid eyes on him.

Abbie

Although Nora felt absolutely certain that Reid had been having an affair for some time, doubt still lingered. I simply could not believe (maybe I didn't want to believe) that my husband and one of my friends had been screwing each other behind my back. Somehow, I managed to put all thoughts of Reid and Rose out of my mind while I cooked the girls their dinner, spent time with them in the evening, then put them to bed. Despite my desire to simply push those thoughts from my mind, images of the two of them embracing—as well as other things—continued to creep into the edges of my consciousness. Once I was certain the girls were asleep, I knew I wasn't going to be able to keep those thoughts at bay any longer.

It was time to do a bit of research.

I grabbed my laptop, a wine glass, and a bottle of wine and sat down on the couch. No sense in getting up for a refill tonight. I knew I'd be here for some time and when I finally stood up, the bottle would be empty.

Opening up the laptop, I clicked on the icon to open internet explorer. Then I paused. What exactly what I looking for? And where was I going to look for it? Was I absolutely certain that I wanted to find out anything? I mean, Reid was gone; he'd left our family telling me he no longer wanted to be a part of our marriage. Did finding out he was involved—had been involved—with another woman really make a difference?

Maybe not. But I was consumed with a desire to know everything, despite the amount of pain it would cause me.

I still wasn't sure exactly how I was going to prove or disprove what Nora had told me. In lieu of nothing else to do, I opened my email account and began to clear out the countless messages I receive daily from The Gap, Old Navy, Michaels—

just to name a few. Then I decided to peruse Facebook, something I rarely have time to do.

And then it hit me.

I clicked on the search bar at the top of the page and typed in Rosemary Fuller. Actually, I didn't even finish typing her name before the computer pre-filled it for me. Once I was on her page, I began to look at all of her posts, searching for any hints that anything was going on between her and Reid. I wasn't exactly certain what I hoped to find….until I found it.

There was a picture of four feet intertwined together. Two feet, clearly female, had toes painted a forest green and the other set were clearly the feet of a man. The picture looked like it had been taken from a seated position with the legs splayed out in front. Behind the feet, both water and sand were visible. The caption read, "Neither one of us wants to leave."

I peered closer to the pic and realized I knew those feet. Quite well, in fact. The right ankle of the male feet had a bump that only someone who knew those feet intimately - say, a wife—would know. I was that wife. And those were Reid's feet. I'd know that bump anywhere. It was the result of a rather nasty break in his ankle that never quite healed completely, thereby ending any hopes he had of a career in football—not that he had the skill to make it, but still.

The date of the photo was nearly four months before Reid told me he was leaving.

And the women's feet? Well, let's just say that the shade of polish on those toes wasn't a color I'd ever had in my possession.

I felt like I'd been run over by a truck. Here was the proof of what Nora had told me earlier. Somehow, this information managed to inflict pain on me all over again. Sure, I was devastated to hear that Reid was involved with someone so quickly after our separation. I was shocked to discover that it was someone I knew, someone close to me. But this? This was nearly more than I could bear. The evidence of an affair was right in front of me and based on the picture I was looking at, it had been going on for quite some time.

There is nothing, nothing like the feeling of finding out your spouse has been unfaithful. As if the separation wasn't painful enough. This? Well, there are no words to describe what I was feeling. I felt as though all the air in the room had been sucked out at exactly the same time my heart was broken into millions of tiny shards. I was trying to breathe and my heart was trying to beat but it felt as though neither were working.

I felt certain I was actually going to die of a broken heart. And given the pain I felt at that moment, death would have been a welcome relief.

After several moments, I realized death was not going to come for me so I began to peruse more of Rose's posts. Now that I knew what had been going on, the posts that I'd only glanced at during the prior months now had new meaning. There was a picture of two cups of coffee on a table. In the background was the shirted chest of a man I now knew for certain was Reid. I recognized the shirt since I bought the damn thing for him. There were numerous posts that mentioned her happiness, or how she was missing someone. As I read more and more, I felt the bile creep up into my throat and I had to force it back down. There were so many pictures, so many captions, so many indications on her page that up until this very moment seemed like nothing. But now, given what I knew, her posts had taken on an entirely new meaning.

I had to hand it to her, she'd been brilliant at posting everything while posting nothing. Unless you knew exactly what was going on, as I did now, you would have no idea she was involved with someone.

But I knew.

And I realized I wanted to know everything, despite how painful it all was.

I opened up another browser and then signed in to

Facebook once again. I now had my account open in two separate pages. On the first one, I went back to the most recent posts on Rose's page. On the second one, I went to Reid's page. I flipped back and forth, checking to see how often they were in the same town at the same time. I had a hunch they might have been traveling together but wanted to see if was even a possibility.

Sure enough, Rose would post her status, normally with a selfie, practically every day. Reid hardly ever did that but he did mention things like which town he was flying to or where he'd eat lunch. His posts weren't nearly as frequent as hers but it didn't take me long to figure out that wherever Reid was, Rose was with him.

That bastard!

I was suddenly so angry I couldn't see straight. The anger seemed to clear my head just enough for me to recall so many things—things I hadn't paid attention to before. There were nights I'd called Reid's cell phone and it went to voice mail. There were times I'd ask for flight information and he'd brush me off, saying he'd get it to me or he hadn't made a reservation yet. And the travel...the travel had gotten to be so much more than it had ever been before. Ever since Christmas, I've been feeling like I was a single parent. I couldn't help but wonder if he'd travel more and more so that he could spend time with Rose.

But my memory had fully kicked in. Things sprung to my mind that, at the time, I hadn't even given a second thought to. There was the passcode on Reid's phone that had never been there before. The long hours working while at home; was he on the phone with her? Texting her? And then there was the trip to the mountains for the "team building" exercises where spouses weren't allowed. A trip that now I felt certain was simply a way for Reid to spend some time with Rose. And then there was the night that I found Reid running—actually running—on my treadmill. God, was I really that obtuse? Could I have been so wrapped up in my own life that I missed all the signals?

I reached for the bottle and moved to pour myself another glass. When I lifted it, I found it was lighter than I thought it was. Upon further inspection, I found the bottle to be empty. A quick glance to the clock on the wall told me that I'd been sitting on the couch for the better part of three hours, stalking my soon to be ex-husband and his mistress.

And now I had to pee. Desperately.

After taking care of business, I went back to the couch and sat down. Slowly, I opened the laptop and stared at the picture of Rose on her Facebook cover photo. I knew that now since Reid had left me, the pics of the two of them would be more open. I knew there would be more pictures, more comments, more captions. I wasn't sure if I could take it. Thought a small part of me *wanted* to see it all. I wanted to see how the relationship progressed, despite the pain I knew it would cause me each and every time I saw a picture of the two of them with their head tilted together, smiling into their goddamn, K&M paid for cell phones.

Despite my own warped sense of curiosity, I knew that what was best for my mental well-being was to not watch the relationship progress. I leaned forward and stared at her face smiling back at me. I knew what I had to do. But was I strong enough to do it?

I had no idea.

My finger moved the cursor over the "unfriend" button and hovered there. I knew I had to unfriend so that I would remove the ability to see all her posts. I had to do it. But actually clicking that button was the hardest step. It was also the first step of my healing process. It took me several minutes to do it, but I did. I unfriended her, which meant I could no longer see her posts, or anything that had she posted for only her "friends" to see. Of course, if she tagged him in her photos, I'd be able to see that. I just hoped she wasn't one of those women whose maturity level had stopped progressing around the age of sixteen, thereby ensuring she would post a selfie of herself with her new boyfriend every time they did anything together. Good lord, didn't they realize what a fool they were making of themselves? Posts of every moment spent, including weeknight dinners at some local Mexican restaurant where the best items on the menu were the chips and salsa you got just for sitting down at a table.

Without a doubt, these women would post things like "Good dinner. Great company!" along with a pic of herself cuddled next to her boyfriend in an attempt to show everyone she had a boyfriend. To anyone who had matured beyond the level of high school girl, the post simply screamed "I HAVE NO SELF ESTEEM AND WILL BE COUNTING LIKES WHEN I GET HOME TO MAKE SURE EVERYONE SEES THAT I HAVE A BOYFRIEND!!!!"

Blech.

Those photos are the high school equivalent of getting everyone to sign your yearbook, as though that's any barometer of success at that moment or any moment in the future. It is these women that think in order to be successful, you've got to be dating someone.

And of course, they're never alone. Because they can't be.

Fucking ridiculous.

I sighed heavily. Was it appropriate to unfriend the father of your children? My girls didn't have a Facebook page so it wasn't like they'd see whether or not their father and I were friends, yet still I hesitated. I knew in my head that unfriending him would mean that I wouldn't see these posts but another part of me felt compelled to watch the train wreck as it happened. Not that Reid was very active on social networking sights but I knew that if Rose took any selfies of the two of them, posted them to her page and tagged him, I'd see it. And given her age and what I now realized was her immaturity level, I felt certain there would be a selfie of anything they did, especially since I felt certain she's been prevented from taking any incriminating photos during the past several months.

Ugh. I knew with absolute certainty there would picture after picture of the two of them doing all sorts of mundane things. At least now she'd be able to show his face.

Curiosity got the better of me and my "friendship status" with Reid alone.

As I looked over his page, one thing jumped out at me. In the "About" category, there is a relationship status section. Reid's relationship status now reflected a "single" status.

Ouch.

I remember first becoming active on Facebook and completing that section for myself. When I indicated "married" to Reid Hamilton, a message popped up telling me that Facebook would ask Reid to confirm his marriage to me. I now found it interesting that Reid had to confirm our marriage but I was not required to confirm the end of it.

Well played, Mark Zuckerberg....well played.

Slowly, I close the computer, unable to look at the posts any longer. It is now without question: my husband had been having an affair with someone I considered a friend. Not only that, but she is his employee and thirteen years my junior.

Suddenly, my life is one big fucking cliché. I should've had Rose babysit our children, then Reid would have touched upon every cliché out there.

Bastard.

How did I not see what was going on right under my nose? Christ, that woman was in my home! She has met my children. Good Lord, how am I going to explain this to Hannah and Caroline? Surely, Reid is going to introduce the girls to Rose. How am I supposed to answer their questions?

How do I answer questions about something I'm not even sure of myself?

Rose

The weekend after Reid and I signed our lease—and I love saying that, by the way... our lease—Reid and I went out to grab some lunch. For whatever reason, he has this penchant for the hole-in-the-wall places that serve barbecue and pretty much nothing else. While I tolerated it before, we're going to have to start expanding our menu options. A girl can only take so much of this brownish, chopped-up pork crap.

Anyway, we got our sandwiches and began to talk about the new place—when we could move in, what furniture we'd have, whether or not we'd want to paint anything—when Reid suggested we finish our lunch and head into High Point to look for some furniture.

"What are you looking for?" I asked, forcing the last of my sandwich down.

He looked at me pointedly. "A bed."

"What do we need a bed for?"

"Rose," he said. "I cannot continue to sleep in a queen sized bed with you. You may not realize it but you are a bit of a kicker when you sleep."

"What?!! I am not!"

He laughed, then reached over to pay my hand tenderly. "You're a kicker. Just own it. If I don't get some space pretty soon, people are going to think you beat me."

"Oh, stop..."

Reid bent over the table and lifted up the bottom of his shorts, revealing a rather large bruise on his upper thigh. When I spotted it, I grimaced.

"I did not do that. Did I?"

"Three nights ago," he replied, grinning.

Great, I think. Yet another unattractive quality I have. Let's just hope Reid finds this one endearing somehow.

After lunch, we head to High Point and make our way down the main strip where all the furniture stores are located. It's a pretty unique area in that this section of the town appears to be just another part of a run down city. It's only when you stop and happen to notice the furniture signs in the cloudy windows that you realize there is something more to be seen. We spent the better part of the afternoon going in and out of more stores than I care to recall. Finally, we found this store that was one of those outlet or scratch and dent places. Reid pulled in before I even saw the sign. When he parked the car I looked at him as though he'd lost his mind because it appeared as though he'd pulled in front of an abandoned warehouse.

The outside of the building was gray cement that had seen better days and the brick siding was cracked. The few windows that I saw were dimly lit from the inside and were so dirty, I wondered if they served any purpose at all. Despite the appearance of the exterior, I followed Reid inside, hoping what I saw in the building would be more appealing.

It was not.

Like the exterior of the building, the interior was just as run-down. There was a rickety desk just inside the front door with papers scattered all over and one of those old rotary phones on the corner. There was a chair located near the desk with a leather seat but the leather was cracked and worn and clearly had seen better days. I looked around for any indication that someone actually worked there but saw no one. Reid barely glanced at the desk before heading further into the building.

It was then that I noticed all the furniture. And there was a ton of it. It was stacked in makeshift aisles from one end of the building to the other. There were wooden shelving units on the right side that were stacked to the ceiling with an assortment of home décor items. Piles of rugs were next to the shelving units and in the center were tables, bureaus and bed frames leaning precariously, one on top of the other.

I wondered what you'd do if you wanted one of the frames underneath that pile of wood. How would you get it out of there?

The condition of the building didn't seem to concern Reid at all since he wandered through the aisles as though he had a purpose. When he reached the bed frames, he began to lift up each headboard one by one, and inspect them before lying them down on the opposite side. After he viewed several of them, he held one up and looked at me.

"What?" I asked.

"What do you think of this one?"

I glanced down at and much to my surprise, found that I liked what Reid was holding in his hand. It was a dark wood, perhaps mahogany and had a a design on it that while intricate, wasn't too ornate. The more I looked at it, the more I liked it.

"It's nice...very nice, actually," I replied, running my hand over the detail work on the headboard.

"I think I saw a bureau somewhere that might be the match to this piece. Help me slide this out, would you?"

We lifted and shoved the headboard until it was free of the pile, then Reid gently re-stacked the other headboards back into their original position. He grabbed my hand and led me through the aisles once again until he found what he was looking for.

"Look," he said, pointing to what appeared to be the match to the headboard we found.

I shook my head. "I have no idea how you found two matching pieces in this warehouse of crap but you're right. It's perfect!"

"Wanna get it?"

"Ummm...sure," I replied. I'll admit to being worried at this point. Reid had just signed a lease on our new home without even batting an eye and now we were buying furniture. Despite this being a warehouse of what appeared to be discards, the furniture we were looking at was quite expensive-more expensive than I was accustomed to buying. I was a little nervous that Reid was going to ask me to purchase the furniture since he'd paid for the first and last month's rent at our new place. I figured the furniture would be my contribution.

But I was wrong. Once we located one of the employees and told him we wanted to purchase the two pieces we'd found, Reid grabbed a form from the top of the desk and applied for their in-store financing. All I had to was sign and fill in my social security number. It was a huge relief. I doubted any of my credit cards could handle a charge of this size.

It was then that I realized Reid and I, while incredibly attracted to each other, hadn't discussed any of the "real" aspects of a relationship—finances, religion, kids. I'd been so wrapped up in having him all to myself that it hadn't occurred to me to ask about the subjects that cause most couples problems. I hadn't a clue how much money he made, how we were going to do our budget, how we'd spend our money, or even if we'd put our money into joint accounts. Truth be told, there were lots of things I didn't know about Reid, and for just a moment or two, I worried about it.

I quickly brushed those thoughts from my mind, however, figuring we had the rest of our lives to figure it all out. We'd just take it day by day and tackle each issue as it presented itself For now, I was happy to let Reid purchase items for our new home.

God knows I couldn't afford it.

Reid folded the receipt and tucked it into his wallet, then grabbed my hand and guided me out the front door. He was grinning from ear to ear.

"You seem awfully happy," I said as I climbed into the passenger seat. He closed the door behind me and I watched as he skipped in front of the car making me giggle.

He slid in behind the wheel and started the engine. "What's not to be happy about?" He said, glancing in my direction. "Once that bed is delivered, I'll be out of your kick zone."

"I am not a kicker!" I laughed out loud, then made a move to punch him in the thigh. Reid was quicker than I and instead of allowing me to hit my target, he grabbed my hand and held it is his own. As we pulled out of the parking lot, Reid looked at me, lifted up my hand and brought it to his lips.

Though I never saw the truck that hit us, I will never, ever forget the sound of it as it smashed into us and dragged our car through the intersection.

Abbie

My children had to watch as their father was laid in the ground today. And while I wanted to be strong for them, there was a part of me that kept my eyes and ears open, waiting for that woman to show up at either the funeral home or the cemetery.

I'm not sure what I would have done if she'd had the balls to show up. I like to think I would have remained calm and stood beside my children, mustering all the grace I'd like to think I possess but the reality of it is, I probably would have lost it.

And not even Nora's tight grip on my arm would have prevented me from physically assaulting that woman.

Do I blame her? You're damn right I do. Though even I know that part of the reason I've shifted all of the blame to her is because Reid is no longer here for me to be angry with. For whatever reason, she survived. The woman who destroyed my family survived that horrific car crash while my husband, my children's father, was killed instantly.

Christ, he didn't even have a pulse when the first responders showed up at the scene.

I'm not exactly sure how I did it, but somehow, I've managed to get both girls to lie upstairs in their bedrooms. Though given the day's vents, I feel certain both of them will fall asleep without too much effort. At least I hope they will. Burying your father is enough to make anyone need a nap and given the heartache my girls have gone through, I hope they can sleep, even if only for a little while. God knows it's the only time their loss isn't foremost in their minds.

Despite Nora's insistence on it being the right thing to do, I simply refused to have anyone to the house after the service. I

235

just couldn't put my girls through countless strangers commenting on their loss. I have been to those events after a funeral and quite frankly, they've never made much sense to me. The people closest to the deceased sit around in a daze while everyone else tries to force them to eat one of the countless casseroles that are placed on any flat surface in the home. It boggles my mind, this tradition. I don't know of a single person who craves turkey tetrazzini or broccoli casserole after they lose a loved one. I myself haven't eaten more than a bite or two since I received the phone call telling me that Reid had been killed.

I still cannot fathom what God had in mind when he ripped Reid from this earth and allowed that woman to remain. But I have got to stop this. I will never understand any of this and the hatred I feel isn't doing me or anyone else any good. But there is a teeny (Okay, average size) part of me that relishes in imagining all the horrific ways she could die.

I can feel my stress building inside of me just thinking about it and I realize I'm only upsetting myself. I walk into the kitchen and pull out my prescription of Xanax. I found that after Reid told me he was leaving, I was unable to sleep, eat or even function remotely like a human being. Since I had two little ones to take care of, I broke down and asked my doctor to give me something so I could do what was required of me. Xanax was the answer. I hate to admit it, but it does help. It enables me to be a bit more calm, less angry at the world, and miraculously, I'm able to stop crying and care for my children. As an added bonus, I'm able to fall asleep and remain that way for several hours.

I pop one of the tiny pink pills into my mouth and wash it down with some water. Maybe it's just the placebo effect, but I immediately feel the tension ease from my shoulders. I walk back into the living room, stopping at the stairs to listen for any noise from above. There is none, thankfully and I think the girls might actually be sleeping.

I collapse onto the couch and kick off my heels, turning my ankles around and around. Given all the stress of the past few days and the little, pink pull I just took, I begin to think a nap might be possible for me as well. After all, I'd love an hour or so when I don't have to think about all we've been through. It's just as I'm about to lie down on my side that I hear a sharp knock on the front door. I sigh heavily, then heave myself up off the couch and pad in my stocking feet to the front door.

As I pull open the front door open, my jaw drops open.

"Rose," I say. The anger wells up inside of me and I wonder when I will ever be able to look at this woman without feeling such animosity and betrayal. Certainly, today isn't the day. "What are you doing here?" My words are short and clipped. I can't help it but I glance at the stairs behind me, making sure the girls are not anywhere to be seen.

"I need to talk to you."

I stand there for several minutes just looking at her. I can't help but noticed the bruises on her face and neck. Once again, I wonder how this woman managed to walk away from an accident that killed my husband. I saw the car, for God's sakes! No one should have survived.

What the hell can this woman possibly have to say to me at a time like this? I'm completely dumbfounded at the size of this woman's balls.

Seriously. Cantaloupe-sized balls made of titanium.

"What is it that you need to say?" I ask. My voice comes out sounding incredibly bitchy, but quite frankly, I think I've earned it.

"Can I come in?"

I cross my arms over my chest and glare at her. Do I really want this woman in my home? What can she possible say to me inside the house that she can't say outside on the porch?

Oh, who gives a shit, I think. I wave my hand to the expanse of the living room in the universal 'come in' gesture and she steps inside. I close the door behind her, then lead the way into the living room. Good manners dictate that I offer her coffee or a drink of some sort but I won't do it. I will not sit politely with the woman who destroyed my family and have a glass of iced tea. I feel certain Emily Post would side with me on this one.

I motion to the couch, then take a seat in the chair opposite from her. "So what is it? What did you want to talk to me about?"

"Well…." She pauses and licks her lips, probably a nervous habit. Then I wonder if she's trying to tell me she's thirsty but I will not offer this woman something to drink. If she's hot and uncomfortable, all the better. "I was uhh-"

"What, Rose?" I interrupt. "What is it you came here for?"

She jumped at the sound of my voice; even I was a bit surprised at the venomous tone. Quite frankly, I didn't know I had it in me.

She shrugs, then looks away. "I was hoping we could be friends…"

My jaw drops. "We already were friends. But you fucked that up when you decided to start screwing my husband." I laughed angrily. "Did you really come here today expecting I would accept your little proposition? That I'd just forget what you did to me? To my family?"

"No," she replied. "I didn't think you'd forgotten. I guess I just thought that after all we've been through-"

"We," I pointed between the two of us, "haven't been through anything. You've put me and my family through hell. Do not for one minute think that you and I have been through anything together. How dare you come to my *home* after everything you have done to this family and ask for my friendship. As if I'd just forget about the hell you put me and my children through! You've got some nerve coming here."

I was fuming. It was all I could do to sit there and look at the face of the woman who'd ripped my family apart. And to make matters even more infuriating, Rose just sat there while I yelled at her, releasing all the anger I'd kept pent up inside of me. And I will admit, it helped. Whoever thought up the idea of "being the better person" or "turning the other cheek" or "forgive and forget" must have been crazy. I hadn't felt this good in a month!

I looked at Rose, sitting there on my couch. She was calm, despite my breakdown. Her hands were folded in her lap and her gaze was focused forward about three feet in front of her. At least she had the decency not to meet my gaze. I'm sure at that point, she would have been afraid at the anger stored there. Windows to the soul and all…

The girls were still asleep upstairs and save for the gentle tic-toc coming from the clock on the wall, the house was silent. Rose leaned back, almost as if she were becoming more relaxed. The thought of it angered me and I brought my gaze back to her. For the first time, I took the opportunity to truly look at her and it was then that I noticed the difference in her appearance. Though I hadn't seen her nearly a month, the change in her appearance was striking. I knew her to be in her mid-twenties but today she looked closer to thirty or more. There were fine lines around her mouth and eyes and her skin lacked the youthful dewiness I'd noticed when we first met. Her hair, normally shiny and full of bounce, hung in loose, erratic curls to just below her shoulders. Clearly the result of air-drying her naturally curly hair, which I knew she only did when forced to do so because of lack of product or time. And it seemed to me that now, she had an abundance of time on her hands.

She was wearing an oversized Pearl Jam t-shirt that I wondered if she'd bought while at a concert with Reid. Again, anger flared inside of me and I wondered for probably the millionth time if I'd ever be able to put this betrayal past me. As I stared at the t-shirt, something finally clicked. There was something all too familiar about the way she had her arms placed. I'd sat in much the same way nearly eleven years ago and then again, nearly nine years ago.

It was universal, it seemed; the way a woman sits with her hand ever so slightly curved around her belly, almost as though she were protecting the life that was growing inside of her, which of course, we were. Seeing Rose sit in that position that had, at the time, been the happiest in my life, made me angrier than I'd ever been before, if that were even possible.

Rose was pregnant. Of this, I was certain.

Before I knew what was happening, I laughed. For the first time in more than a month I laughed. A full, hold your belly until it hurts kind of laugh. I went on and on laughing, not even worrying that I would wake the girls up. It was all clear now. I knew exactly why Rose had come today. I knew what she wanted, and it certainly wasn't friendship. She wanted to make sure her child was taken care of.

After several moments, I managed to contain my laughter. Of course, by now tears were streaming down my face. I wiped my fingers across my cheeks, not caring if my makeup was smudged or if my face was red and splotchy. I didn't care how I looked. That laugh was the best possible medicine for me.

When I finally managed to focus on Rose again, she was looking at me with an expression of pure confusion. "Just what is so funny?" she asked.

Smiling, I put my head in my hands and pressed my lips to the inside of my palms, trying to prevent yet another bout of laughter. When I felt I had control of myself, I looked up at her. "You," I said, pointing at her belly, "You are pregnant!"

She inhaled sharply and raised her eyebrows. "How could you possibly know that? I'm barely eight weeks along!"

I chuckled and shook my head. "Once you've been through it yourself, you tend to recognize it others."

"Wait," she said. "Is that why you were laughing?"

I nodded.

"I don't see what's so funny about it."

"Hmmmm...No. I guess not. Pregnancy in and of itself

isn't funny." I was being evasive and I knew it.

Rose crossed her arms over her chest tightly. "So why don't you tell me why you were laughing?"

I mirrored her position and sat back against my chair, resuming my earlier position. "Why don't you tell me the real reason you came here today?"

She glanced away quickly; almost too quickly. I will give her credit though, her gaze returned to mine almost immediately. "What do you mean? I told you. I came here because I'd hoped we could be friends."

I snorted.

"You don't believe me?"

I leaned forward and placed my elbows on my knees. "No, Rose, I don't believe you. I don't believe you for one minute. Now why don't you tell my exactly what you had in mind when you knocked on my door."

She sat across from me for several moments in stunned silence. I watched calmly as her gaze flitted all over the room, not once focusing on me. I waited, arms crossed over my chest, completely relaxed. I had all the time in the world. Finally, after several minutes, she began to speak. "It's just that…well, it's just that I found out I'm pregnant and now that Reid is gone, I don't know…."

"You don't know how you're going to provide for this child. Is that about right?"

She nodded. "Reid and I took out a lease on a townhouse and bought this furniture for the place and now there's the baby to consider…"

"You and Reid signed a lease," I said slowly. "Together. So you're responsible for the rent." It was all falling into place for me now.

She nodded.

"So, the real reason you came here today was to ask for some sort of financial help for that child you're carrying."

Again, she nodded. This time, however, her nod was much

slower, almost as if she was unsure if she should not at all.

I leaned forward slowly, keeping my gaze locked on hers the entire time. "Why in the HELL would I provide any financial assistance to you whatsoever?" I leaned back and crossed my arms over my chest once again, waiting for the shock to settle in. It didn't take long. I could almost watch as my words made their way up to her stupid little brain. When she finally comprehended what I was telling her, her jaw dropped open and she stared at me, dumbfounded.

"Close your jaw, Rose. You'll catch flies."

Slowly, she closed her mouth. "I'm only asking for what is rightfully mine. Only what Hannah or Caroline would have."

I bristled at the sound of my daughter's names coming out of the mouth of this woman. "How you *dare* you even mention my daughters. You keep them out of this. This is between you and me."

"And my baby," Rose retorted.

Her chin had lifted up ever so slightly, making her appear a bit indignant, which made me clench my fists at my sides, thereby preventing me from knocking that stupid look off her face. I could feel my fingernails piercing the skin of my palms and knew I had to calm down.

After several deep breaths, I was able to speak.

"Yes," I replied evenly. "*Your* baby. Yours and yours alone. That child has nothing to do with me or my children." The venom that was spewing out of my mouth was even shocking to me. I'd never been one to be anything other than happy at the news of an impending birth. As a matter of fact, at the first news of a friend's pregnancy, I'd been known to begin purchasing items for the baby shower, despite it being months away. When the big day finally arrived, I'd have enough items to fill several bags. But this? This was too much. There was no way I was going to let Rose continue to harm my family.

"How can you say that? This child has everything to do with you! Reid is going to have another child. Your children are going to have a baby brother or sister."

I leapt up, unwilling to listen to anything else that came out of her mouth. I stood over her, loomed over her is probably a better description, and watched as she leaned back and looked up at me. I will admit, I felt a good deal of pleasure when I saw the fear reflected in her eyes.

Taking a deep breath, I began. "Let's get one thing clear right now. You are going to get your *ass* up off my couch and leave this house. You will never come back here. And you will never, EVER utter my children's names again. Do I make myself clear?"

"But what about the baby? How can you turn away your husband's child?"

"Easy," I spat out. "You and I both know that the child you are carrying isn't Reid's. That child is of no relation to my daughters."

She lifted her chin up at me in a show of defiance. "How can you be so sure?"

I sat back down slowly, enjoying every second of this exchange. I wanted to be looking at this woman eye to eye when I delivered this life-changing information. I wanted to see the look of shock on her face,then meet her gaze at the exact moment she realized she'd never see a penny of Reid's money.

"You stupid, stupid girl. You probably should have done some research before you came here today."

She looked at me, clearly not understanding anything I was saying.

"Reid had a vasectomy six months after Caroline was born." I sat back, crossed my arms over my chest and waited for her to connect the dots.

Her eyes widened as she realized she'd never see a penny. Her mission here today was a complete and total failure.

I couldn't have been more pleased with myself.

Though truth be told, I really didn't do anything. Rose did it all to herself. She ripped my husband from his family and couldn't even be faithful to him for the short time she had him. Despite it all, even Reid didn't deserve that.

"Now get the hell out of my house."

Abbie

Like most friends would do for each other, Nora checked in with me nearly every day. She knew better than to make a casserole or something too fancy. She did, however, bring the basics. That is—milk, cream, cereal and of course, herself.

Oh, and wine. Lots and lots of wine.

The girls and I were slowly healing. I knew it would be some time before things were back to normal, though I had no idea what our normal would look like. Perhaps we'd have to create a new normal. Something that was perfect for the three of us.

One weekend, about a month or so after Reid's death, Nora came over for dinner. I felt up to cooking, which I'd not done in some time. The girls and I had been subsisting on things we could heat up quickly and devour. Eating for us had simply become something to do in order to survive.

After we'd eaten whatever we could find, we'd cuddle on the couch or watch a movie together snuggled under a blanket. Hannah, it seemed, relished our time together even more than her baby sister and if there was any silver lining in this whole fiasco, it was that I was able to hug my eldest as much as I wanted to, much like when she was younger.

On this particular night, I felt up for something more substantial than macaroni and cheese or hot dogs. I was feeling like an actual meal—a meatloaf, some chicken, or maybe some steaks on the grill. In the end, I decided to bake a chicken. Having Nora at our table, I knew, would eliminate the spot left by Reid, if only for one meal.

I've often wondered if the reason I didn't cook much during the few weeks after Reid's death was because I couldn't bear the thought of my girls looking at the empty chair, knowing their father would never sit in it again. Although he'd been gone for sometime prior to his death, there had always been the possibility that he would return, even if it was only for a meal or two. Now, the finality of it all was staring us in the face every time we sat at the table together; our family, minus one.

Nora, true to form, arrived earlier than I'd expected. I think she wanted to make sure I wasn't going to lose my mind by the simple act of preparing dinner.

If cooking a dinner for one's family was enough to make someone lose it, most women would have gone bonkers by now. Besides, after all I'd been through, I felt certain I could handle pretty much anything that came my way without losing it.

Nora strolled into my kitchen and made herself at home by pouring us each of us a glass of wine. She placed my glass in front of me and sat down at the bar while I prepped the chicken.

"It's good to see a bit of your old self," she said softly, taking a sip of the chardonnay.

"I'm trying," I replied. "I really am. I think it'd be easier if it was only me. But the girls?" I shook my head from side to side. "When I think about all they've lost, it just makes me sad and I begin to hurt all over again."

"You're a great mom and a very strong woman. You'll help them through it."

I nodded, feeling the tears well up in my eyes. Quickly, I focused my attention to the chicken. I washed it off, dried it with a paper towel and then placed it in the roasting pan. After I moved it to the top of the stove, I began to rifle through the spices in the cabinet above the stove.

"Whatcha looking for? Spices for the chicken?"

"Yeah," I replied. "Any suggestions?"

"I've used a bunch. Rosemary works really well."

Slowly, I turned to look at Nora, who had gone pale. I don't either of us made the connection between Rose's name and the spice until that moment. She got up and made her way over to me slowly, almost tip-toeing. It was as if she thought any sudden movements might cause me to collapse onto the floor in a heap. She wrapped her arms around me, pulling me close. "Oh my God," she whispered. "I am so sorry."

I pulled back so that I could look her in the eyes. "You know," I said, a smile beginning to form on my lips. "I think that woman may have ruined the spice for me forever."

Nora clasped my shoulders and laughed out loud. "I've missed you, Abbie. It's good to have you back."

"I've missed me too."

She pulled me into another tight embrace, then released me. When her gaze once again met mine, she smiled. "Abbie Hamilton, you're going to be just fine."

And I was. We all were.

For the first time in a long time, I was sure of it.